Charles Johnson

Middle Passage

A Novel

A Work from the Johnson Construction Co.

SCRIBNER CLASSICS

New York   London   Toronto   Sydney   New Delhi

SCRIBNER
An Imprint of Simon & Schuster, Inc.
1230 Avenue of the Americas
New York, NY 10020

This Scribner hardcover edition July 2015

SCRIBNER and design are registered trademarks of The Gale Group, Inc.,
used under license by Simon & Schuster, Inc., the publisher of this work.

For information about special discounts for bulk purchases,
please contact Simon & Schuster Special Sales at 1-866-506-1949
or business@simonandschuster.com.

The Simon & Schuster Speakers Bureau can bring authors to your live event.
For more information or to book an event, contact the Simon & Schuster Speakers
Bureau at 1-866-248-3049 or visit our website at www.simonspeakers.com.

Manufactured in the United States of America

1 3 5 7 9 10 8 6 4 2

The Library of Congress has cataloged the Atheneum edition as follows:
Johnson, Charles Richard, 1948–
Middle passage / Charles Johnson.
p. cm.
I. Title.
PS3560.03735M5 1990
813'.54—dc20 90-32713
CIP

ISBN 978-1-5011-1052-8
ISBN 978-1-4391-2503-8 (ebook)

To Joan
for the last twenty-two years

INTRODUCTION

What Charles Johnson has—and can do with it—is much easier to say than to replicate or imitate. Actual artists have always been that way, able to create something so original and so futuristic, shaping the reading backward to myth and forward to the stations of timeless dreams, but in a seemingly effortless way. William Faulkner said that what one attempts to do is to bottle the flame and presence of life which is always moving even though sitting still on the page.

I was with Charles Johnson at the Plaza Hotel the night he won the National Book Award for *Middle Passage*. He spoke quite generously about Ralph Ellison on that storied night. The marvelous Saul Bellow also attended, as did our most productive writer of high class and adventurous fiction, Joyce Carol Oates.

It is hard to go wrong when attempting to deal with a writer such as Charles Johnson who combines the physical realities with the internal mysteries of sensibility so well. His command of the language is so omni-directional that he creates a nineteenth-century seaman and adventurer, a curious minded man in a time when the world was made to heel before technology, mystic explanations, and the intertwined facts of slaving and slavery. Any character on a slave ship from New Orleans in the 1840s had to face all of that and muse over multiple meanings, inevitable among all humans, even men making their living selling other men.

Melville and Twain went into that struggle and left the opposition—chaos—with some serious wounds within the aesthetic context. Their greatest heir may well have been William Faulkner, who understood that facing the weight and airborne force of the sometimes-subterranean black American was essential to getting a full grip on American literature. That actual Negro brought the dream of originality to the writer willing to work the imagination in that direction, which is what Charles Johnson has done in this book now celebrated for over twenty-five years.

Middle Passage is a tale about slavery at both ends, at the home front and the bush of a primitive land. The novel fulfills Faulkner's description of an aim available to every writer, "The aim of every artist is to arrest motion, which is life, by the artificial means and hold it fixed so that a hundred years later, when a stranger looks at it, it moves again since it is life. Since man is mortal, the only immortality possible for him is to leave something behind him that is immortal since it will always move."

Johnson's writing stands up well against expensive parlor tricks because of his poetic imagination, the truest defender of human sensibility. The reader is pushed into another world that could or might not have ever existed but seems to have because we *recognize* all of the people, all of their preferences, and the ongoing fact that each sits atop a gaggle of experience that always remains in place, whacky, wilted, or sporadic—open to other beliefs or systems of human organization. Sailors like those in *Middle Passage* had to understand that there was always what is now called "diversity." Johnson shows that anyone believing in complete purity is basically a complete fool—and has been since time immemorial. Early in *Moby-Dick,* Ishmael speaks up for human variety because the tale he is telling was as full of various types as any mythic tale.

Johnson steps away from Melville through his harsh and beautiful rendering of his hero's romance with his wife, a relationship determined by her intelligence, sweet words, and ordinary looks; no great wonder woman of attraction, she still has him before he knows it and is perfectly convincing to the reader. Her understanding of the essential importance of charm avoids the clichés of our time and is well handled by Johnson. He puts a woman and her sailor husband on another level, in which we respect the young seaman's taste, but understand as well his adolescent qualities that *must* mature if he is to make it through forthcoming adventures.

Twenty-five years after being as graceful on the page and humorously savage as Johnson was, the younger and less decidedly shocking for the fun of it, our champion writer tried as Faulkner did and Ellison did to show American writers that race is only a luminous spot on the page if the writer brings a broad enough scope to speak now and forever for human interest, the greatest subject of them all.

Stanley Crouch
December 31, 2014

Homo est quo dammodo omnia
                    Saint Thomas Aquinas

What port awaits us, Davy Jones'
or home? I've heard of slavers drifting, drifting,
    playthings of wind and storm and chance,
    their crews
    gone blind, the jungle hatred
    crawling up on deck.
                    Robert Hayden
                    "Middle Passage"

Who sees variety and not the Unity wanders
on from death to death
                    Brihad-aranyaka Upanishad

Laud Deo

Journal of a Voyage intended

by God's permission

in the *Republic*, African

from New Orleans to the Windward

Coast of Africa

Entry, the first
JUNE 14, 1830

Of all the things that drive men to sea, the most common disaster, I've come to learn, is women. In my case, it was a spirited Boston schoolteacher named Isadora Bailey who led me to become a cook aboard the *Republic*. Both Isadora and my creditors, I should add, who entered into a conspiracy, a trap, a scheme so cunning that my only choices were prison, a brief stay in the stony oubliette of the Spanish Calabozo (or a long one at the bottom of the Mississippi), or marriage, which was, for a man of my temperament, worse than imprisonment—especially if you knew Isadora. So I went to sea, sailing from Louisiana on April 14, 1830, hoping a quarter year aboard a slave clipper would give this relentless woman time to reconsider, and my bill collectors time to forget they'd ever heard the name Rutherford Calhoun. But what lay ahead in Africa, then later on the open, endless sea, was, as I shall tell you, far worse than the fortune I'd fled in New Orleans.

New Orleans, you should know, was a city tailored to my taste for the excessive, exotic fringes of life, a world port of such extravagance in 1829 when I arrived from southern Illinois—a newly freed bondman, my papers in an old portmanteau, a gift from my master in Makanda—that I dropped my bags and a shock of recognition shot up my spine to my throat, rolling off my tongue in a whispered, *"Here, Ruth-erford is home."* So it seemed those first few months to the country boy with cotton in his hair, a great whore of a city in her glory, a kind of glandular Golden Age. She was if not a town devoted to an almost religious pursuit of Sin, then at least to a steamy sexuality. To the newcomer she was an assault of smells: molasses commingled with mangoes in the sensually damp air, the stench of slop in a muddy street, and, from the labyrinthine warehouses on the docks, the odor of Brazilian coffee and Mexican oils. And also this: the most exquisitely beautiful women in the world, thoroughbreds of pleasure created two centuries before by the French for their enjoyment. Mulattos colored like magnolia petals, qua-droons with breasts big as melons—women who smelled like roses all year round. Home? Brother, for a randy Illinois boy of two and twenty accustomed to cornfields, cow plops, and handjobs in his master's hayloft, New Orleans wasn't home. It was Heaven. But even paradise must have its back side too, and it is here (alas) that the newcomer comes to rest. Upstream there were waterfront saloons and dives, a black underworld of thieves, gamblers, and ne'er-do-wells who, unlike the Creoles downstream (they sniffed down their long, Continental noses at poor, purebred Negroes like myself), didn't give a tinker's damn about my family tree and welcomed me as the world downstream would not.

In plain English, I was a petty thief.

How I fell into this life of living off others, of being a social parasite, is a long, sordid story best shortened for those who, like the Greeks, prefer to keep their violence off-stage. Naturally, I looked for honest work. But arriving in the city, checking the saloons and Negro bars, I found noth-ing. So I stole—it came as second nature to me. My mas-ter, Reverend Peleg Chandler, had noticed this stickiness of my fingers when I was a child, and a tendency I had to tell preposterous lies for the hell of it; he was convinced I was born to be hanged and did his damnedest to reeducate said fingers in finer pursuits such as good penmanship and playing the grand piano in his parlor. A Biblical scholar, he endlessly preached Old Testament virtues to me, and to this very day I remember his tedious disquisitions on Neoplatonism, the evils of nominalism, the genius of Aquinas, and the work of such seers as Jakob Böhme. He'd wanted me to become a Negro preacher, perhaps even a black saint like the South American priest Martín de Porres—or, for that matter, my brother Jackson. Yet, for all that theological background, I have always been drawn by nature to extremes. Since the hour of my manumission—a day of such gloom and depression that I must put off its telling for a while, if you'll be patient with me—since that day, and what I can only call my older brother Jackson's spineless behavior in the face of freedom, I have never been able to do things halfway, and I hungered—literally *hungered*—for life in all its shades and hues: I was hooked on sensation, you might say, a lecher for perception and the nerve-knocking thrill, like a shot of opium, of new "experiences." And so, with the hateful, dull Illinois farm behind me, I drifted about New Orleans those first few months, pilfering food and picking money belts off tourists, but don't be too quick to pass judgment. I may be from southern Illinois, but I'm not stupid. Cityfolks lived by cheating and crime. Everyone knew this, everyone saw it, everyone talked ethics piously, then took payoffs under the table, tampered with the till, or fattened his purse by duping the poor. Shameless, you say? Perhaps so. But had I not been a thief, I would not have met Isadora and shortly thereafter found myself literally at sea.

Sometimes after working the hotels for visitors, or when

I was drying out from whiskey or a piece of two-dollar tail,
I would sneak off to the waterfront, and there, sitting on
the rain-leached pier in heavy, liquescent air, in shimmering light so soft and opalescent that sunlight could not fully
pierce the fine erotic mist, limpid and luminous at dusk, I
would stare out to sea, envying the sailors riding out on
merchantmen on the gift of good weather, wondering if
there was some far-flung port, a foreign country or island
far away at the earth's rim where a freeman could escape
the vanities cityfolk called self-interest, the mediocrity they
called achievement, the blatant selfishness they called individual freedom—all the bilge that made each day landside
a kind of living death. I don't know if you've ever farmed
in the Midwest, but if you have, you'll know that southern
Illinois has scale; fields like sea swell; soil so good that if you
plant a stick, a year later a carriage will spring up in its place;
forests and woods as wild as they were before people lost
their pioneer spirit and a healthy sense of awe. Only here, on
the waterfront, could I recapture that feeling. Wind off the
water was like a fist of fresh air, a cleansing blow that made
me feel momentarily clean. In the spill of yellow moonlight,
I'd shuck off my boots and sink both feet into the water.
But the pier was most beautiful, I think, in early morning,
when sunlight struck the wood and made it steam as mois-
ture and mist from the night before evaporated. Then you
could believe, like the ancient philosopher Thales, that the
analogue for life was water, the formless, omnific sea. Busi-
nessmen with half a hundred duties barnacled to their lives
came to stare, longingly, at boats trolling up to dock. Black
men, free and slave, sat quietly on rocks coated with crus-
tacea, in the odors of oil and fish, studying an evening sky
as blue as the skin of heathen Lord Krishna. And Isadora
Bailey came too, though for what reason I cannot say—her

expression on the pier was unreadable—since she was, as I soon learned, a woman grounded, physically and metaphysically, in the land. I'd tipped closer to her, eyeing the bead-purse on her lap, then thought better of boosting it when I was ambushed by the innocence—the alarming trust—in her eyes when she looked up at me. I wondered, and wonder still: What's a nice girl like her doing in a city like this?

She was, in fact, as out of place in New Orleans as Saint Teresa would be at an orgy with de Sade: a frugal, quiet, devoutly Christian girl, I learned, the fourth daughter of a large Boston family free since the Revolutionary War, and positively ill with eastern culture. An educated girl of twenty, she thought it best to leave home to lighten her family's burden, but found no prospects for a Negro teacher, and female at that, in the Northeast. She came south by coach, avoiding the newfangled trains after reading an expert say that traveling at over twenty miles an hour would suffocate all aboard when the speed sucked all the air from the cars. Once in New Orleans, she took a job as a nursery governess for the children of Madame Marie Toulouse, a Creole who had spent her young womanhood as the mistress of first a banker, then a famous actor, a minister, and finally a mortician. Why these four? As Madame Toulouse told Isadora, she'd used the principle of "one for the money, two for the show, three to get ready, and four to go," and they'd left her generous endowments that she invested in a hotel at Royal and Saint Peter's streets. But Isadora was not, I'm afraid, any happier living in a Creole household than I would have been. They were beautiful; she was bookish. They were society here; she was, as a Northerner, the object of polite condescension—the Toulouses, in short, could afford the luxury of stupidity, the blind, cowlike, chin-lifted hauteur of Beautiful People.

And such luxury Isadora had never known. You had the feeling, once you knew her, that she'd gambled on knowledge as others gambled on power, believing—wrongly, I think—that she had little else to offer. She let herself get fat, for example, to end the pressure women feel from being endlessly ogled and propositioned. Men hardly noticed her, pudgy as she was, and this suited Isadora just fine. She had a religious respect for Work. She was a nervous eater too, I guess, the sort of lonely, intelligent woman who found comfort in food, or went to restaurants simply to be treated kindly by the waiters, to be fussed over and served, to be asked, "Is everything all right here?"

Yet she *was* pretty in a prim, dry, flat-breasted way. Isadora never used make-up. At age five she had been sentenced to the straightening comb, and since then kept her hair pinned back so tightly each glossy strand stood out like wire, which also pulled back the skin at her temples, pushing forward a nose that looked startlingly like a doorknob, and enlarging two watery, moonlike eyes that seemed ever on the verge of tears. No, she wasn't much to look at, nor was the hotel room where she lived with eight one-eyed cats, two three-legged dogs, and birds with broken wings. Most often, her place had a sweet, atticlike odor, but looked like a petshop and sometimes smelled like a zoo. Isadora took in these handicapped strays, unable to see them left unattended, and each time I dropped by she had something new. No, not a girl to tell your friends about, but one reassuring to be with because she had an inner brilliance, an intelligence and clarity of spirit that overwhelmed me. Generally she spoke in choriambs and iambs when she was relaxed, which created a kind of dimetrical music to her speech. Did I love Isadora? Really, I couldn't say. I'd always felt people fell in love as they might fall into a hole; it was something I thought a smart man avoided.

But some days, after weeks of whoring and card games that lasted three days and nights, I found myself at her hotel room, drunk as Noah, broke and bottomed out, holding a bouquet of stolen flowers outside her door, eager to hear her voice, which was velvety and light like water gently rushing nearby. We'd sit and talk (she abhorred Nature walks; claiming that the only thing she knew about Nature was that it itched), her menagerie of crippled beasts crawling over her lap and mine. Those afternoons of genteel conversation (Isadora wouldn't let me do anything else) we talked of how we both were newcomers to New Orleans, or we took short walks together, or we'd dine at sidewalk cafés, where we watched the Creoles. My earliest impressions of the Cabildo, the fancy-dress quadroon balls and slave auctions arranged by the firm of Hewlett & Bright each Saturday at the new Exchange Market (ghastly affairs, I must add, which made poor Isadora a bit ill), were intertwined with her voice, her reassuring, Protestant, soap-and-water smell. Aye, she was good and honest and forthright, was Isadora. Nevertheless, at other times she was intolerable. She was, after all, a *teacher*, and couldn't turn it off sometimes, that tendency to talk in propositions, or declarative sentences, to correct my southern Illinois accent, with its squashed vowels and missing consonants, and challenge everything I said on, I thought, General Principle.

"Rea-a-ally, Rutherford," she said one afternoon in her sitting room, her back to a deep-silled window where outside a pear tree was in full bloom, its fruit like a hundred green bells draped upon the branches. "You don't think you can keep this up forever, do you? The gambling and girl-chasing?" She gave her gentle, spinster's smile and, as always, looked at me with a steadier gaze than I could look at her. "You have a *mind*. And, if what you tell me is true, you've lacked for nothing in this life. Am I right in saying this? Neither in childhood education nor the nourishment of a sound body and Christian character?"

I gave her a nod, for this was so. Though a slaveholder, Reverend Chandler hated slavery. He'd inherited my brother and me from his father and, out of Christian guilt, taught us more than some white men in Makanda knew, then finally released us one by one, except that Jackson stayed, more deeply bound to our master than any of us dreamed. But I am not ready just yet to talk of Jackson Calhoun.

"So you were," Isadora asked, toying with her teacup, "blessed with reasonably pleasant surroundings and pious counsel?"

I nodded again, squirming a little. Always, and eerily, I had the feeling that Isadora knew more about me than I did.

"Then aren't you obliged, given these gifts, to settle down and start a family so you can give to others in even greater measure?" Her eyes went quiet, closing as if on a vision of her and me at the altar. "My father, you know, was a little like you, Rutherford, or at least my aunties say he was. He stayed in Scolley Square or in the pubs, looking for himself in rum and loose women until he met a woman of character—I mean my mother—who brought out his better instincts."

"What's he doing now?" I rested my teacup on my knee. "Your father?"

"Well . . ." She pulled back, pausing to word this right. "Not much just now. He died last winter, you know, from heart failure."

Wonderful, I thought: The wage of the family man was coronary thrombosis. "And," I said, "he was how old?"

"Forty-nine." Then Isadora hurried to add, "But he had people who *cared* for him, daughters and sons, and a wife who brought him down to earth. . . ."

"Indeed," I said. "Quite far down, I'd say."

"Rutherford!" she yipped, her voice sliding up a scale. "It *hurts* me to see you in such ruin! Really, it does! Half the time I see you, you haven't eaten in two days. Or you're hung over. Or someone is chasing you for money. Or you've been in a fight! You need a family. You're not—not *common!*"

Ah, there it was, revealed at last, the one thing inside Isadora that made me shudder. It was what you heard all your blessed life from black elders and church women in flowered gowns: Don't be common. Comb your hair. Be a credit to the Race. Strive, like the Creoles, for respectability. Class. It made my insides clench. Oh, yes, it mattered to me that Isadora cared, but she saw me as clay. Something she could knead beneath her tiny brown fingers into precisely the sort of creature I—after seeing my brother shackled to subservience—was determined not to become: "a gentleman of color." The phrase made me hawk, then spit in a corner of my mind. It conjured (for me) the image of an Englishman, round of belly, balding, who'd been lightly brushed with brown watercolor or cinnamon.

"No, Isadora." I shook my head. "I don't believe I'll ever get married. There's too much to do. And see. Life is too short for me to shackle myself to a mortgage and marriage." I was a breath away from adding, "And a houseful of gimped cats," but thought it best to bite my tongue.

Her eyes took on a woebegone, persecuted look, a kind of dying-duck expression she had now and then: She stared at me for the longest time, then flashed, "You just won't act *right*, will you?" Touching her handkerchief to the doorknob nose, she stood suddenly, her cat leaping from her enskirted knees and bumping blindly into a candlestand. Isadora took three paces toward the door—I thought she was about to throw me out—then turned to pitch her voice back into the room. "Suppose you *have* to get married, Rutherford Calhoun!" Now her eyes burned. "What about that?"

What Isadora meant by this was a mystery to me. She couldn't be pregnant. Not her. At least not by me—she twisted my fingers whenever I reached for her knee. *Have* to marry her? It made no sense that afternoon, but less than a fortnight later her meaning became horribly clear.

Near the waterfront, after a day of dodging my creditors and shooting craps, I turned a corner and found myself facing a Negro named Santos, a kind of walking wrecking crew who pretty much ran things down on the docks for a Creole gangster known by the name of Philippe "Papa" Zeringue. Some masters, as you know, groomed their slaves to be gladiators: the Africans with a reach, or thickness of skull, or smoldering anger that, if not checked, would result in slave rebellion. So it was with Santos. He'd been a dirt-pit wrestler on a Baton Rouge plantation, and made his master, John Ruffner, a fortune in bare-knuckle fights he arranged for him with blacks from other farms. Freed by Ruffner, undefeated, and itching for trouble, he'd next come to New Orleans, and fell, as many did, into the orbit of life upstream. You have seen, perhaps, sketches of Piltdown man? Cover him with coal dust, add deerskin leggings and a cutaway coat tight as wet leather, and you shall have Santos's younger, undernourished *sister*.

This upright disaster was in the oval light of a lamppost on Royal Street as I passed. He was gnawing a stolen ham. Behind him two policemen stood, tapping their nightsticks on their palms. "Come along now, Santos," said one. "Don't make trouble. That ham'll cost you a month in the Calabozo." Santos went right on chewing, his small, quick eyes half-seeled in gastronomic bliss. And then, without warning, both policemen smashed him full on both sides of his temples with their nightsticks. They'd each taken half steps back too, putting their waists and full weight into the swing. One nightstick broke with a sickening crack, the other vibrated in the officer's hand as if wood had struck wood. As for Santos, he only looked up sleepily. Said, "Now what'd you do that fo'?"

No fools, the policemen flew past me, Santos's eyes on their flapping waistcoats until his gaze lighted upon me. "Illinois!" he said—or, rather his sweaty voice rumbled and rattled windows along the street. "Ain't you Rutherford Calhoun from Illinois?"

I shook my head and took a step backward.

"Dammit, you *are* Calhoun! Don't lie! Papa been lookin' fo' you, boy!"

I touched my chest. "Me?"

"Yes, *you*, nigguh." He came forward, seizing my arm. "He wants to *talk* to you 'bout somethin' you owe him." I told him that surely he was mistaken, that indeed I owed several people within a mile circumference of the city— my landlady Mrs. Dupree; Mr. Fenton the moneylender; and the vendors too—but I'd never *met* Papa. How could I owe him? None of this washed with Santos, a man with whom you didn't argue, because he looked exactly like what he was: an athlete gone slightly to seed, with maybe thirty pounds of muscle alchemizing to fat on his upper body. He'd be dead by forty from the strain on his heart—the extra bulk had scrunched down his spine, I heard, shortening him by two inches, but no matter. He was bigger than me. Silently he steered me, his right hand on the back of my collar, to a tavern owned by Papa on Chartres Street, a one-story building of English-bond brickwork, with sunken, uneven floors, and windows with old, diamond-paned lattices, pushing me through the door to a table at the rear of the room where Papa sat eating a meal of drop-biscuits and blueberries with—my heart jumped!—Isadora! Of a sudden, I had that special feeling of dread that comes when you enter a café and stumble upon two women you used to sleep with—who you'd have sworn were strangers but were now whispering together. About *you*, by God! She looked up as I scuffed jelly-legged to the table, and her eyes, I tell you, were indecipherable.

"Isadora," I gulped, "you *know* these people!"

She gave Papa, in fact, a very knowing smile.

"We just met to discuss a business arrangement that affects you, Rutherford. I'm sure you'll be interested to hear what Mr. Zeringue and I have decided." Isadora touched a napkin to her lips, then stood up. "I'll wait for you outside."

She seemed to take all the available air in the room with her as she sashayed outside, mysteriously happier than I'd seen her in months. For an instant I could not catch my breath. Papa sat with a napkin tucked into his collar. He was holding a soup spoon dripping with blueberry jelly in his right hand when I extended my hand and introduced myself; this spoon he slapped against my palm and, having nothing else to shake, I shook that. Santos roared.

"Sir, you wanted to see me abo—"

"Don't say nothin', Calhoun."

If there were musical instruments that fit this man's voice, that would ring from the orchestra, say, if he appeared on stage, they would be the bull fiddle, tuba, and slide trombone (Isadora was all strings, a soft flick of the lyre), a combination so guttural and brutish, full of grunts and deep-throated notes, that I cannot say his voice put me at ease. Nor this room. It had the atmosphere you feel in houses where some great "Murder of the Age" has taken place. My worst fears about him were confirmed. He was, in every sense of the word, the very Ur-type of Gangster. Fiftyish, a brown-skinned black man with gray-webbed hair, he dressed in rich burgundy waistcoats and had a princely, feudal air about him, the smell of a man who loved Gothic subterfuges and schemes, deceits, and Satanic games of power. Yet, despite his wealth, and despite the extravagant riverboat parties I heard he threw—bashes that made Roman bacchanals look like a backwoods flangdang—he was a black lord in ruins, a fallen angel who, like Lucifer, controlled the lower depths of the city—the cathouses, the Negro press, the gambling dens—but held his dark kingdom, and all within it, in the greatest contempt. He was wicked. Wicked and self-serving, I thought, but why did he want to see me?

"I suppose," said Papa, as if he'd read my mind, "you wanna know why I had Santos bring you heah."

Indeed, I did.

"It's simple—you owe me, Illinois." I started to protest, but his left hand flew up, and he said, "First thing you gotta learn, I reckon, is that it's *rude* to talk when I'm talkin', and that I don't mind gettin' rid of people who have the bad manners to cut me off in mid-sentence. Most people are so confused, you know, 'bout life and what's right that it ain't completely wrong to take it from 'em." He paused as a waiter came to the table, topping off his coffee, then drilled his gaze at me. "Now, you ain't one of them people, I kin tell."

"Nossir," I said.

Papa's brow went dark. "You just did it again, Calhoun."

Quietly, biting my lips, I thought, *Sorry!*

"'Bout this debt now." He began working a grain of food from his front teeth with his fingernail. "You know that li'l boardinghouse for cullud folks run by Mrs. Dupree?"

I didn't like where this was leading, and found myself disliking him too, but gave him a nod.

"I own it." His eyes narrowed. "Fact is, I own *her*, and

she tells me you're three months behind in yo' rent. And that li'l moneylender Fenton—you know him?"

I bobbed my head.

"I own him too, so you might as well say I'm the one holdin' the bad paper, promises, and IOUs that you been handin' out like flyers. It comes to mebbe fifty thousand francs, I figure, and we all know a farthing-and-sixpence hoodlum like you can't even afford the down payment on a glass of lemonade." Looking square at me, he shook his head. "If all cullud men was like you, Calhoun, I 'spect the Race would be extinct by now."

Papa offered me a cigar, but my hands trembled so violently that I used four locofocos before the flame took to the end. "Now, a man *should* pay his debts, it seems to me." He placed a finger thoughtfully on one side of his nose and ordered me to sit down. "That's how worldly things work, Calhoun. The Social Wheel, as I unnerstand it after forty years in business for myself, is oiled by debts, each man owing the other somethin' in a kinda web of endless obligations. Normally," he added, "if a man welched on me like you done, he'd find hisself on the riverbottom. But you are truly blessed, Calhoun. I daresay you have divine protection. You are indeed watched over and loved by one of God's very own angels."

This was all news to me. "I am?"

"Uh-huh. That schoolteacher Miss Bailey has saved yo' behind. Out of the goodness of her heart, she has come forward and offered to liquidate yo' debts with her meager savings, provided you agree—as I know you will—to the simple condition of holy matrimony."

"But that's *blackmail!*"

"Yes," said Papa, nodding. "Yes, it is. I'm acquainted with the technique, son."

"She can't do this!" I sat biting my fingers in rage. "It's . . . it's criminal!"

Santos raised his eyebrows. "Look who's talkin'."

"And it's done," said Papa. "Tomorrow you and Miss Bailey will be wed. I *wouldn't* miss that ceremony, if I was you. It would cancel our arrangement, and I'd have to return Miss Bailey's money, and you'd be in debt again." His eyes bent slowly up to me. "You *do* wanna erase yo' debts, don't you?"

"Nossir . . . I mean, yessir!" I eased back off my chair. "But you say the wedding is *tomorrow?*"

"At noon. And I'll be givin' Miss Bailey away. Santos heah will be yo' best man." His factotum grinned. Papa reached his ringed fingers toward my hand and pumped it. "Congratulations, Calhoun. I know you two are gonna be happy together."

For the rest of that day, and most of the night, I had cold shakes and fits of fear-induced hiccuping. Stumbling from the tavern, I felt light-headed, ready to fall, and slapped one hand on the wall outside to steady myself. Isadora came up behind me. She threaded her arm through mine, supporting me as I walked, dazed, toward the waterfront. Yes, I'd underestimated her. She'd wiped my nose with my own handkerchief; with my own bread she'd baked me a tart. "Tell me"—she squeezed my arm—"what you're thinking."

"You are not . . . hic . . . to be *believed*, Isadora!"

"Thank you." She hugged my arm tighter and rested her head on my shoulder. "I'm doing this for your own good, Rutherford."

"The hell you are! I'm *not* getting married! Never!"

"Yes, you are." Her voice was full of finality. "And someday when we are very old, have grandchildren, and you

look back upon this rackety free-lance life you've led from
the advantage of the comfortable home and family we've
built together, you will thank me."

"I will . . . hic . . . *despise* you! Is that what you want?
You're twisting my cullions, but you haven't won my con-
sent!" I grabbed her arms and shook her hard enough to
dislodge her hat and send her hair flying loose from its pins.
"Why are you *doing* this?"

Bareheaded like that, with hair swinging in her eyes, the
change came over Isadora, a collapsing of her lips inward
against her teeth, the blood rising to her cheeks as if I'd suddenly struck her. One by one, she peeled my fingers off her
arms, then stepped away from me, drawing up her shoulders, her hair wilder now than that of a witch.

"Because I love you . . . you fool! . . . and I don't know
what to *do* about it because you don't love *me*! I know that!
I'm not blind, Rutherford." She began gathering hairpins
off the boardwalk, sticking them any which way back into
her head. "It's because I'm not . . . not pretty. No, don't
say it! That *is* why. Because I'm *dark*. You'd rather have a
beautiful, glamorous, light-skinned wife like the women in
the theaters and magazines. It's what all men want, someone they can show off and say to the world, 'See, look what
I'm humping!' But she'd worry you sorely, Rutherford—I
know that—you'd be suspicious of every man who came to
the house, and your friends too, and she'd be vain and lazy
and squander your money on all sorts of foolish things, and
she'd hate having children, or doing housework, or being
at your side when you're sick, but *I* can make you happy!"
We were drawing a crowd, she noticed, and lowered her
voice, sniffling a little as she tried to push her hat back into
shape. "I'd hoped that you'd *learn* to love me the way I love
you . . ."

"Isadora," I struggled. "It's not like that. I *do* love you. It's just that I don't want to marry *anyone* . . ."

"Well, you're getting married tomorrow, or I'm taking back my money." Isadora rammed her hat, hopelessly ruined, down over her ears, her eyes still blazing. "You choose, Rutherford Calhoun, whichever way you like."

And there she left me, standing by the docks in a lather of confusion. Never in my life had anyone loved me so selflessly, as the hag in the Wife of Bath's Tale had loved her fickle knight, but despite this remarkable love, I was not, as I say, ready for marriage. If you must know, I didn't feel *worthy* of her. Her goodness shamed me. I turned into the first pub I found, one frequented by sailors, a darkly lit, rum-smelling room about fourteen feet square, with a well-sanded floor and a lamp that hung within two feet of the tables, stinking of whale oil. The place was packed with seamen. All armed to the eyeballs with pistols and cutlasses, scowling and jabbering like pirates, squirting jets of brown tobacco juice everywhere except in the spittoons—a den of Chinese assassins, scowling Moors, English scoundrels, Yankee adventurers, and evil-looking Arabs. Naturally, I felt pretty much right at home. I sat near the window beside an old mariner in a pair of shag trousers and a red flannel shirt, who was playing with his parrot, an African gray, and drinking hot brandy grog. I ordered a gin twist, then tried to untangle this knot Isadora had tightened around me.

She was as cunning as a Byzantine merchant—that was clear—but I couldn't rightly fault her. She'd known her share of grief, had Isadora. Her mother Viola, she'd told me, died when she was three, which meant that she and her sisters had no one to teach them to think like independent, menless Modern Women—it was something you *learned*, she implied, like learning how to ride a bicycle, or do the backstroke. Certainly her father was no help. Isaiah Bailey was a wifebeater, that's how Viola died, and once she was buried he started punching Isadora and her sisters around on Saturday nights after visiting his still. Yet, miraculously, Isadora had remained innocent. There was no hatred in her. Or selfishness. No vanity, or negativism. Some part of her, perhaps the part she withdrew when Isaiah started whaling on her, remained untouched, a part she fed in the local African Methodist Episcopal Church, and shored up with Scripture: a still, uncorrupted center like the Chinese lotus that, though grown in muck and mud, remained beautifully poised and pure. But shy too. Seeing horses defecate on the street made Isadora blanch. She was constitutionally unable to swear. When she was angry, her lips would form a four-letter word, then freeze, as if she'd been chewing alum. A part of me ached to be with her always, to see that only things of beauty and light came before her. Would marrying her be so bad? That night, a little before dawn, I had a vision of how that union would be in decades to come—eighteen thousand six hundred and ninety-three cups of watery sassafras tea for breakfast, and in each of these I would find cat fur or pigeon feathers. No, it was not a vision to stir a soul that longed for high adventure.

After the gin, five pitchers of beer emptied before me; the sailors thinned out, but still I sat, knowing that each hour brought me closer to the bondage of wedlock. Behind me, I heard first a burp, then the gravelly voice of the now drunken sailor in shag trousers. "Yo-ho, there, young un!" He held up a flagon of grog, his fifth, which he'd only half finished. "Ye can take this, my dear, if you've a mind to. Josiah Squibb's had enough for one night."

"Much obliged . . . Squibb, is it?" I took his flagon in my left hand and his thick, rough hand in my right. "You've put away quite a lot. A man would think you're going to a hanging, friend."

"Worse," said Squibb. "I'm shipping out tomorrow with Captain Ebenezer Falcon. Good as a hangin', that, to hear some men tell it. He's a descendant of Colonel Blood who stole the crown jewels, some say, a buccaneer at heart, and proud of it." Blearily he lit a long-shanked pipe and studied me through eyes too bloodshot, really, to see. "Ye drink a lot y'self, boy. Got problems, have ye?"

"Marriage," I told him. "Tomorrow at noon."

"Blimey!" Squibb sat back, stunned, his chair creaking. "Ye *have* got a problem. Oh, I know about wives all right. Got a couple myself—one in Connecticut, and one in Vermont. That's *why* I ship out. What say I buy yuh a round?"

Josiah Squibb, I learned, had signed on as a cook aboard the *Republic*, a ninety-ton square-rigger that would up-anchor and sail eastward against the prevailing winds to the barracoon, or slave factory, at Bangalang on the Guinea coast, take on a cargo of Africans, and then, God willing, return in three months. "There she be." Squibb stabbed his pipestem toward the window, and the ship he showed me from this distance was strikingly beautiful, a great three-masted, full-rigged bark with a roundtuck hull, grated hatches and bulkheads cut round the deck for circulation. As it turned out, these were the last words from Squibb. Halfway through our last drink, his forehead crashed down upon the table. And his papers . . . ah, these were rolled cylindrically inside his right boot. I thought, *Naw, Calhoun, you can't do that*; but at that selfsame instant I remembered what awaited me at the altar, and I decided most definitely, *Yes, I can.*

"Bad move," said the parrot. "Very bad move."

I said, "Shut up."

Transferring Squibb's papers to my coat, I eased away from the table whilst he snored. "Thief! Thief!" shouted the parrot, but fortunately he could not shatter the cook's heavy-headed sleep. I slipped outside into a shock of cool air and ran down the pier to a cluster of small boats rocking lazily to and fro on the water. I unfastened the rope to one, paddled out toward the *Republic*, then hauled myself hand over hand up a rope ladder to the topgallant bulwark, and over onto a broad empty deck. The crew had not come aboard yet. Standing aft, looking back at the glittering lights ashore, I had an odd sensation, difficult to explain, that I'd boarded not a ship but a kind of fantastic, floating Black Maria, a wooden sepulcher whose timbers moaned with the memory of too many runs of black gold between the New World and the Old; moaned, I say again, because the ship—with its tiered compartments and galleys, like a crazy-quilt house built by a hundred carpenters, each with a different plan—felt conscious and disapprovingly aware of my presence when I pulled back the canvas on a flat-bottomed launch and laid myself down in its hull, which was long and narrow, both hands crossed on my chest. And then waves lapping below the ship gently swung me left then right as in a hammock, sinking me like a fish, or a stone, farther down through leagues of darkness, and mercifully to sleep.

Entry, the second [22]
JUNE 20, 1830

It wasn't the *Republic* sailing east for the Gulf of Guinea, skimming along easily in a six-knot breeze, that awoke me (I've been known to sleep through gunshots and tavern brawls), or even the chatter of Captain Falcon's flea-infested, foul-tongued crew, but rather the cold barrel of a pistol shoved under my shirt and against my belly by Peter Cringle, the first mate and quartermaster, that brought me back to full consciousness from the deepest sleep I'd known in years. An hour out of port, Cringle had thrown back the tarp fashioned from old sail, uncovering me, and I stared up— my mouth and eyes partly sealed and phlegmed by sleep—at a silvery-gray sky aswirl with honking sea gulls, the elaborate webbing of the foremast entangled with low-bellying clouds, and the faces of five men you'd hardly care to stumble upon during an evening stroll: black eyepatches, I saw, beards like tangled bushes, hooks where hands should be—I speak the truth—and they had, like the monocular witches outwitted by Perseus, only two good teeth among them all. "A black stowaway, is he now, Mr. Cringle?" said one, whose mouth could have doubled for the Black Hole of Calcutta. "Let us 'ave him, sir. We'll throw the blighter overboard and save you the powder—we wouldn't want you exertin' yerself too much, y'know, you bein' first mate and all."

Laughter exploded round me, but the mate's expression did not change.

"On your feet, you," Cringle ordered, and I obeyed because of all the faces present his seemed the most sympathetic. In other words, his was the only one not pitted by smallpox, split by Saturday night knifescar, disfigured by Polynesian tattoos, or distorted by dropsy. Indeed, First Mate Cringle's whole air spoke of New England gentility. He was tall and straight as a ship's door, a gentleman from his unwrinkled shirt right down to the spit-polished boots that reflected back winces and deadeyes on deck. His skin was as white as wax, which made him seem like nothing less than a tightly wound toy soldier. "You've less than a minute," said he, shaking with rage, or more like fear, "to explain what you're doing aboard this ship."

Quickly I pulled Squibb's papers from my waistcoat, unfolded them, then thrust them toward him. "I didn't mean to be asleep, sir," I said, maneuvering. "I'm ready now to report for work."

Cringle frowned irritably down the first page. The other sailors, that blustering, braying gang of tormentors, looked over his shoulder like an infernal chorus and seemed to enjoy the agitation my discovery brought him; they watched him more closely than they watched me, elbowing each other and winking, like bullies having fun at the expense of a new boy—a sissy in short pants—at school. Above us birds veered, then vanished into diaphanous layers of mist high as the mizzenpole. The deck was silent, so quiet I could hear blood hammering in my ears and the hungry gurgle of gastric fluids in my belly. At length Cringle shut his eyes. He crumpled the papers in his fist.

"Josiah Squibb is down *below*, you bloody impostor!"

"Oh." My breath stopped. "Odd coincidence, that. Imagine! Two of us with the same na—" He leveled the firelock straight at my forehead, but less to frighten me, I thought, than to make a point with the others. "Sir, my name isn't Squibb. You've guessed that already? Uh, right. It's Rutherford Calhoun, and I only came aboard to return these papers to—"

"Hold your tongue." He faced around to the others. "And stop your row, all of you, and get back to work. I can handle this myself."

Under Cringle's stare the crew turned back, laughing less at me than at the mate, to their business—belaying sheets and halyards—and Cringle's bunched shoulders lowered a little. He put away his pistol, wiped his forehead with his sleeve, whispered, "Hoodlums, every one of them," then shoved me toward Captain Falcon's cabin. "It's the Devil, I do believe, that sends us the bloody flux, contrary winds, and rumpots like these!" We passed small pens of chickens and Berkshire pigs the captain kept on board for himself, but as we neared the cabin door my stomach dropped. I felt uneasy in my spine. Sweat began to stream into my clothes. The deck beneath me dipped and rose dizzily, and with that motion my center of gravity was instantly gone. My last meal, too, over the railing, which I ran to and gripped with all my strength as the ship—or so my confused inner ear told me—careened left. "Now, that's a pretty sight. And you say you're a sailor, eh? I think you're a farmer, Calhoun."

Between heaves, I said, "Illinois!"

A softening and a sort of pity came into Cringle's voice. He withdrew his handkerchief, handed it to me, then watched as my belly turned inside out, like a shirt cuff. "But you'll feel a lot worse if the skipper's in a mood for cobbing. What on earth prompted you to stow away on a ship run by Ebenezer Falcon?"

"Debts," I said, my eyes still swimming. "A woman. Maybe a jail sentence, or . . ."

Cringle smiled, and from out of his flash of even white teeth there flowered the relaxed, boyish grin, it struck me, of a young Presbyterian minister, or someone who'd grown up with a great deal of wealth, privileges, or personal gifts, and felt guilty about them in the presence of those who hadn't: a man who'd maybe been a concert pianist at age five, or at twelve entered Harvard, or at fifteen solved some theoretical enigma in physics that had puzzled scientists twice his age, and who never spoke of these things without a touch of endearing humiliation because he hated not to be "regular," yet who, it was clear, carried a core of aloneness within him that nothing on shore could touch. Cringle had, I was to learn, an almost psychotic total recall of everything he'd read. Had he been a woman—he certainly had a feminine air—he'd be the kind who could do Leibnizian logic or Ptolemaic astronomy but hid the fact in order not to frighten off suitors; or, if a slave, one who could bend spoons with his mind but didn't so white people wouldn't get panicky.

"Half the crew's here for those reasons, or some other social failure on shore," he laughed. "But I'll tell you true: Jail's better. Being on a ship *is* being in jail with the chance of being drowned to boot."

"I can't go back . . ."

"None of us can. Come along. Maybe the captain can use someone in the galley. Can you cook?"

"Yes."

"Liar," said he. "Doesn't matter, though. We've all gotten used to the taste of maggots in everything."

At the captain's door, which had three bullet holes in it, Cringle tried the latch. It was unbolted, but he decided against barging in and rapped instead, and a good thing this was, because from within the cabin, whose curtained windows were pulled shut, I heard the squeaking of mattress springs, then a stifled whimper, and at last a venereal moan so odd in its commingling of pleasure and complaint that I had, of a sudden, the vision of being not aboard ship but instead in a bordello. It made no sense then, those Venusian groans, that gasping yip of orgasmic stings, but soon enough it would. "Has he a woman aboard?" I looked to Cringle for an answer, but the mate wouldn't look me in the eye; he chewed the inside of his cheek and politely pulled the door shut. "Didn't I say this was worse than prison?" For another minute we stood waiting, looking at the door, at each other, and finally it opened and a heartbreakingly handsome cabin boy, with curly hair like wood shavings, young but hardly in long pants (and barely in these, for he was pulling up his striped duck pantaloons, tripping on the cuffs), came scrambling out, closing the door behind him, his jerkin unfastened, his face drained of color, and eyes crossed by what he'd been through.

"Good day to you, Mr. Cringle." He kept his eyes low.

Cringle rubbed his face with one hand, peeking at the boy through his fingers.

"Are you and the captain finished, Tom?"

"Yessir. . . . I'm sorry, sir, you can go in now."

The mate forced a smile that must have been harder to lift than a sledgehammer, looking down at the boy as you might a younger brother (or sister) you'd just glimpsed in a stranger's set of pornographic pictures, pained by his shivering and rubbing his arms and standing bowlegged as if his bum was cemented shut by dried semen, as it probably was. Cringle tousled the boy's hair, his lips tight, and moved Tom aside. "Tell Squibb"—his voice quivered—"I said he's to fix you the finest meal he can, Tom." And then to me: "Of course, you'll say nothing of this to anyone."

"Of course," I said.

"It would not help morale, if the men knew . . ."

"I've seen nothing," I said, "but I wonder: Is my silence worth a word in my favor with the captain?"

His fingertips pushed the door inward. "Just go inside, Calhoun." Ducking my head, I stepped down into a low-studded room, aware of Cringle's breath and bodily warmth behind me, but of little else, for the cabin of Captain Falcon had the dank, ancient dampness of old ships, or a cave—that, and the clamlike, bacterial odor of tabooed pleasures. The air was denser inside, difficult for my throat-pipes to draw. To my left, a small voice, like that of a genie in a jug, said, "Draw the curtains a bit, Mr. Cringle," and when the mate did so, suddenly raying the room with bright light, a high-post bedstead with valances and knotted with dirty sheets sprang forth in the glare. Now I was rivering sweat. From the ceiling a pyramid-shaped poop lantern with horn windows swung low enough to crack your head, and to the right of that were a washbasin and clawfooted bathtub bolted to the floorboards—perhaps the only other landside luxury in the room. Across from these was a cluttered chart table. Seated at this, with his back to me, a big-shouldered man was barricaded in by maps of the sea and the African bush. On his table lay a gilded, ornamental Bible, a quadrant, chronometer, spyglass, and the log in which I now write (but this months later after mutiny and death, the reporting on which I must put off for a while). He kept to his business, refusing to turn, and said in that shocking voice thin and shrill and strung like catgut, "All right, stand at ease and state yer business."

Cringle cleared his throat, coughing into one hand.

"We found this boy in the longboat, Skipper. He says he's Rutherford Calhoun, a friend of Squibb. I thought perhaps—"

"You've rung the bell to change watch?"

The mate paused. "I was about to when I discovered th—"

"See to it, then. And shut the door behind you."

The mate left, glancing helplessly at me. Standing alone, looking at the back of Captain Falcon's sloping head, shining my boots on the back of my breeches to polish them, I thought that maybe racial savvy might see me through this interview. Maybe I shouldn't say this, but we all know it anyway: namely, that a crafty Negro, a shrewd black strategist, can work a prospective white employer around, if he's smart, by playing poor mouth, or greasing his guilt with a hard-luck story. At least it had always worked for me before. In my most plaintive voice I told the captain how desperate I was for work, that I'd stowed away because gainful employment was systematically denied black men back home, that New Orleans was so bigoted a Negro couldn't even buy vanilla ice cream.

"So?" said Falcon.

I told him about my mother's death from overwork in the fields of Illinois when I was three. (She died in bed, actually, but I could trade on this version and liked it better.)

"So?"

And then I related the hardships I'd received at the hands of my religiously stern master, Peleg Chandler, who gave all his slaves two teaspoons of castor oil *every* Saturday morning, whether they were sick or not, and called that "preventative medicine." (It may not seem like much to you, but to me, at age twelve, it was torture.)

"So?" he said again, this time swiveling full around to

face me, his elbows splashed on the leather arms of the chair, and as his gaze crossed mine in the crepuscular cabin light, as I saw his face, I felt skin at the nape of my neck tingling like when a marksman has you in his sights, because the master of the *Republic*, the man known for his daring exploits and subjugation of the colored races from Africa to the West Indies, was a *dwarf.* Well, perhaps not a true dwarf, but Ebenezer Falcon, I saw, was shorter even than the poor, buggered cabin boy Tom. Though his legs measured less than those of his chart table, Captain Falcon had a shoulder span like that of Santos, and between this knot of monstrously developed deltoids and latissimus dorsi a long head rose with an explosion of hair so black his face seemed dead in contrast: eye sockets like anthracite furnaces, medieval lines more complex than tracery on his maps, a nose slightly to one side, and a great bulging forehead that looked harder than whalebone, but intelligent too—a thinker's brow, it was, the kind fantasy writers put on spacemen far ahead of us in science and philosophy. His belly was unspeakable. His hands, like roots. More remarkable, I'd seen drawings of this gnarled little man's face before in newspapers in New Orleans, though I never paid them much attention, or noted the name. He was famous. In point of fact, infamous. That special breed of empire builder, explorer, and imperialist that sculptors loved to elongate, El Greco–like, in city park statues until they achieved Brobdingnagian proportions. He carried, I read, portraits of Pizarro and Magellan on every expedition he made.

Now . . . yes, now I remembered those stories well. Falcon, the papers said, knew seven African coastal dialects and, in fact, could learn any new tongue in two weeks' time. More, even, he'd proven it with Hottentot, and lived among their tribe for a month, plundering their most sacred religious shrines. He'd gone hunting for the source of the Nile, failed, but even his miscarried exploits made him raw material for myths spun in brandy and cavendish smoke in clubs along the eastern seaboard. He'd translated the *Bardo Thodol*—this, after stealing the only scroll from a remote temple in Tibet—and if the papers can be believed, he was a patriot whose burning passion was the manifest destiny of the United States to Americanize the entire planet. Really, I wanted to take off my hat in his presence, but I hadn't worn one. Never mind that his sins were scarlet. He was living history. Of course, he stood only as high as my hips, and I had to fight the urge to pat him on his head, but I was, as I say, impressed.

"Sit," said he, motioning to the chair at his chart table. "I don't like people looking down at me."

I could understand that; I sat.

Falcon toddled over to his washbasin, poured water from a bucket half his size, and began to sponge-bathe under his nightshirt, speaking over his left shoulder at me. "And, generally speaking, I don't like Negroes either."

"Sorry, sir." He was frank; I liked that. With bigots a man knew where he stood. "But I can't help that, sir."

Falcon half-turned, his eyebrows lifting.

"I *know* you can't, Calhoun. It's one of the things I learned about Negroes after living with the Lotophagi on the African coast. You don't think too well, or too often. I don't blame you for stowing aboard." He squeezed out his sponge. "Poor creature, you probably thought we were a riverboat, didn't you?"

I fell back against the seat. "This *isn't* a riverboat?"

"I thought so." Falcon wet his hands, then finger-combed his hair, shook off the water, and carried his basin to the door, throwing it out on a man who began cursing like . . . well, like a sailor until he saw the captain's face, and meekly tipped his hat. Slamming the door, Falcon fixed me again with both eyes. "'Tis a *slaver*, Mr. Calhoun, and the cargo awaiting us at Bangalang is forty Allmuseri tribesmen, hides, prime ivory teeth, gold, and bullocks, which comes to a total caravan value of nearly nine thousand dollars, of which the officers and I have a profitable share—quite enough to let me retire after this run or finance an expedition I have in mind to Tortuga or, if I've a mind, see my share tripled at the gaming tables of Franscatis in Paris. But if you sail with us to Guinea—that is, if I don't decide to nail your feet to the floor—it will have to be without pay. Do you see that, Calhoun?"

"Yessir." I nodded. "Thank you, sir."

"Good." After toweling his hands, he took a shirt with frills down the front and a pair of pantaloons from a chest by the door. "I don't hold it against you for being here. Or for being black, but I believe in *excellence*—an unfashionable thing these days, I know, what with headmasters giving illiterate Negroes degrees because they feel too guilty to fail them, then employers giving that same boy a place in the firm since he's got the degree in hand and saying no will bring a gang of Abolitionists down on their necks. But no"—he looked pained—"not on my ship, Mr. Calhoun. Eighty percent of the crews on other ships, damn near anywhere in America, are *incompetent*, and all because everyone's ready to lower standards of excellence to make up for slavery, or discrimination, and the problem . . . the *problem*, Mr. Calhoun, is, I say, that most of these minorities aren't ready for the titles of quartermaster or first mate precisely because discrimination denied them the training that makes for true excellence—ready to be mediocre mates, I'll grant you that, or middlebrow functionaries, or run-of-the-mill employees, but not to *advance* the position, or make a lasting breakthrough of any kind. O, 'tis a scandal on the ships I've seen, and hardly the fault of the poor, half-trained Negro who hungers like anyone else these days for the glamour of titles and position." He was grimly quiet for a second, lost in thought, and though it troubles me to tell you this, I almost saw his point, yet only for an instant, for what he said next was enough to straighten a sane man's hair. "Now that I think of it, you remind me of a colored cabin boy named Fortunata who was aboard on my first trip to Madagascar."

"He's aboard now?"

"Hell, no . . . Christ, no." Falcon's brows slammed together. "We ate him."

Slowly I sat forward in my chair. "Sir?"

"Don't look at me like that. I believe in Christian decency and doing right as much as the next man. I have a family, you know, in Virginia, and the man-eating savages I've seen, who make it a practice, disgust me. But there's not a civilized law that holds water"—Falcon's smile flickered briefly—"once you've put to sea." He held the slow, hurt, sidelong look he'd given me, then began finger-stuffing his nightshirt into breeches that might have been tailored for a child. "We ran into a Spanish galleon and sank her, thank God—we'd have swung for smuggling if we hadn't—but she left us damaged and with half the crew dead. The foremast was gone, the main yard sprung, and our rigging hung in elflocks. 'Twas an awful fight, I tell you, and we drifted for days without food or fresh water." Falcon squirreled closer to me, his eyes brighter, wilder than I had yet seen them. "The sea does things to your head, Calhoun, terrible unravelings of belief that aren't in a cultured man's metaphysic. We ate tallow first, then sawdust, stopped up our noses and slurped foul water from the pumps before barbecuing that Negro boy." Falcon added—sadly, I thought,

"He was freshly dead, of course, crushed by a falling mast. He tasted . . . stringy."

Shivering, I rubbed my arms, wondering if just maybe the crew list for this voyage and the menu might be the same thing for this man. "I'm sorry."

"So was I."

It was silent then, Captain Falcon peering back into his memory of deep-sea cannibalism, a faintly bitter smile twisting his lips and jaw to one side, and I saw something— or thought I did—of myself in him and hated that. Cannibalism at sea was common enough, I knew, but he *enjoyed* telling this tale—enjoyed, as I did, any experience that disrupted the fragile, artificial pattern of life on land. Once at home, I realized, he would probably boast of his "experiences" at sea, use them to pull rank on those more timid and less vital than himself, interrupting a dinner with his wife's parson—some psalm-singing milquetoast—to say, "I've no taste for chicken dumplings tonight after eating cabin boy, dear," and they would be forced to look at him in both horror and fascination; yes, this above all else did Captain Falcon and his species of world conquerors thrive upon: the desire to be fascinating objects in the eyes of others.

Even then, as he quietly reflected and paced, tapping the end of his nose, he sneaked a look at me to see with how much reverence or revulsion—it didn't matter either way since both fed the ego—I regarded him. More of the latter, I daresay, but for a man like this—who was so full of himself that he could not speak slowly or without collapsing one sentence into another, the words spilling out in a rush of brilliant confusion—for an American empire builder even my revulsion was enough to make him feel singular, special, unique.

"Have that mama's boy Mr. Cringle find you a hammock," said he, "and tell Squibb to put you to work in the kitchen. You'll be his shifter and keep the coppers supplied with water and clean. You won't turn a guinea on this trip, Calhoun, but I'll wager you'll be a man's man when we dock again in New Orleans."

"Thank you, sir." I extended my hand. "Like you, sir?"

"Like me?" It seemed to startle him. "Don't be silly." He barely touched my palm with his fingers. "No, never like me, Calhoun."

That was reassuring to me, though he would never realize it. I turned and walked slowly to where Cringle stood on watch, for I was still very weak in the knees, and my stomach had not stabilized either, continuing to chew upon itself as the mate led me through a hatchway on the main deck, then farther down, well below the ship's waterline, to a soggy pit that assaulted my senses with the odor of old piss riding on the air beside the sickly-sweet stench of decaying timbers. This wet cavity had a name: the orlop, an ammonia-smelling hold with little light and less air, where hammocks swung from mildewed beams and where cargo—sea chests and cable—was stored. He gave me a footlocker and gear, and showed me how to fashion a hammock from sailcloth, but seeing these berths I felt sicker than before. Isadora's cat-ridden rooms were intolerable, no question of that, but in the *Republic*'s orlop only an inch of plank separated my boots from the bottom of the sea. "It's bloody dangerous below," Cringle said, and you didn't need a degree in maritime science to see why.

Down there, in the leaking, wishbone-shaped hull, the fusty hold looked darker than the belly of Jonah's whale; it was divided into a maze of low, layered compartments much like the cross section of an archaeological dig—level upon level of crawl spaces, galleys, and cramped cells so small we barely had enough room to turn around—and, once the forge was going, the forecastle cookroom, where I was to work, was hotter than the griddles of Hell. Cockroaches I saw everywhere. And rats. All this, however, was like a hotel suite when compared to the head. It consisted of twelve splintery boards in the bows—a shipboard *pissoir* impossible to use in a rough sea because the foul, malarial soup of human feces from intestines twisted by flux flew up round your feet and splattered overhead when the ship met a head sea. "Either this," Cringle said, keeping his mouth covered with one hand, "or swing your black arse over the side, as the skipper and I do." His eyes watering, he motioned me to climb back up. "After a month that side of the ship's so rank the authorities at Bangalang make us clean it before we can put to port."

All in all, she was a typical ship, I learned those first few days from Cringle, and by this he meant she was stinking and wet, with sea scurvy and god-awful diseases rampant; but even queerer than all this—strange to me, at least—the *Republic* was physically unstable. She was perpetually flying apart and re-forming during the voyage, falling to pieces beneath us, the great sails ripping to rags in high winds, the rot, cracks, and parasites in old wood so cancerously swift, springing up where least expected, that Captain Falcon's crew spent most of their time literally rebuilding the *Republic* as we crawled along the waves. In a word, she was, from stem to stern, a process. She would not be, Cringle warned me, the same vessel that left New Orleans, it not being in the nature of any ship to remain the same on that thrashing Void called the Atlantic. (Also called the Ethiopic Ocean by some, owing to the trade.) And a seaman's first duty was to keep her afloat at any cost.

His second duty was to stay drunk. Every man "knew

the ropes"—specifically, the sheets and halyards that controlled the sails; each knew the ship's parts and principles, and any one of them, from the boatswain's mate to the cabin boy Tom, could undertake the various duties involved— to hand, reef, or steer—but only a fool would stay sober when he wasn't on watch. The whole Middle Passage, you might say, was one long hangover. It had the character of a four-month binge. And the biggest sot of all, I discovered, the most pitiful rumpot, was Josiah Squibb. Stepping timidly into the grimy cookroom after Cringle left me, my arms over my head in case Squibb pegged something at me for stealing his papers, I found the adjacent spirit room open and Squibb as polluted as I'd left him in the tavern. The poor devil's head lay on a long table littered with strips of salt pork and bricklike biscuits double-baked back on shore. His parrot was drunk too, but his voice was not as faint as Squibb's, who was in that advanced stage of alcoholic stupor that severs mind from body, both his eyeballs large as eggs, and glaring blankly into a mug of warm beer, as drunks often do, talking to his reflection. "Josiah," he sniffed. Then answered: "Yes?" "If yuh wants respect, darlin', yuh got to leave the ruddy cup alone, yes yuh do. Yuh wants 'em to respect yuh now, don't yuh?" "Yes," he said, "yes, I do. . . ."

"'H'lo?" I stepped closer. "Mr. Squibb, are you all right, sir?"

"Do I *look* all right?" He sat scratching under one arm, squinting to see me more clearly. "I'm a wee bit drunk with dinner to fix, and so help me I can't *do* it!" The movement of looking up tipped him backward (the ship veering larboard didn't help either), and I was obliged to catch him under his armpits, then pitch him forward. He let his head hang. "Fix me some blackstrap, will ye, then finish up this mess."

"But I've never—"

"*Do* it." Squibb filled his cheeks with wind, then he swallowed. "I'll show ye how."

Following his orders, I helped him prepare mess, and mess it was, for the biscuits were hard and full of weevils ("I left two teeth in one of 'em this morning," said Squibb), the salt beef tasted of the barrel in which it had been packed, not being helped very much by the onions and peppers I added, and would have been intolerable if not for the beer—each crewman, he said, consumed a gallon a day, but in Squibb's case it was more like three. He was, had been, an alcoholic since his first voyage at the age of eleven, though he wasn't exactly certain of his age, and precious little else when he was pickled, which was every waking hour, as it turned out. His lips kept the set smile of a lush. There was no risk in his recognizing me from the tavern; he had trouble keeping track of my identity from one hour to the next. And, sad to say, this was probably Squibb's last voyage. Only a slaver would have him. His right foot was dead. He'd drunkenly stepped off a mizzentop during his last trip, having forgotten where he was, fallen twenty feet, and miraculously landed on his right foot. Which shattered. Where bone had been, Squibb now had a metal rod. He limped, of course. Like most fat people he wore his shirt outside his trousers whenever possible. He was slow, useless except in the cookroom, with lumps and udders in his face from liquor; a liability at sea, but what sailor could not see in Josiah Squibb his own portrait in years to come if Providence turned her back? As for his parrot, he was more or less the cook's shadow, having his bawdy humor, and even asked me occasionally, "You had any lately, mate?"

"Aye," said Squibb, sipping blackstrap as I slopped salmagundi into buckets to haul to the great cabin. "I've *seen* some things, laddie. Reason I look so bad is 'cause I've been livin'."

That made me pause in the doorway. Like Captain Falcon, like me and so many other people (except Isadora), he seemed to hunger for "experience" as the bourgeois Creoles desired possessions. Believing ourselves better than that, too refined to crave gross, physical things, we heaped and hived "experiences" instead, as Madame Toulouse filled her rooms with imported furniture, as if *life* was a commodity, a *thing* we could cram into ourselves. I was tempted to ask about his "experiences," to have him share and display them before me like show-and-tell at school. Instead, I asked:

"Was it worth it?"

He flinched. "How do you mean?"

"Are you a better man for all that fast living?"

Squibb stared at me, growing sober now. "Yer a strange one, Illinois. Naw, darlin', I can't say better." He laughed suddenly, but with little humor. "Ask my wives—all five of 'em—and they'd probably say I'm worse for it."

"Five, is it now?"

"Or six." Squibb shrugged. "I lose count. I gets drunk, ye know, and I forgets I'm married, and a woman comes along, and before I knows it I've proposed again, and do ye know what's odd? I keeps fallin' in love with the same kinda woman ovah and ovah again. They all look like my wife Maud—God rest her—when we first met. She was a pretty li'l thing. She ruined me, ye know. Spoiled me. I mean, Maud didn't even mind when I broke wind under the bedsheets: you *know* that's love, darlin'. She had long, dark hair, a waist no bigger than that"—he snapped his fingers—"and eyes dark as wine—they all do. They could be her sisters, for all the diff'rence, and damned if I don't slip sometimes 'n' call 'em by the pet name I give her—Stinky." He sighed, perplexed, and rapped his temples with the heel of his palm, as if to shake his brain back in place. "Ain't the quantity of experiences that count I sometimes think, Illinois, but the quality. It's sorta like I keep lookin' for Stinky when she was seventeen so I kin do right by her this time."

I left him still mumbling into his cup, and Squibb, I'm sure, didn't notice my absence for an hour. But what he'd said stuck to me like a barnacle. It seemed so Sisyphean, this endless seeking of a single woman's love—the vision of the first girl who snared his heart—in all others, because they would change, grow old, and he'd again be on a quixotic, Parmenidean quest for beauty beyond the reach of Becoming. Yet he seemed ironically faithful too, despite his several wives, his devotion to Stinky as deep as any monk's for the Virgin. A peculiar man, this Josiah Squibb, I thought, though really no stranger than the others in Captain Falcon's ragtag crew. We were forty of a company. And we'd all blundered, failed at bourgeois life in one way or another—we were, to tell the truth, all refugees from responsibility and, like social misfits ever pushing westward to escape citified life, took to the sea as the last frontier that welcomed miscreants, dreamers, and fools. Only one sailor the mate warned me to stay away from, a dark, clean-shaven fellow, with thin brown hair and the air of a parson about him. Cringle pointed him out to me as he tied deadeyes down the deck from where we stood. "That'll be Nathaniel Meadows," whispered Cringle, "and I'd not cross him, if I were you."

I turned to give him a better look; Cringle swung me around.

"Don't *stare* at him, fool!"

"He doesn't look dangerous," I said.

"Then," said he, "your judgment of character is worse than your cooking. Meadows signed on to escape the authorities in Liverpool. He murdered his whole family while they slept, according to the skipper. Axed them all. The family dog, two cows, and a goat too."

I tried to swallow. Failed. "Why?"

"D'ye care to stroll up 'n' ask him?"

"Oh, no . . . wouldn't think of prying. Hardly my business, you know, that sort of thing . . ."

The mate smiled. "Smart boy."

Slowly, I gained my sea legs. By and by, I learned to keep down my dinner and keep up my end in the cookroom and on deck with this crew of American degenerates and dregs; but there's little point in describing individually the other men on board, for the voyage to Africa was uneventful, the men on ship capable at their specialties, and not one of them would live to see New Orleans again.

Only Cringle, I suppose, sensed what was coming. He had a sixth sense about disaster. Ankle-deep in deckwash, he'd stand by the bowsprit some nights in the light of a single lantern, wearing a woolen fearnought to blunt the teeth of the wind, and stare. Just stare. The fact is that Cringle, more than all the others, was out of place: an officer by accident, I would learn, whose precise speech the crew saw as pomposity, whose sensitivity Captain Falcon read as weakness. The *Republic* was, above all else, a ship of *men*. Without the civilizing presence of women, everyone felt the pressure, the masculine imperative to prove himself equal to a vague standard of manliness in order to be judged "regular." To fail at this in the eyes of the other men could, I needn't tell you, make your life at sea quite miserable. It led to posturing among the crew, a tendency to turn themselves into caricatures of the concept of maleness: to strut, keep their chests stuck out and stomachs sucked in, and talk monosyllabically in surly mumbles or grunts because being good at language was womanly. Lord knows, this front was hard to maintain for very long. You had to *work* at being manly; it took more effort, in a way, than rigging sails. The crewmen had drinking contests nearly every day. They gambled on who could piss the farthest over the rail, or on whose uncircumcised schlong was the longest, and far into the night lie awake in their hammocks swapping jokes about nuns sitting on candles. (And some of these, I must confess, weren't all that bad, even memorable, such as one Squibb told one night.

Q: What's the difference between a dog and a fox?

A: About four drinks.)

But Cringle kept his distance; the competition to prove the purity of one's gender, I'm guessing, made him uncomfortable, even melancholy, and this cost him the respect of the others, who claimed the mate, at age twenty-nine, was a virgin. Little wonder then that he was relaxed only when alone, there on watch, or reading, or talking with me once he learned that I'd grown up in the household of a (Thomist) theologian.

"They can't feel it," he said the night before we sighted land, looking back from the rail to where two men were carousing around a lantern. His gaze drifted from me back toward row after row of white-maned, foamy waves. That night the sea was full of explosions, rumblings deep as the earth tremors I'd learned to fear in southern Illinois, like the Devil knocking on the ground's thin crust. "Three quarters of the world's surface," said Cringle, "is covered by that formless Naught, and I dislike it, Calhoun, being hemmed in by Nothing, this bottomless chaos breeding all manner of monstrosities and creatures that defy civilized law. These waters are littered with wrecked vessels. And I've seen monsters, oh, yes, such things are real down there." He laughed bleakly. "Down there, reality fits more the dreams of slugs and snakes than men. 'Tis frightening to me sometimes," he added, looking from me to his feet, "that all our reasoning and works are so provisional, so damned fragile, and someday we pass away like the stain of breath on a mirror and sink back into *that* from whence we've come." He fumbled through his pockets for his pipe, then puffed hard to get it going. "They skim along the surface, the others; they have no feeling for what the sea *is*." He gave a slow, Byronic sigh. "Sometimes I envy them for their stupidity."

When he talked like this he frightened me. I wondered if the others were right about his being weak, or enfeebled somehow, and I hardly knew how to reply. "We'll be on land soon enough. I heard Squibb say we'd put to at the factory within the week."

The mate smiled gently as if I'd said something stupid. "We're taking on Allmuseri tribesmen, Calhoun. Not Ashanti. Nor even Kru or Hausa—them, at least, I can understand. Have you ever seen an Allmuseri?"

I had to admit that I had not.

"Don't feel bad." His smile vanished. "Few men have. Arab traders will bring them from the interior, I'm told, because no European has been to their village and lived to tell of it. They are an old people. Older, some say, than the !Kung Tribe of Southern Africa, people who existed when the planet—the galaxy, even—was a ball of fire and steam. And not like us at all. No, not like you either, though you are black. In all the records there is but one sentence about these Allmuseri, and that from a Spanish explorer named Rafael García, whose home is now an institution for the incurably insane in Havana." He was silent again, biting down hard on the stem of his pipe. "I do not feel good about this cargo, Calhoun."

"That sentence," I asked him. "What did García say?"

Cringle stared back to the sea, leaning on the rail, his voice blurred, then obliterated by the wind; I had to strain to hear him. "Sorcerers!" he said. "They're a whole tribe—men, women, and tykes—of devil-worshiping, spell-casting wizards."

Entry, the third
JUNE 23, 1830

Forty-one days after leaving New Orleans, we coasted in
on calm waters, a breeze at our backs, and the skipper set
all hands to unmooring the ship, bringing her slowly like a
hearse to anchorage alongside the trading post at Bangalang.
It was a rowdy fort, all right. Cringle told me the barracoons
were built by the Royal African Company in 1683—one of
several well-fortified western forts always endangered by
hostile, headhunting natives nearby, by competing merchants, and over two centuries residents at the fort had
fought first the Dutch, then the French for control of Negro
slaves. Lately, it had fallen into the soft, uncallused hands of
Owen Bogha, the halfbreed son of a brutal slave trader from
Liverpool and the black princess of a small tribe on the Rio
Pongo. He was a sensualist. A powdered fop and Anglophile
who dyed his chest and pubic hairs blond and, as did other
men of the day plagued by head lice big as beans, shaved
his pate and wore perfumed wigs. Educated in England, this
man Bogha, who greatly enjoyed wealth and the same gaming tables played by Captain Falcon in Paris, returned to
take advantage of his father's property and mother's pres-
tige in Bangalang, overseeing from his great hilltop home
the many warehouses, bazaars, harems, and Moslem car-
avans that crawled from the interior during the Dry Sea-

son. The skipper stayed at his home most nights, consuming stuffed fish and raisin wine, and giving Bogha news of "civilization" back in England and America—he was starving for news, claimed Bogha, in this filthy, Godforsaken hole. And Cringle, being an officer, was invited too, but said he couldn't abide flesh merchants; in fact, he abhorred everything about Bangalang, and slept instead with the rest of the crew on deck in the open air to escape the heat below.

As for myself, I was simply glad to be ashore. It had been unsettling and claustrophobic, out there with the ship cleaving waves the color of root medicine, soughing wind that broke the spider-web tracery of rigging like thread, and the sky and sea blurred together into a pewter gray gloom without a stitch, without outlines, without a bottom to their depths, and sometimes, when we could not see the horizon and sailed through endless fog and shifting mist, I'd felt such dizzying entrapment—of being deprived of such basic directions as left and right, up and down—that I screamed myself awake some nights, choking on the rank male sweat that hung around my hammock like wet clothing. I ached from cleaning pots in the cookroom, and I'd grown tired of my clothes being so perpetually wet from deckwash, the slap of rainwind, and leaks in the orlop that once I had the feeling that the toes on my left foot were webbed. On top of that, Cringle had shouted at me so often for being slow, or asleep during my watch, that I could tell you which of his teeth had been worked on in Boston or Philadelphia, pulled in another city or by a dentist in New Orleans. I wished in vain for dry breeches, floorboards that didn't move, a bowl of warm milk at bedtime, and sometimes—aye—for Isadora. Worse, I kept a light cold, and my incessant coughing gave me headaches. Even so, I could not join the others in their banter after we lowered anchor, or even drink with much gusto—stale beer gave me the johnnytrots—but simply lie quietly in my bunk, wondering if in a single fantastic evening I had become Captain Ebenezer Falcon's shipboard bride.

I could express this fear to no one, and I beg you to keep it to yourself. His courtship of me, for so it must be called, began the night Falcon caught me rummaging through his cabin. This was not an easy situation to explain away. Especially after what I learned from his papers, ledgers, and journal. Somehow I'd miscalculated. According to his schedule, the skipper should have been at the fort all evening, unloading four skiffs freighted with clothing and beads, liquor, and utensils of brass and pewter for the notorious Arab trader Ahman-de-Bellah, whose first caravan of captured Negroes from eight, maybe nine tribes, was herded into Bangalang a few hours before. Falcon's curtains were drawn. His door was padlocked. Of course that presented no problem for me.

Slipping away from my watch and into his room, easing his door shut with my fingertips, I felt the change come over me, a familiar, sensual tingle that came whenever I broke into someone's home, as if I were slipping inside another's soul. Everything must be done slowly, deliberately, first the breath coming deep from the belly, easily, as if the room itself were breathing, limbs light like hollow reeds, free of tension, all parts of me flowing as a single piece, for I had learned in Louisiana that in balletlike movements there could be no error of the body, no elbows cracking into chair arms in a stranger's space to give me away. Theft, if the truth be told, was the closest thing I knew to transcendence. Even better, it broke the power of the propertied class, which pleased me. As a boy I'd never had enough of anything. Yes, my brother Jackson and I lived close to our master, but on the Makanda farm during the leaner years, life was, as old bond-

women put it, "too little too late." At suppertime: watery
soup and the worst part of the hog and so little of that that
Jackson often skipped meals secretly so I could have a little
bit more. If you have never been hungry, you cannot know
the *either/or* agony created by a single sorghum biscuit—
either your brother gets it or you do. And if you *do* eat it,
you know in your bones you have stolen the food straight
from his mouth, there being so little for either of you. This
was the daily, debilitating side of poverty that no one speaks
of, the perpetual scarcity that, at every turn, makes the simplest act a moral dilemma. On a nearby farm there lived a
slave father and his two sons who had one blouse and pair
of breeches among them, so that when one went off to work
the others were left naked and had to hide at home in their
shed. True enough, Jackson and I fared better than they,
but in linen handed down by Reverend Chandler or by his
pious friends—who no doubt felt good about the very char-
ity that annihilated me—in their scented waistcoats and
smelly boots I whiffed the odor of other men, even heard
their accents echo in the very English I spoke, as if I was no
one—or nothing—in my own right, and I wondered how in
God's name you could *have* anything if circumstances threw
you amongst the *had*. Ah, me. The Reverend's prophecy
that I would grow up to be a picklock was wiser than he
knew, for was I not, as a Negro in the New World, *born* to
be a thief? Or, put less harshly, inheritor of two millennia of
things I had not myself made? But enough of this.

On ship I decided against my usual signatures of defi-
ance: pooping amiddlemost a local politician's satin pillow,
for example, or fabricating for his wife—some blue-blooded
snob—a love letter from their black chambermaid that was
worthy of James Cleveland, or simply scrawling on their
parlor wall in charcoal from their hearth, as I often did, "I

can enter your life whenever I wish." No, I did none of this, there in Falcon's quarters. All I wanted was to know his heart (if he had one) and to walk off, as was reasonable, with a tradable trinket or two.

I drifted from object to object at first, just touching things with sweat-tipped fingers as a way to taint and take hold of them—to loose them from their owner—but ever more slowly, for I soon found that Falcon's room was ingeniously rigged with exploding, trip-lever booby traps. He'd filled ordinary rum bottles on his shelf with liquid explosives (each detonated by a pull-friction fuse in the cork), and two of his calabash pipes had stems packed with gunpowder. Also he kept all the ship's weapons in his cabin under lock and key. These security measures (or perhaps they spoke of Falcon's insecurity) I expected, but not what I found next. His biggest crates of plunder from every culture conceivable, which he covered with tarp at the rear of the room, were wrenched open, spilling onto the sloping floor bird-shaped Etruscan vases, Persian silk prayer carpets, and portfolios of Japanese paintings on rice paper. Temple scrolls I found, precious tablets, and works so exotic to my eyes that Falcon's crew of fortune hunters could have taken them only by midnight raids and murder. Slowly, it came to me, like the sound of a stone plunked into a pond, that he had a standing order from his financiers, powerful families in New Orleans who underwrote the *Republic*, to stock Yankee museums and their homes with whatever of value was not nailed down in the nations he visited. To bring back slaves, yes, but to salvage the best of their war-shocked cultures too.

More carefully, then, I moved on, slipping a few doubloons down the front of my blouse, and even more into the crotch of my breeches. The moon's pull on waves beneath us rocked the ship so suddenly I was thrown off balance and cracked my head on a crossbeam. Then I found his chart table with my kneecap. After striking a match, I saw his journal winged open to pages written in the cramped yet even script we associate with scriveners, each page more unusual than the last, revealing in this age of tepid personalities a Faustian man of powerful loves, passions, hatreds: a creature of preposterous, volatile contradictions. From what I was able to piece together, the nation was but a few hours old when Ebenezer Falcon was born, its pulpits and work places and pubs buzzing with talk of what the new social order should be. He was the only child of a close-mouthed Nantucket minister, one of the Sons of Liberty, and a pale, lonely woman of polite education who could discuss with her husband neither the books she loved nor theater, politics or her past in the colonies. Therefore, she poured stories about El Dorado and the Fountain of Youth, her feelings and fantasies into Ebenezer. She placed maps before him, and music boxes; like most doting mothers of this sort, she lived vicariously through her son. For his part, Falcon grew up determined to outperform his father (and most other men) and bring her gifts from all the lands she would never see. He was that sort of son. Aye, small enough to miss in a crowd, but with the bantam spirit for fighting and over-compensating that many men of slight stature possess. Her death when he was fifteen, off on his first stint as a cabin boy, changed nothing; he, like the fledgling republic itself, felt expansive, eager to push back frontiers, even to slide betimes into bullying others and taking, if need be, what was not offered. Needless to say, he made enemies. Under another name, one of his several aliases, he was wanted for murder or treason in three states. The first charge was produced by a duel at daybreak over gambling debts in Philadelphia; the

second by a proposition he had made during the last war
to Anthony Merry, the British minister in Washington, to
divide the western region of the continent into empires separate from the United States, one of which the skipper hoped
to shape himself, establishing there not a kingdom—for he
hated men like George III—but a true American utopia, a
dream nurtured by more than one man after the Revolution. By nature he was anti-British, and anti-Jeffersonian as
well after the ill-planned Embargo Act that threw seamen
and shipbuilders out of work, and he agreed more than any
sane man should with Pierre-Joseph Proudhon's devilish
idea that social conflict and war were, in the Kantian sense,
a *structure* of the human mind. These feelings he shared only
with a few co-conspirators who had served with him under
Captain William Bathbridge when their ship, the *Constitu-
tion*, engaged the British frigate *Jaya* off the coast of Bra-
zil and battered her into submission. These were friends
injured, as he was in that battle, and passed over for com-
missions. Embittered, they saw the war against England as
mismanaged, an embarrassing study in military blunders
so astonishingly stupid (the nation did nothing to upgrade
its fleet, so merchantmen with muzzle-loading cannons
strapped on their decks single-handedly took on the world's
greatest navy) that the only sane course for common sailors
who valued their skin was to escape being used as cannon
fodder and to profit as best they could from international
confusion. As it turned out, the time for slaving was good,
boosted by the South's cotton boom after planters adopted
Whitney's cotton gin and the demand for Negro slaves doubled. No matter that in 1808 the trade was outlawed. Like so
many others with a seaworthy ship and crew of grumbling
tars disillusioned by their country's inability to keep the seas
free from piracy and British impressment, Falcon turned to

piracy himself, then to a contraband market that many these days served clandestinely. In other words, in a dangerous world, a realm of disasters, a place of grief and pain, a sensible man made *himself* dangerous, more frightening than all the social and political "accidents" that might befall him. He was, in a way, a specialist in survival. A magister ludi of the Hard Life.

The man who emerged in these journal entries possessed a few of the solitary virtues and the entire twisted will of Puritanism: a desire to achieve perfection; the loneliness, self-punishment, and bouts of suicide this brings; and a profound disdain for anyone who failed to meet his nearly superhuman standards. He attributed his knack for survival in uncertain times to a series of exercises he'd developed, written in Latin, French, and Greek—for he thought simultaneously in all three languages—under the heading "Self-Reliance."

Outside, shoe leather struck the deck near Falcon's door. Someone coughed, then cursed the skipper safely since he was not there, and I recognized his voice as that of the boatswain, Matthew McGaffin. Long seconds passed while McGaffin pissed on Falcon's door, expelling the sea within himself; then he moved drunkenly on, and I read of our captain's personal regimen—training himself to read six lines of any book in one snap, to work while others slept, to withstand extremes of heat and cold in case of shipwreck, to find everything in his cabin blindfolded, to ignore pain, to live on as little as a single biscuit, and to do calisthenics to strengthen his eyes and make bifocals unnecessary. Culture, in his view, came from an Icarian, *causa sui* impulse I found difficult to decipher. Not surprisingly, he saw himself as profoundly misunderstood, his deeds as terribly underrated. According to one day-old notation, the demands he made on others had someone plotting to kill him—he suspected first Squibb, then Cringle—by dropping arsenic and thallium sulfate into his dinner, though this could simply be the mistrust of an unpopular captain who kept knives concealed in every cabin, and whose imagination, I swear on this, was artistically limited to the finely wrought workmanship of pistols, the blunt simplicity of well-balanced, hand-crafted weapons. Maybe the reason for this was his being a natural marksman. From birth he'd lacked binocular vision. All his life he'd been squinting shut his left eye, so that when someone put a pistol in his hand at eighteen, he naturally sighted his targets and began blowing them away effortlessly. Yet, for all this obsession with survival, he had the air of a man who desperately wanted to die, which made his position on ship—his power over the others—all the more frightening.

Few mates wanted to share his company. Some nights he would step up timidly behind a circle of joking men, there in Bangalang, and instantly feel them stiffen, grow silent, then shuffle off to other business. Or he would hover at the periphery of his foremast hands as they worked, fingers shoved into his waistcoat like a new boy at school, hoping they would invite him into their banter about work and women. But no one did. They knew better. They were common folk. Most could not read, in contrast to Falcon, a polyhistor who spent twenty hours a week pouring over old tomes when the weather was fair—this, because as captain he could not bear having anyone, especially his first mate, correct him. He and Cringle argued bitterly, of course, about his pushing the crew too hard. Some nights their shouting in Falcon's quarters could be heard by all on watch. It became clear, by and by, that as in a house divided at the helm where both parents bicker, the crew benefited by keeping the officers at odds. If Falcon denied extra rations, Cringle might approve them. If Falcon brushed off a lighthand's complaints of feeling poorly, the mate might let him lie abed. Still, the skipper needed an audience. Try as he might, he could not win what he wanted most once we landed in Africa: the loyalty of his crew. Thus, he had few allies. Only hypocritical lickspittles like Nathaniel Meadows, who smiled in his face for favors and bad-mouthed him behind his back. As you might expect, the crew was perpetually angry and dissatisfied. What was odd in this was that it wasn't *their* anger at all—it was Falcon's. His emotions permeated the ship like the smell of rum and rotting wood, and these feelings—as is always true of groups confined together in small quarters, or of couples—the men picked up, believing the directionless rage they felt to be their own. All this explained (for me) Falcon's webwork of traps, the spring-released darts coated with curare. But little else, for in his concluding entry he spoke of plans to purchase forty Allmuseri tribesmen and something else Ahman-de-Bellah lost five servants capturing, a colossus he felt he could sell for a king's ransom in Europe. Of this creature, he wrote no more, only noting he could not bring it aboard until the *Republic*'s carpenters reinforced leg-irons and planking in the hold.

Standing there, peering at these pages to make sure I'd read them right, feeling as though I had fallen into another man's nightmare, and sweating in the heat of his locked room since no air was circulating, I was so absorbed I failed to hear the doorlatch turn and became aware of company only when air rushed in suddenly, altering the room's pressure and clogging my left inner ear. My right had a ringing sound. The edges of my eyes felt blurred. Then just as suddenly the sensation was gone and I heard a shrill, adenoidal voice that swallowed most of its soft consonants say, "Whatever you're lookin' to steal, 'tis gone."

"Cap'n," says I, "this isn't what it looks like. All I wanted was a lantern. I guess I made a mistake."

"'Deed you have."

Silhouetted as he was, his wild hair like rope yarn, skin drier than scales, and beard nearly an ell from top to bottom, his face looked, so help me, like five miles of bad Louisiana road. Rum came reeking, like a slap, off his clothing. A gun hung low in his belt. Yet his eyes were in-turned, icy, as he pushed by me into the room, swaying on his feet like a damaged rig, drunk and barely registering my presence at all. He lowered his rump onto the cushion of his chair, one hand squeezing the armrest, the other pressed against his chest; then he lifted his chin slightly, to the left and away from me, to let a belch of volcanic proportions bubble free. "Light a candle, please. And bring me that jug in the corner and a clean cup—bring one for yourself too." Instantly, I felt ill, but hastened to obey, each step I took causing the doubloons in my crotch to jingle. By rights, he could have me birched or keelhauled or lashed to the capstan bar. But even worse than that, I realized he might *lecture* me again, beginning as he often did with a personal anecdote that might go on *forever*, embellishing each line of dialogue and taking every part in the story for my instruction. Even worse, he might decide to demonstrate esoteric Chinese jointlocks he'd learned while living for a year in King Miu village, using *me* as his hypothetical opponent in lessons that resulted in my neck aching for days thereafter. Carefully, I poured him a cup of merry-go-down. Then I took a step back, gauging my distance from the door.

"Shall I leave now, sir? I've found the lantern."

"D'you now? A lantern, was it? And nothin' else?"

"On my word."

Color was climbing high in Falcon's neck and face. His

exhalations were loud, pursive, and again he pressed his palm against his middle, as though mashing down some deep, recurring pain or intestinal burn he'd somehow learned to live with. His face ritched left in a frown. "You weren't heah to murder me in my sleep and jump ship?"

"No! Of course not, sir!"

"Six men tried that tonight on shore. Not an hour ago, Mr. Calhoun." His glass empty, he took the jug from me, lifted it and splashed more rum straight down his throat, his whole body shuddering for a second; then his eyes gave me a rum-soaked glare. "I was unarmed, 'cept for these boots I'm wearin'. D'you like 'em?"

"Yessir, and fine boots they are, Cap'n."

"Naw, you don't truly *see* 'em, boy." He lifted one foot, pointing the toe toward me. "You're not supposed to! That's the point of boots like these. The toes are reinforced with steel plates. I'm not a big man, as you may have noticed, and as a lad I was bullied by taller boys. 'Deed, I was. Nary a day passed in my childhood that somebody didn't single me out for a beatin' or some cruel jest. Nearly broke me mum's heart, that did, but I'll tell you true: Nowadays when I kick a swab's shins he seldom walks again. I advise you to fix yourself a pair of such useful boots for the voyage back. Have you got a pistol?"

"Nossir."

"Then we must find one for you." From among the contents of his chest Falcon selected a 45-percussion Kentucky pistol. "Lovely, isn't it? I've adjusted the sights, added precision rifling in the barrel, and damned if this beauty don't feature one of my own concoctions. See how heavy the handle is? There's a magnet inside. It locks down the trigger so no man kin fire it, or snatch it from you, who isn't wearin' magnetized rings such as I wear, even when I sleep." Falcon unscrewed from his third finger, right hand, a metal band, pushed it on my finger, then snapped around my waist a holster of his own design. "You'll notice," says he, stepping back to study me, "that spare ammunition fits into three pouches on the sides and the small of your back. The holster has a thumb-break snap, so you kin draw back with one smooth motion to push away your blouse. From now on you'd do well to follow a formula I've developed. Every few seconds pat yourself: knife, guns, keys, in that order, to make sure you've got everything. A light touch now and then is all it takes; then it'll become instinctive. I'd advise you not to let any of the blacks get too close when we bring 'em on board—'specially the women. They'll get right up in your face—they love to do that when talkin'—so keep 'em at arm's length, with your holster facin' away from 'em. Don't eat or drink anythin' they give you. If you have to shoot one, use small shot 'stead of ball. 'Tis a wee bit more merciful. And when we bring 'em up from below for exercise, work in pairs—Cringle and Meadows, for example. Squibb keeps an eye on Fletcher. And you and me watch out for one another." His eyes slid up, blinking. "You're not gonna blow your damned foot off, are you?"

"I think I'll get the hang of it. But, Cap'n, why do I need all this?"

He began to undress slowly, the moonlight and candles doubling his shadow against the wall. Falcon's buttonless blouse gave him trouble when he tried pulling it over his enormous head; its collar caught under his beard, leaving him hooded for a moment (I believe I could have shot him then, and I even pointed the pistol at his head to see how this might feel) with both his arms helplessly in the air. "Give me a hand here, Mr. Calhoun. I hope you can see that I trust you. I need a colored mate to be my eyes and ears once the

Africans are on board. Same with the crew. I want to know what each man's thinkin'." Against my better instincts to gun him down right there, I helped the skipper pull his shirt free. Now he was dressed for bed in his nightshirt and steel-toed boots. "Once weekly I'll want a full report. If there's any talk, you'll tell me."

"Be your Judas?" I asked. "A spy?"

His eyes filled with hurt, slipped to a corner of the room, as if the correct word he wanted was there. "Nay, a friend! I need someone to keep his eyes open and tell me of any signs of trouble." He lay back on his bed, drinking straight from the jug now, and began bellyaching more to himself than to me about his officers, bitterly relating personal things about each I never dreamed of and did not wish to know. He was clearly breaking confidences, betraying every one of them in a voice so venomous I wanted to cover my ears. I felt uncomfortable. More: I felt unclean as he described in detail all the dirt and gossip, weakness and shortcomings, of every mother's son on board. Everyone, it seemed, had a secret. A shadow. A buried past so scandalous that I was nervous for the rest of the night. Why was he saying these things? I could only speculate that something was seriously wrong with the ship—he never specified what—and his solution was the oldest and simplest in the world. Divide and conquer. Poison each man's perception of the other. By *making* me hear of each man's faults (I had no choice) he subtly compromised me, made me something of a betrayer too, and I sighed and shut my eyes, thinking of Isadora, who would say these things were sent to try us. Moments later he was asleep. I leaned over him, wanting to empty into his head the pistol he'd given me, but found myself transfixed by the crude ring twinned on his left hand and mine, as if, heaven help me, we were married, and the very thing I'd

[58]

escaped in New Orleans had, here off the unlighted coast of Senegambia, overtaken me.

Sleep and I were strangers that night. All that evening, moaning and sharp cries such as only Negro women can make drifted on the wind from the warehouse, where Africans living, dying, and dead were thrown together. Hoping to steady my thoughts, twisted worse than rigging after a storm, I shook awake Squibb, there on deck, and asked him about our cargo. Sailors, I know, can be careless with the truth, but he told me the first caravan of Allmuseri were being separated for the morrow's sale: husbands from their wives, children from their parents, the infirm from the healthy, each parting like an amputation or flaying of skin, for as a clan-state they were as close-knit as cells in the body. "First, Ahman-de-Bellah will have his people shave off their body hair. That's the first humiliation, makin' 'em smooth as babies from the womb, like mebbe they was born yestiday. He'll have them bathed, soaked in palm oil to make their black hides glisten like leather, then they'll get a feast to fatten 'em for tomorrow's buyers."

In the darkness I said to the shadowy lump he was on deck, "Like cattle?"

"Like Allmuseri," he replied. "They'll get what Africans are used to eatin'. Roots like, cooked green or else dried and made into flour, then mashed or stewed into porridge. They'll get a tasty sauce with it too, and probably some honey beer made from maize to wash it down." He lifted his hips a little, then broke wind gently, a faint ripple of sound as if he'd tightened his sphincters to soften the sound of it. "We should eat so well, darlin'."

"Squibb!" shouted Cringle. "If you do that again, you pig, I'll make you sleep below, or on the other side of the ship!"

[59]

"Pardon *me*, sir, but that's Nature, yuh know. A man shouldn't keep it inside, and that. 'Tain't healthy, me wife Maud used to say. It's bad for the heart, she says. Why, when we first got married Maud usta say—"

"I don't *care* what she said! I'm not your bloody wife, man!"

"Aye"—he winked my way—"thank God fer that."

Quietly, under his breath, Cringle repeated one of his Scriptural passages, then rolled over and slept, as did Squibb, flat on his back with his parrot on his belly, like a sea gull atop a whale in a tropical current.

Next day I joined them in the landing party that went ashore. The *Republic* lay at anchor a distance of ten cables from the fort, with McIntosh at the helm, and slip ropes on her cables, the ship ready to spread canvas and sail if for some reason Bogha betrayed us. By the time the last Allmuseri caravan arrived it was full dark. A balmy night. Squibb and I bloated ourselves on beer in the town square, tossed coins to beggars crippled at birth by their parents to make them better panhandlers, and watched one turbaned harem girl whose figure and veiled face filled me with such longing that I felt as if my life's blood splashed to the ground each time she sashayed by, so fascinating was this girl, and so long had I felt coltish and unwillingly celibate at sea. I knew my hungry gaze must have burned her, for her brown fingers, long and thin with bones frail as a bird's, gently brushed my hand the fourth and fifth times she refilled my mug. By that time my heart was bouncing off my ribs, and I barely saw two African boys sprint past us, announcing the approach of a caravan from the interior. I stood, felt unsteady, then sat again, hearing gunshots from afar. Behind us the fort's many guns replied, so thunderously the air shook. Abruptly, all was confusion. Cries went out from every merchant.

From every bazaar the coffle's arrival was cheered. I looked around for the lass, but she was gone. I stood to see better. Squibb yanked me back to my seat.

"Better yuh keep your noodle down, Illinois." He was instantly sober, his grip on me tight as a winch. "Or yuh'll be sold too. Stolen right off ship, I'm sayin', and pressed into a gang. It's happened before." He tugged a little at my sleeve. "These blokes don't know you're a sailor. And they don't care."

He needn't have told me twice. I squeezed back a little into the shadows, watching Bogha's servants light palm-oil lamps atop the fort's walls. Cautiously I eased back into the crowd to see better, sweat streaming inside my blouse, puddling at the back of my spine above my belt. I sighted Cringle off to one side and, sidling up behind him, caught him talking to himself, tapping his chin with his pipestem and appraising the Allmuseri tribesmen shackled in twos at their ankles. As I'd heard, they were a remarkably *old* people. About them was the smell of old temples. Cities lost when Europe was embryonic. Looking at them, at their dark skin soft as black leather against knee-length gowns similar to Greek chitons, you felt they had run the full gamut of civilized choices, or played through every political and social possibility and now had nowhere to *go*. A tall people, larger even than Watusi; their palms were blank, bearing no lines. No fingerprints. But all Allmuseri, I had been told, had a second brain, a small one at the base of their spines. A people so incapable of abstraction no two instances of "hot" or "cold" were the same for them, this hot porridge today being so specific, unique, and bound to the present that it had only a nominal resemblance to the hot porridge of yesterday. Physically, they seemed a synthesis of several tribes, as if longevity in this land had made them a biological

repository of Egyptian and sub-Saharan eccentricities or—
in the Hegelian equation—a clan distilled from the essence
of everything that came earlier. Put another way, they might
have been the Ur-tribe of humanity itself. I'd never seen
anyone like them. Or felt such antiquity in the presence of
others; a clan of *Sphaeriker*. Indeed, what I felt was the presence of countless others *in* them, a crowd spun from everything this vast continent had created.

Past the barbican to the broad piazza of the receiving
house, Ahman-de-Bellah, a froglike, vast-bearded Arab who
was notorious for drawing out the brains of his enemies with
an iron hook, herded the Allmuseri to stand before Bogha and
Captain Falcon, who met Bellah with the cracking-fingers
greeting of the coast. There, off to one side of the trees, his
people put up their tents, then forced the Allmuseri toward
the warehouses.

"Poor bastards," said Cringle, seeing me squeezing my
fists and unable to swallow. "Their villages were destroyed
by famine." He banged his large calabash pipe on the Bible
he carried, bound in pressed pigskin, to shake loose the dot-
tle. "Ahman-de-Bellah took them without a fight. Their
rivers dried up. The drought's lasted a decade, I believe,
which means they'll never survive the voyage back, if that's
what you're wondering. The skipper won't find three in ten
healthy enough to spend two months in the hold. Better,"
said he, "to be dead in a ditch than in their shoes."

"Peter, what's happening on ship?"

"How do you mean?"

"The captain, he gave me a talk I cannot untangle. He
asks me to help him—"

The mate shook his head two, three times. "Stay away
from him, Rutherford. He's mad"—Cringle touched two
fingers to his left temple—"and if you hope to see New

Orleans again, the best thing is to separate yourself from Falcon now." The muscles around his eyes knotted. "He will sink this ship and take us with him. He doesn't *want* to return. Did you know that? That's why he goes to sea. Haven't you noticed how nothing is ever right for him? How even when he jokes, it is a jeering kind of humor? No one knows this, but he's been married thirty years and he still plays with himself. His wife, Molly, a beldam if ever there was one, makes him wash his hands and dingus before they fornicate. She picks her nose when they make love, she's that bored. Little wonder he doesn't want to return to *her*. When she is angry, I hear, she sews all his clothing together. In their wedding portrait, which I have seen, she is thin enough to be a model for El Greco. Now she's dumpled enough to pose for Peter Paul Rubens. And that's the least of his complaints about life. He is vain. And therefore self-pitying. And vicious, lad. He keeps a list of personal affronts, insults and abuses he's received, or believes he's received, and *dates* them—he reviews them when he's drunk, keeps them alive, and always watches for a man's weaknesses once he's signed on. He knows mine is Tommy, that I cannot stand his treatment of the boy." Cringle stood pitched forward as if in a stiff wind, a habit he'd formed at sea. "Out there, on the ocean, in Africa, or during some 'adventure,' he hopes something will do for him what he cannot do himself."

"Then you're saying we won't get home?"

"Not with what he's bringing aboard."

"The Allmuseri?"

"No," said Cringle, "the other thing . . ."

"What?"

"I don't know what it is! It has no name. All I know is that it belongs to the Allmuseri and has no business in our world." He looked away, out toward the distant ships whose dactyloid masts favored a dark stretch of winter trees on the water, then away again. Ever since we'd come ashore he had been twitchy as a squirrel. So tense any clock he came close to ran, by my reckoning, forty seconds faster. "Are you with me and the few of our chaps who stand against him?"

"I guess, I don't know—"

"Decide soon," he said. "Falcon has friends here, but we will act as soon as we put out to sea."

Then he was off, called away by Captain Falcon to help in the hellish work of inspecting the cavity-ridden teeth, shaved skulls, and stippled privates of four men for whom the skipper paid 100 bars each (a bar being worth half a dollar, a pound of powder, or a fathom of ordinary cloth); then the women over twenty-five (Bellah gave Falcon a 25 percent reduction on these); and finally the children who, like trout, had to measure four feet four inches or they would be thrown back into the bush. And Falcon was furious. Ahman-de-Bellah had passed at least one doctored black off on him, an old man medicated with some unknown drug that bloated his skin. He oozed oniony-smelling sweat from powder treatments. When Falcon pressed a finger against his teeth, bubbles of pus oozed from the man's gums. Lemon juice had been swabbed along his body to give it a glossy appearance, but it made no difference. He died, delirious, before Falcon could get his money back. The captain, of course, was no paragon of honesty. The cotton bales he used for barter were hollow at their centers, the whiskey carefully watered down, and the gunpowder was of an inferior stock. Captain Falcon grew edgy, I guess, that this deceit might be discovered, and kept us busy most of the night transferring his cargo from the boats to the ship's belly. In his "rough" log (the one a ship's master edited to produce a more polished book for his employers), which I would see later, he wrote:

3,500 hides	$1,750
19 large and prime ivory teeth	1,560
Gold	2,500
600 pounds of small ivory	320
15 tons of rice	600
40 slaves	1,600
36 bullocks	360
Sheep, goats, vegetables, butter	100
900 lbs beeswax	95
Total caravan value	$8,885

The skipper's share or "lay" of the profits was a handsome 25 percent of the take. The crew received a pitiful twelve dollars per month, a thing increasingly offensive to most hands when talk of Falcon's mysterious find—loaded last of all onto the ship in a crate big enough to carry a bull elephant, its price omitted from his log—moved, like an electric shock, from one mate to another. Added to which, and perhaps worst of all, our ship's carpenters grumbled of water in the frowzy hold. Once the Allmuseri saw the great ship and the squalid pit that would house them sardined belly-to-buttocks in the orlop, with its dead air and razor-teethed bilge rats, each slave forced to lie spoon-fashion on his left side to relieve the pressure against his heart—after seeing *this*, the Africans panicked. Believe it or not, a barker told us they thought we were barbarians shipping them to America to be eaten. They saw us as savages. In their mythology Europeans had once been members of their tribe—rulers, even, for a time—but fell into what was for these people the blackest of sins. The failure to experience the unity of Being everywhere was the Allmuseri vision of Hell. And that was where we lived: purgatory. That was where we were taking them—into the madness of multiplicity—and the thought of it drove them wild. A one-handed Allmuseri thief attacked Cringle with a belaying pin and was shot by the mate. (I should explain that lopping off a thief's right hand was this tribe's punishment for stealing, because the Allmuseri ate with their right hands and wiped their arses with their left; by depriving this man of his right hand, they forced him into the indignity of eating and scraping off excrement with the selfsame limb.) A woman pitched her baby overboard into the waters below us. At least two men tried to follow, straining against their chains, and this sudden flurry of resistance brought out the worst in Falcon, if you can imagine that. He beat them until blood came. The male slaves he double-ironed, removing the ladder to the hold and lowering them by ropes so none could climb back up. Women he had sleep in the cabins, young children were jummixed on deck in the longboats beneath sheets of tarpaulin, and if any Negro even looked as if he was thinking of rebellion, that man was to be birched and taught the sting of noose and yardarm.

It was then my hair started going white. Unable to watch, I repaired to sit alone in the cookroom, my head in my hands and back against an oven of such antiquity it was usually hotter on one side than the other, so that Squibb's tipsycakes (so called since he laced them with rum) rose crooked and once they were frosted the top layer would gradually slide off. Clearly, nothing on the *Republic* was as it should be, but it behooves me for the sake of my own character, shabby as this is, to explain how murderous my thoughts became after taking part in the captivity of the Allmuseri. I wondered if the blacks who'd traveled with Balboa and Cortez hated their leaders as much as I did Ebenezer Falcon, if Estéban, the legendary explorer from Morocco, felt as cool toward his companions, three Spanish officers, as I sometimes did toward Cringle, who would never in this life see himself, his own blighted history, in the slaves we intended to sell, or wonder, as I did, how in God's name I could go on after this? How could I feel whole after seeing it? How could I tell my children of it without placing a curse on them forever? How could I even dare to *have* children in a world so senseless? How could . . .

"Mr. Calhoun?"

"Here, sir."

"There's one hour till daylight." Falcon stuck his head into the hatchway. "I've new orders for you."

I stood, brushing off the seat of my trousers. "Sir?"

"We're about to weigh anchor. You're in charge of feeding the Africans in messes of ten at nine in the morning and four, and give 'em half a pint of water three times a day. Squibb handles the crew as before, but no one is to feed the new cargo, or come near it, except me."

"No? Might I ask what it *eats*?"

"Don't ask," says he. "Nothin' from your supplies, so you needn't worry."

That, of course, was a lie.

There was plenty of reason for worry. Captain Falcon revealed to no one the contents of the mysterious crate brought by raft and lowered below by Bogha's servants into a storeroom behind the stemson through a hole cut into the deckbeams, then boarded over. Ere the skipper brought the *Republic* about and headed out to sea, a few of the crew, myself among them, wagered five bob on what his find might be. Squibb claimed it was the Missing Link between man and monkey; Cringle said it was most probably a nearly extinct lizard, maybe intelligent, that would have scholars from Cambridge to Queen's College rewriting natural history; and Meadows, to frighten us all, reported that he had heard someone at the fort say it had fallen from the sky near the Allmuseri villages, which whilom were tucked away in the bush between Cape Lopez and the Congo River and had been protected by them for centuries. We drew lots to see who would be the first to sneak below while the captain slept and wrench open a plank to peer inside. Tommy O'Toole, the cabin boy, pulled the shortest length of string. He shinnied down a rope reef-knotted round his waist so we could pull him up. After ten minutes Squibb tugged and found the rope broken. We were about to lower *him* when the boy crawled back on deck with only half his mind—or could be it was twice the mind he had had before. His skin was cold, all one bluish color as if he had been baptized in the Deep. His face was blank as a pan. And his words, as his mouth spread and closed like a fish's, were strange: a slabber of Bantu patois, Bushman, Cushitic, and Sudanic tongues, and your guess where he learned them is as good as mine. His eyes glowed like deck lights, less solid orbs of color, if you saw them up close, than splinters of luciferin indigo that, like an emulsion, had caught the camphor of a blaze once before them.

With Cringle's waistcoat shawled over his shoulders for warmth, and holding a horn of rum in his hands, he found a space in his sporadic madness to tell how he'd come within three feet of forcing open a door in the crate after the rope broke but was stopped by the density of air around it, a natural defense of the thing inside, which did not so much occupy a place as it bent space and time around itself like a greatcoat. He could force his bare feet to go no farther. This was just as well, for dark coils of the creature's defecation were everywhere, slithering with insects, worms, and sluglike beings that apparently lived inside its bowels. All at once, the crate rocked gently as something crab-walked from one side of the box to the other, scritching its nails on the walls, muttering to itself like a devil chained inside a mountain for a thousand years, its voice gently syllabled and honeyed, as sacramental as a siren's, or peradventure its very breathing was a chant so full of love and werelight, vatic lament and Vedic sorrow, that the boy's heart bade him listen more. He slapped his left hand over his mouth, clamped his right hand over the left, and bent down on one knee, this being a brain-rinsing song the boy somehow felt he knew. Down in that lichened chamber, down in this shrunken air scattered with galleywood and bosun's stores, down in a vault swimming with imponderables, he forgot where he was and why he had come: a sea change nicer than any of us knew, he said; and then the creature's lay whistled from his own lips like the sweetest of fluids whelming through his windpipes, and he was inside the luminous darkness of the crate, himself chained now yet somehow unchained from all else, sadly watching young Tommy O'Toole, sensing as if through the lotic skin of a stingray or crab, and they were a single thing: singer, listener, and song, light spilling into light, the boundaries of inside and outside, here and there, today and tomorrow, obliterated as in the penetralia of the densest stars, or at the farthest hem of Heaven.

When he had finished, his eyes ashimmer after peering into the heart of things hidden and his body swaying to music none but he could hear—after this, there was no sound forward and aft except the creaking of rigging loud as a bonfire. "Blimey." A deck hand ran his fingers through his hair. "It eats people, that's what it eats." Squibb was tight as usual, trying to stand erect, weaving on both feet, tilting first left, then right. He lifted the cross from his neck and, his eyes closed, kissed it. "Saints preserve us." A few chaps shivered, and not simply from the wind's chill gnawing through our coats. All could see the ship's boy would never come about. He was lost to us.

"You can belay that kind of talk," said Cringle, buttoning his coat up on the boy. "I take it you've work to do, so be at it. Prompt, if you please." His arm waisting Tommy, Cringle assured him he would come to no harm. He promised to erase his name from the work roster and, being the sort of quartermaster given to rising at night to pull back the covers on others who'd kicked them off when sleeping, fearing they might be chilled, he led him to his own berth, which the ship's boy was to have for the rest of our voyage home.

Entry, the fourth
JUNE 28, 1830

Homeward bound on May 30, we left the fort with the *Republic* leaking like a sieve, hoping again to cross the Flood, but this time with the sides of the ship bloated, scorched by the sun, and with barnacles clotting her stern-piece. She reached the latitude of 20° south, and longitude 10° west, sailing full and by without serious mishap on North Atlantic trade winds until on the fifteenth day the weather turned squally. Pellets of rain hammered the sails so heavily Captain Falcon was obliged to shorten the main topsail and let the ship sail under bare timber. "Nothing for you to worry about," he told me. "Just see that you and Squibb doublelash the longboats and secure the galley." But his voice wobbled, and I knew he was not telling me the worst. It was the stormy season of the year off West Africa. And during the bleakest nights when curdling fog rolled in, obscuring the stars and sky, making precise calculations of our position impossible, when the wind wheeled unex-pectedly from NW to NNW, twirling us like a matchbox or toy ship of balsa wood—those nights, Falcon and the few men still loyal to him stayed awake through each watch in the skipper's cabin, sipping coffee laced with rum, crimped foreheads tilted together over maps and compasses spin-ning widdershins. Younger lighthands lost their appetites.

Tommy, relieved of all his duties, couldn't hold down as much as a sea biscuit, and neither could I, mainly because Squibb and I cooked the slop and I saw him spit into it when he was angry with the crew. Older sailors swore, suddenly got religion (there are no atheists at sea, as they say), and fingered their crosses, whispering prayers for fair weather, and scheming all the time—anyone could see this—on ways to seize the ship and steal her cargo.

Dependent as we were on each other, hardship brought out small kindnesses as well as cruelty, even from the most unlikely people, among them Nathaniel Meadows, a barber-surgeon who looked, for all the talk of his being an ax-murderer, Biblically meek: a crankled little stretchbelly with fishy eyes and big scarlet ears, who kept his hair slicked back with seal's oil. He had no chin to speak of, his jaws dropping straight down into his neck. He smelled like the dogs on ship. He superstitiously carried a clump of Liverpool sod in his trousers when at sea, a habit shared by many old salts; but unlike anyone I have ever known he had the unsettling habit of blinking rapidly when he spoke. There was a space between his teeth, which gave his *s*'s a faint whistling sound when he pronounced them, as if he'd swallowed a flute but got it only halfway down his trachea. Some deck hands said his mother had been frightened by a field mouse when she was carrying him. That wasn't hard to believe. He looked like a titmouse in human form. And Meadows had no chest at all—that is, in profile his body curved like a question mark, and you'd associate his tamed, quiet manner with, say, reformed alcoholics, or men who're recovering from a stroke. Meekness aside, I still gave him a wide berth.

"'Ello, mate. 'Bout to do my laundry, I am," says he to me. "Just wonderin' if you need anythin' washed, Mr. Calhoun."

His arms loaded down with the wash of others, he approached me by the spanker-boom, where I was biting into the last of my breakfast, a biscuit going bad, on the verge of molding, you know, visibly all right on the outside but, once I sank my teeth in, it tasted as if it was loaded with dust. I tossed it to one of the children in a jolly boat, then put down my kid (eating tub), and stood to the sound of sudden growling behind Meadows's legs. He'd brought one of the dogs with him, a half-starved mongrel who apparently wanted something dark to chew on. I drew back.

"'Ey, don't mind him," said Meadows. "'E's just hungery."

"I can tell." His dog starting sniffling at my crotch, poking his nose between my legs, which convinced me it might be time to do my laundry after all.

"You want your shirt washed or wot?"

I slipped it off and placed it on top of his pile, noticing there one of Cringle's blouses and the ragged cloths a few of the Allmuseri used to cover themselves. "Meadows," says I through clogged sinuses, "you're scrubbing clothes for the slaves too?"

"Aye, might's well. If you're goin' to wash, 'tis better to do a full load, wouldn't you say? Saves on soap 'n' water."

He *was* one to save on supplies, I remembered, being the sort of man who mashed together slivers of soap left by others to make a new, lopsided bar. Watching him leave, I scolded myself for distrusting him and wished the others might be as helpful as Meadows, especially when it came to lightening the suffering of the Africans. As I said, the ship made a great deal of water. Night and day, Falcon kept the pumps working. Even so, the slaves still lay in a foot of salt water in a hold blacker than the belly of Jonah's whale, forced below by the boatswain's cat-o'-nine-tails. Some rested on the laps of others, down there in scummy darkness foul with defecation, slithering with water snakes. Chumps of firewood were given to each for a pillow, which later proved to be a mistake. Up above, the skipper had us cut apertures and grate hatches and bulkheads to provide better air for the Allmuseri, who only came topside (the men) for a few hours each day to have their hair and nails shorn to prevent them from injuring themselves during the fighting for space that inevitably broke out each night. At nine o'clock sharp each morning, when the weather permitted, a mate named Fletcher trotted them out, made them dance a little to music from the cabin boy's flute for exercise, then hurried them below again. It was Captain Falcon's belief that slave insurrections could be prevented if for every ten prisoners one was selected to oversee the others and keep them in line. He issued these shipboard major-domos, one of them named Ngonyama, whom I came to know well those first few weeks, old shirts and tar-splattered trousers, giving them the advantage of being clothed like the crew; they had greater freedom to roam the slippery deck, and Falcon also gave them better food and a few minor tasks such as picking old ropes apart. "The best way to control a rebellious nigger," said he, "is to give him some responsibility."

However, few slaving formulas worked with Ngonyama. Dressed he was now, in tarry breeches and a duck frock, which distinguished him from the others, despite the red bead in his right nostril, and he was quiet during our first fortnight at sea, notwithstanding wind that whipped the sails devilishly and the fact that sometimes the sea ran as high as five houses and our forward deck was invisible underwater, a thing that made the other slaves claw and wail all the more. But Ngonyama, I had the feeling, was waiting. He was so quiet sometimes he seemed to blend, then disappear into the background of shipboard life. Quiet and cunning, I'd say, because he was studying everything—everything—we did, and even enlisted my aid in teaching him a smattering of English and explaining how the steerage worked, in exchange for his teaching me Allmuseri. Of all the players who promenade through this narrative, he was easily the most mysterious. At first he could not distinguish any of the white crew individually, and asked me, "How do their families tell them apart?" I suppose he selected me because I was the only Negro on board, though the distance between his people and black America was vast—his people saw whites as Raw Barbarians and me (being a colored mate) as a Cooked one. And his depth perception so differed from mine that when he looked at a portrait of Isadora I carried in my purse, he asked, "Why is her face splotched with smudges?" by which he meant the *shadows* the artist had drawn under her chin and eyes, for his tribe did not use our sense of perspective but rather the flat, depthless technique of Egyptian art. (He also asked why her nose looked like a conch, if maybe this was a trick of vision too, then saw my anger and dropped the question.)

Sometimes he helped Squibb and me in the cookroom, and the way he carved one of the skipper's pigs stopped me cold. Me, I never could carve. But Ngonyama, his shoulders relaxed, holding his breath for what seemed hours before he started, fixed his eyes as if he could see through the pig, his right hand gripping the cook's blade as if it had grown right out of his wrist. It was eerie, you ask me. It seemed, suddenly, as though the galley slipped in time and took on a transparent feel, as if everything round us were made of glass. Ngonyama began to carve. He slipped metal through meat as if it wasn't there or, leastways, wasn't solid, without striking bone, and in a pattern I couldn't follow, without hacking or rending—doing no harm—the blade guided by, I think, a knack that favored the same touch I'd developed as a thief, which let me feel safe tumblers falling a fraction of a second *before* they dropped, tracing the invisible trellis of muscles, tendons, tissues, until the pig fell apart magically in his hands. He left no knife tracks. Not a trace. The cookroom was as quiet as a tomb when he finished.

"Mirrors!" Squibb whispered to me, stunned. "It's some kinda heathen trick!"

Yet there was no trick to it. In every fiber of their lives you could sense this same quiet magic. Truth to tell, they were not even "Negroes." They were Allmuseri. Talking late at night, blue rivulets scudding back and forth on the deck, our eyes screwed up against the weather, Ngonyama unfolded before me like a merchant's cloth his tribe's official history, the story of themselves they stuck by. Once they had been a seafaring people, years and years ago, and deposited their mariners in that portion of India later to be called Harappa, where they blended with its inhabitants, the Dravidians, in the days before the Aryans and their juggernauts—"city-destroyers"—leveled the civilization of Mohenjo-Daro overnight. Between 1000 B.C. and 500 B.C. they sailed to Central America on North Equatorial currents that made the voyage from the west coast of Africa to the Caribbean only thirty days, bringing their skills in agriculture and metallurgy to the Olmec who, to honor these African mariners, stamped their likeness in stone and enshrined in song their prowess as warriors. Specifically, their martial-art techniques resembled Brazilian *capoeira*. Over time these elegant moves, which Ngonyama taught me when we had time for rest, had become elements in their ceremonial dance.

I must leave their fighting arts for later, because more fascinating than their globe-spanning travels in antiquity and their style of self-defense was the peculiar, gnomic language the Allmuseri practiced. When Ngonyama's tribe spoke it was not so much like talking as the tones the savannah made at night, siffilating through the plains of coarse grass, soughing as dry wind from tree to tree. Not really a language at all, by my guess, as a melic way of breathing deep from the diaphragm that dovetailed articles into nouns, nouns into verbs. I'm not sure I know what I'm saying now, but Ngonyama told me the predication "is," which granted existence to anything, had over the ages eroded into merely an article of faith for them. Nouns or static substances hardly existed in their vocabulary at all. A "bed" was called a "resting," a "robe" a "warming." Furthermore, each verb was different depending on the nature of the object acted upon, whether it was vegetable, mineral, mammal, oblong or rotund. When Ngonyama talked to his tribesmen it was as if the objects and others he referred to flowed together like water, taking different forms, as the sea could now be fluid, now solid ice, now steam swirling around the mizzenpole. Their written language—these Africans had one—was no less unusual, and of such exquisite limpidity, tone colors, litotes, and contrapletes that I could not run my eyes across it, left to right, without feeling everything inside me relax. It consisted of pictograms. You had to look at the characters, Ngonyama taught me, as you would an old friend you've seen many times before, grasping the meaning—and relation to other characters—in a single intuitive snap. It was not, I gathered, a good language for doing analytic work, or deconstructing things into discrete parts, which probably explained why the Allmuseri had no empirical science to speak of, at least not as we understood that term. To Falcon that made them savages. Just the same, it seemed a fitting tongue for the most sought-after blacks in the world.

Compared to other African tribes, the Allmuseri were the most popular servants. They brought twice the price of a Bantu or Kru. According to legend, Allmuseri elders took twig brooms with them everywhere, sweeping the ground so as not to inadvertently step on creatures too small to see. Eating no meat, they were easy to feed. Disliking property, they were simple to clothe. Able to heal themselves, they required no medication. They seldom fought. They could not steal. They fell *sick*, it was said, if they wronged anyone. As I live, they so shamed me I wanted their ageless culture to be my own, if in fact Ngonyama spoke truly. But who was I fooling? While Rutherford Calhoun might envy certain features of Allmuseri folkways, he could never claim something he had no hand in creating. I respected them too much to insult them this way—particularly one woman and her eight-year-old daughter, Baleka, who'd caught a biscuit I tossed her one day when talking to Meadows. Her mother snatched it away. She studied it like a woman inspecting melons at a public market, her face growing sharp. She smelled it, she tasted it with a tiny nibble, and spat it out the side of her mouth into the sea. Presently, she stumped across the deck and dropped it back onto my lap. Sliding up behind her, half hidden behind Mama's legs, Baleka stuck out her hand. Her eyes burned a hole in my forehead. Her mother's finger wagged in my face, and in the little of their language I knew she sniffed that her baby deserved far better than one moldy biscuit. I could only agree. To square things, that night I shared my powdered beef, mustard, and tea with Baleka: a major mistake. Her expectation, and that of Mama, for sharing my *every* pan of food became an unspoken contract no less binding between us than a handshake. By and by, we were inseparable. This was how Mama wanted it, having decided her child's survival might depend on staying close to the one crew member who looked most African, asking me to decipher the strange behavior of the whites and intercede on their behalf. Thus, the child stayed at my heels as I spun rope and, when I was on larboard watch by the taffrail, leaned against my legs, looking back sadly toward Senegambia.

Thus we were at five bells in the forenoon of June 11. The wind blew hard, the sea ran high, filled with thunder rumbles and white tendrils of lightning from the southeast. At my post I was for a time hypnotized by tumbling, opaline blades of ocean, by its vortices that were mirrored in me since we were mainly made of Main, by the way—as the mate said—it seemed to be some monster of energy, without start or finish, a shifting cauldron of thalassic force, form superimposed upon form, which grew neither bigger nor smaller, which endlessly spawned all creatures conceivable yet never consumed itself, and contained a hundred kinds of waters, if one could but see them all . . . so hypnotized by this theater of transformations my head spun and eyes slipped after staring too long, my belly trembled, and this was the condition I was in when gusts of strong, skirling wind galed and swung the *Republic* broadside to windward, pointing her *back* the way we had come. Loose ropes, carpenter's tools, and unfastened casks of beef flew everywhere like cannon shot, cracking more than a few skulls. The skipper, who'd been sprawled out, stewed to the gills on his cabin floor, clawed his way topside, shouting "Gangway!" and looked wildly around at those awaiting his orders. Said: "Secure all loose gear." Cringle shouted back that the helm would not respond. "Mr. Fletcher," ordered Falcon, "see if the cords are entangled." The sailmaker checked them and made answer that they were not. "Damme," said Falcon, "she blows hard." His fingers clenched fishbelly white, then faintly blue, on the helm, and in his state he was a pitiful sight, hunched forward, pulling the wheel so hard his temples bulged, barely able to stand. The men saw this. His movements were slower than a man's submerged, like a mime mocking normality. He was that soused, that unsteady on his feet, and said, crestfallen, aware of his condition, "You have to help me here, Mr. Cringle." And then it was full upon us: a sea hot with anger, running in ranges like the Andes or the Rockies, and be damned if in the topgallant sails I didn't see forks of blue lightning. The forecastle was hidden behind curtains of spray. The bows were deep in water. At this point, screams came from the hold. With one hand I clung to the foremast, my head pressed in tightly against Baleka, squeezing her close enough to cut off her wind. And fairly windless was I myself. In this squall, some of the deck hands panicked. Ran from their posts, which was wrong, fell, scrambled below to their hammocks and pleaded with their shipmates to strap them down, screamed again. Others tied themselves to gratings, to the yawl, and to each other. "Hard alee." The wheel spun in the captain's hands. "Keep her hard to leeward." Before long the swirling air and sheets of breaching water overwhelmed him. He relinquished the wheel to Cringle and shouted into a hundred-horsepower wind, "Heave to." For five minutes nothing could be seen of the ship's hull—only shaking masts rising like a forest above foamy meerschaum, the sky stretched above like a gridelin scar, and the *Republic* broaching badly in the wind, popping her nails, her boards creaking like those in an old house, a shrinking casket. Cringle's lips were skinned back against his teeth. "Heave to it is, if you say so, sir."

Falcon's face was crabbed. "Are you makin' sport of me?"

"No—no, sir!"

What came upon us next is not clear. The instant Cringle spoke, the ship swung around with her face to the west, plunging into a trench, as if into Hell, below water columns that broke over us to the height of the crosstrees—two solid walls on either side, held still as when Moses parted the Red Sea. The sun stood still. The moon stayed. My heart stopped. It has never worked exactly right since, because when the roily waves spanked back, shaking the ship to her ribs, I saw two boys catapulted overboard to drown instantly in the shoal. Therewhile, half the Allmuseri children and women—Baleka's mother among them—five of Falcon's sheep, his hogs and fowl, were swept from the deck. The larboard quarterboat was torn away to disappear into the swell.

Then—

Miraculously, the wind shifted to the old quarter, the storm passed away, and we were through it as though it all had been a conjurer's trick. The ship labored back on course, the spell broken, though still the Atlantic thundered. Half the crew ran to the grog room and proceeded to get drunk. Our one Moslem on board dropped to his knees, banged his head on deck hard enough to break bone, and wept, "Inshallah! There *is* no Majesty and there *is* no Might save in Allah!" However that might be, three younger lighthands, too frightened to move, lost the power of speech and looked stupefied at the vacant stations where their lost mates had stood. Entangled in the twisted rigging above hung three bodies upside down. Matthew McGaffin, the boatswain, a pig-jawed former circus strong man with a walrus mustache, black eye patch, and a big, hectoring voice, swore the storm proved the ship was cursed by its black chattel and infernal cargo. Nathaniel Meadows, shaking, one fist in his mouth to stanch a scream, fouled his breeches. Twice. Without speaking, we all clapped our hands together as one company—thirty-two sopping-wet cutthroats black-toothed rakes traitors drunkards rapscallions thieves poltroons forgers clotpolls sots lobcocks sodomists prison escapees and debauchees simultaneously praying like choirboys, our heads tipped, begging forgiveness after this brush with death in Irish, Cockney, Spanish, and Hindi for a litany of collective sins so long I could not number them. Besides, I was too busy peeking through my fingers and promising God I would be good forever if He would quit playing games like that one. Had it lasted a bit longer, we knew, the ship would have been torn to pieces. More: such storms induced madness in seamen; triggered acute appendicitis, respiratory attacks, and suicide in their aftermath—the sorts of gales you tell your grandchildren about, if you live to see them, when they visit on holidays. Yet, standing hard by me, watching the dripping crew cross themselves and offer their first-born whelps to the priesthood, staring with a calm, distant gaze, was the quiet, catfooted Ngonyama. He was dry. Not a drop had touched him. He was coolness itself. Like actors I'd known in New Orleans (all unemployed), he had the unsettling ability to stare at you, or deliver a long speech, without once blinking his eyes or looking away. Maybe this was a trick he'd cultivated, but it struck me that he'd known the storm was coming, and I flinched, afraid of him, as he caught me by my sleeve, and said in his cracking, high-register version of English:

"Lay yourself forward or below tomorrow at noon."

"What?"

"If you have any friends on this ship"—he glanced at Baleka, who refused to release the fingers on my left hand—"tell them to lay below too."

He was gone before I could draw sense out of him. After he left to join his tribesmen below, I stayed for a time by the gunport, the girl's grip on me stronger than before. "We'll be all right," I said, though I didn't believe a word and was troubled by what Ngonyama, that crafty bastard, had told me, and furious at the cryptic tone he used sometimes. Really, when he talked like that, with a wink in his voice, it put me in a mind to clobber him with a caulking iron for his own good. "Universal Native," I'd call it, the high-flown, inscrutable way whites made the Cherokees talk in dime novels, or the Chinese in bad stage plays. It certainly wouldn't serve him well back in the States, or endear him to the slave lords who awaited him in Louisiana. Nonetheless, his warning bothered me. I half believed him; half I did not. But we had only a few hours or so of daylight before the impenetrable darkness of the ocean sank over us. Accordingly, the skipper was lashing the crew to make repairs—"You men get aloft!"— hauling them one by one to their feet to secure all the sails with spare gaskets. "And keep a bright lookout." Others to report on damages below, and double-breech the lower decks. And still others to make fast the boats and haul unnecessary cargo—but not his prized crate—to the rail and pitch it over to lighten us. Erewhile, his lighthands went feverishly to work at the pumps, but their hearts were hardly in it; they worked nervously, waiting for the sea to throw its next seizure. A few deck hands talked of quitting the ship, taking to the remaining boats, and abandoning the blacks who—the boatswain claimed—had caused this troublesome gale and boiling sea to turn us back to Bangalang.

"Steady up there," said Cringle icily when he overheard them. "And you can stow that kind of talk right now. The captain says he'll haze any man that tries to leave the ship."

"Then"—the boatswain spat inches from the mate's boot; he pushed his low-crowned black hat back on his head, its ribbon hanging over his left eye—"we're dead already."

[83]

"Maybe you didn't *hear* me, McGaffin!"

Cringle's right hand touched the owlhead pistol in his waistband. The boatswain only exhaled, then spat again, this time hitting the mate's leg. "You're the one who kin stow it, Cringle—or shove it mebbe, and that self-servin' rummy Falcon too, cose water was me woman before you was in long pants, and I know trouble when I see it. Them niggers is weird. A tribe of witches and strangelings. They kin *do* things. And if you ain't noticed, *sir*, there's water under the keelson, one of the bloody winches is broken, *sir*, and the hand pumps are chokin' up. You're as good a shipmate as ever put a hand to sail, Mr. Cringle, I don't doubt that, but sometimes I think you come to be quartermaster by crawling through the cabin-house window instead of through the hawseholes like the rest of us. God almighty, man, any tar on board'll tell you the skipper can't get this rotten piece of driftwood home—he'll drown the lot of us—and it's your business, I'm sayin', to put things right before it's too late. D'you know what I'm arstin' you to do? D'you have enough skin for it? Cose if you're too fish-hearted to do what you promised, some of us who've had enough *will* do it. See if we don't!"

Cringle could not reply. This list of problems stole the mate's wind. He looked flustered and put out, his lips pressed in hard. Like that, he spun away. Me, I had business of my own to tend to in the galley, and perforce hurried below, Baleka hanging onto my dripping shirttails like a barge in tow.

By nightfall Squibb and I had the galley in "shipshape," if you'll pardon the expression. The steward was feeling pleased with himself. Actually, he was probably squiffy from the genial influence of a tot of rum. Baleka had finally fallen to sleep in a corner, and the cook and I were on our knees, swabbing and squeegeeing when McGaffin, peeling off his oilskin coat, came through the hatch, followed by Cringle and five men as grim as any I'd seen, the terror of the storm still upon them. I saw their boots first as they slid past me, dirtying the floor. Silently, they took seats on the benches as a jury might, or men come for a hanging. I noticed immediately they were armed with cutlasses, knives, ship's tools easy to convert to bludgeons. McGaffin sat on the edge of the galley dresser, a little higher that way than the rest, his big hands with curly black hair on the backs folded on his hips. Cringle closed the door, the quietest of clicks as wood kissed metal. Squibb dried his hands slowly on his apron, rose up on one knee, then the other, and gave me a glance, his whole air saying *Careful!* as he filled a mug of tea for each of them. "Illinois, I think mebbe yuh should leave."

"No," said Cringle. "We need every man we have here."

"Do we now?" McGaffin paused with the mug just below his mouth. "Every man, I'll agree, but this one ain't no sailor, he's a stowaway, remember? A workaway. I been watchin' him since you found him in the longboat. I didn't see him sign any articles. He ain't got no stake in all this."

"In what?" I asked.

"The ship, boy! You come along fer the ride, I reckon. But after you've gone back to farmin' or fogle-huntin', the rest of us got to think about our future and families, God love 'em, if we live to see land again, which I'm startin' to doubt more 'n' more every day." He set his mug down. "You got a family?"

I thought of my brother and said, "No."

"You got a gel?"

I thought of Isadora and said nothing.

"See, then? It don't matter wot happens to *you*, does it?"

Right then, Cringle's hand cutting through the air for McGaffin to stop made the candles affixed to the wall behind him flicker, casting his own face in shadow. He coughed, clearing his throat, and said, "Rutherford, we're here to decide the best way to put this ship back on a steady course. A crew has to trust its captain. Those of us here don't. We think it's time to change leadership."

"You mean mutiny?"

"I didn't call it that."

McGaffin frowned. "That bother you?"

Their eyes, full of hardness, bit into and held me to see if it did; stares aimed like shotguns, gazes so steady and critical I felt as if I were on stage or had the square frame of an oil painting around me. To my left, firewood crackled in Squibb's oven, splashing an eerie coralline light on their faces, and a peculiar warmth on my legs, for my clothes were still damp, except there on my trouser legs, where the heat made the cloth stiff. All this time I stood motionless, unsure what to say. Silence, never doubt it, was equally a sin in their eyes—eyes I had seen before, I realized, under the sun-blackened brows of slaves: men and women who had no more at stake in the fields they worked than these men in the profits of a ship owned by financiers as far away from the dangers at sea as masters from the rows of cotton their bondmen picked. No less than the blacks in the hold these sea-toughened killbucks were chattel. McGaffin's gaze drifted to my left hand.

"That queer ring he's wearin', d'you see it? I only seen one like it afore. It's on the flipper of the scoundrel who almost sank us this evenin'. You know," he said to the others, "I think I was wrong. This one ain't no stowaway, he's a blinkin' spy."

"No! I stole the ring."

"Oho! Then you hold no brief for Ebenezer Falcon?"

"None at all."

"You wouldn't grieve none, or pour ashes on your head if, by some unexpected but nat'ral nautical accident at sea, the Old Man came to a sudden and tragic end?"

"No."

"Or mebbe"—he leaned forward, touching flame to Kentucky burley in his potbowl pipe—"if *you* was the cause of that?"

"Hold your tongue," sighed Cringle. "We must keep our heads. Rutherford is on *our* side."

"Yes," I said quickly. "How can I help?"

"Right, how *kin* you help? He's driftwood, this one. A fugitive and a vagabond. He's got nothin' to lose. If we poach this ship, you, Mr. Cringle, or Fletcher there, or that bedswerver Josiah who got more wives than a Mormon elder—it's plain we'll swing for piracy. The brokers Falcon works for will have us hunted from Chesapeake Bay to the South China Sea. Our wives'll be widowed. Our sisters, poor darlin's, will have to go out on the twang to turn a coin. And our wee li'l ones? They'll be orphaned, I tell you, or sold to the workhouse. But suppose *he* done it? Suppose we tell 'em a stowaway done in the skipper? Well, what *abaht* that? Huh? Once we reach New Orleans the rest of us kin sign on to other ships, and Calhoun'll go his own way, like he's always done, believin' in nothin', belongin' to nobody, driftin' here and there and dyin', probably, in a ditch without so much as leavin' a mark on the world—or as much of a mark as you get from writin' on water."

I said, "Now, just a minute—"

But the others were nodding. One said, "That could work, Mr. Cringle, if you'd take the helm—"

"And," said another, "maybe the captain's share of the cargo'd be spread amongst alla us. You could see to that, couldn't you, sir, seein' as you'd be captain when we got home?"

"Yes, I'd see to that." He was rubbing his forehead, breathing deep through his nose. One nostril whistled, clogged by something best left unsaid. He took out his handkerchief, pressed a finger to one side of his nose, and blew. "But what about Calhoun?"

"What abaht him?" said McGaffin.

"Does he get a share?"

"Aye, if he does like I said. It'd prove where his loyalties lie. For once in his life he'd be doin' somethin' useful." He looked sideways at me. "You ever cut a man's throat, Calhoun?"

"Oh, all the time."

"Leave him be." Cringle blew again. "Nothing says we have to *harm* the captain. I'm not a bold man, but I despise him as much as all of you do. Mutiny"—he turned to the boatswain—"doesn't bother me either. God knows, to *be* a Yank is to be mutinous. The goddamn country was born out of rebellion. But, to be fair, Falcon's carried us this far safely." He paused bleakly, folding his handkerchief. "That counts for something."

"Give him a launch, then." Fletcher stroked his long-chinned face. "I say put the bugger and a few provisions in a gig when we go by an island. Most likely he'll land on his feet thataway, knowing him."

"That's what I was thinkin' meself," said a boy in the back, a carpenter's mate generally quiet who brought this out only after stoking up the courage to speak. Their eyes coming his way made him color. More softly, as if taking back what he'd just said, he added, "Maroon him?"

McGaffin made a contemptuous snort. "Aye, and knowin' the Old Man, he'll come through, raise another crew, hoist the Jolly Roger, and track every one of us down. Naw, I don't like it."

"But it's fair," said Cringle. "At least he'll have a chance. That much we owe him."

The boatswain disagreed, but saw each man shift to Cringle's side. "All right. If that's how you want it. But I don't see nobody volunterin' to *put* him in that launch."

Fletcher turned his head away; a few others looked at the floor.

Quietly, a catch in his voice, Squibb said, "There are seven of yuh."

"Sure, Josiah, and twice as many blokes who'll take his side, like Meadows, once the shit hits the orlop ceilin'." McGaffin bent his brows deeply. "You'd have to disarm the bugger first, or draw him away from the rest, get him alone somehow, or when he's sleepin'. Trouble is, he sleeps light. You all know that. And his cabin's got more fykes and infernal traps than I seen red men lay down. Naw, he ain't got this old and ugly and evil by bein' stupid, not on your life." For a few moments he sucked his pipe, blowing columns of smoke that collected in layers on the floor at his feet. Then: "Calhoun?"

"What?"

"You nicked that ring, you say?"

"That I did."

"From where'd you nick it?"

"The Old Man's cabin."

There was silence, a collective shock commingled with suspicion, as though maybe they thought I was lying. Which I was. As a general principle and mode of operation during my days as a slave, I always lied, and sometimes just to see the comic results when a listener based his beliefs and behavior on things that were Not. But don't judge me harshly; it was one of the few forms of entertainment bond-men had. However, if I'd known where this lie would lead, I'd not have said a word.

Cringle leaned forward. "You were *inside?* You got past all those locks? All those latches?"

"Yessir." That much at least was true.

"So," said McGaffin, "if he broached cargo once, he kin do it again. This time, though, let him unload grape from the captain's guns when he's out, dampen his powder, dis-connect all them security wires, and our lads kin slip in as easy as you please. Mebbe Squibb kin put a li'l somethin' in his dinner."

"No." The cook shook his head. "I believe in what you're doin', but don't ask me that."

McGaffin spat a string of tobacco onto the floor. "Josiah, you make me sick. You know that?"

"Say what yuh want. I ain't doin' it."

"Half a mo', guvnuh. Wot day we talkin' 'bout?" asked Fletcher. "Needs to be soon, I'd say."

"Tomorrow at six bells," said McGaffin. "See, we find some bothersome task to keep Falcon aft, somethin' he'll need to supervise, like overseein' the blacks when they're brought up to give 'em air—he's allas there fer that—then Calhoun has the time he needs. We kin put Falcon over the side that night. Cringle kin make sure we're the ones on evenin' watch tomorrow."

Fletcher's lips burst open in a goatish laugh. "Tell the others he *fell* overboard."

"Drunk as the parson's wife, eh?" McGaffin slapped his leg. "I like that. What say *you*, Mr. Cringle? Are you in this?"

"I'm in. But if Rutherford is caught . . ."

"Aw, he's a *thief*," said McGaffin. "Nobody'll think nothin' if he's caught. It's his nature to be in places he ain't supposed to be. Worst come to worst, he'll get a few stripes, that's all."

Cringle's eyes softened, the most sympathetic I'd seen them in days. Unlike the others, he did not drink, but moved among them with a mug in his hand, so as not to offend, lifting it to his mouth occasionally but never taking a sip. "Can you do it, lad?"

In a narrow room filled with grizzled, desperate sea rovers, all in agreement (and armed), except for Josiah Squibb, standing a little off to one side and behind the others, pulling at his fingers and swinging his head side to side for only me to see—encircled by conspirators such as these with the nerve tips of my index finger throbbing where I'd nervously torn off a nail, I could only do as they wished and say, "'Tis done."

Thus things stood when the meeting ended. Each sailor cut a notch in his thumb, dripped blood into McGaffin's mug, and drank from this, sealing the bond. Did I sip from this cup? Aye. Once they were gone, their lips and teeth stained crimson, Squibb and I set to fixing mess. We worked in silence. One thing I liked about the cook was that he knew when to shut up even when he was mubblefubbled and dying to talk. Occasionally, I felt his eyes, like fishhooks, try to catch mine as we squeezed past one another in the narrow galley, but he kept his thoughts untongued. Personally, I was too pitchkettled to trust my own speech. My eyes began to sting and steam a little; I wiped a sleeve across them, and kept my back toward Squibb, more than a little ashamed for not standing my ground earlier. But here, let it be said, that in

waters strange as these, where any allegiance looked mis-
placed, I could no longer find my loyalties. All bonds, landside or on ships, between masters and mates, women and
men, it struck me, were a lie forged briefly in the name of
convenience and just as quickly broken when they no longer served one's interests. But what were my interests? No
question that since my manumission I'd brought a world of
grief on myself but, hang it, I wished like hell I had someone
to blame—my parents, the Jackson administration, or white
people in general—for this new tangle of predicaments.

"Blame for what?" Squibb stared at me.

"Nothing. I was just thinking out loud."

"Oh."

He was very quiet, was Squibb. He finished carefully
arranging a plate of fresh prawns, earthapples, and kale
he'd bought special for Captain Falcon in Bangalang. No
French chef could have better composed the meal to seduce
a hungry man's eye and mind. To my way of thinking,
that's pretty much what you paid for in fancy-dress New
Orleans restaurants anyway: a skimpy meal that left you
famished hours later but laid out oh so beautifully, as Tin-
toretto might prepare a still life in eye-catching colors and
forms. Added to that, Falcon insisted on the best silver and
a freshly lighted candle with his supper. The funny thing
was that while he demanded, like the rich, meals served in
ever more inventive aesthetic configurations that took the
poor steward hours to prepare, the skipper, after a second of
appreciation, approached the act of eating like a task, falling
to it with silent, single-minded determination, seldom looking up from the table, glopping it down with efficient, steady
forklifts that favored a farmer baling hay. In a trice he was
finished, sprang up from the table, throwing down his soiled
napkin, and was off to see to some shipboard chore.

"Yuh wanna carry this fish 'n' tayters over to him?" Squibb wiped his fingers down the front of his apron. "If yuh're in with them others now, I guess bringin' his chow'd give yuh a chance to look his cabin over a little. Better wipe that stain off yuh mouth first."

I took Falcon's meal and climbed through the hatchway, a clean napkin draped over my forearm. At his door, feeling like a waiter, I rapped three times on wood with my knuckles, the keel and bottom planks beneath me swaying on waves pulsing to the pull of the moon. I heard chair legs scrape on wood. Latches were thrown, a key turned in the lock, and when the door whipped open the Old Man stood before me naked except for his gunbelt and steel-toed boots. Instinctively, I swung my head away and took a step backward.

"Sorry, sir!"

"Don't stand there, man." He sniffed at his food. "Bring it in."

I stayed in the doorway as he went, boat-necked and tattooed over half his body, back to his chart table, his quill, and his logbook. There was meat on this man. It dawned on me, as I waited outside, watching his bare, freckled shoulders hunched over whatever he was writing, that he threw off his habiliments and wrote naked as the newborn for purely literary reasons. I had known a poet in New Orleans who told me he did the same. Rumor had it that Benjamin Franklin was a nudist too. Something to do with inspiration and freeing themselves up. That sort of thing. Naturally, I understood nothing about these matters; I only knew that I had no interest in seeing an empire builder in the raw, and so I stayed in the doorway. Falcon saw my bewilderment, growled something under his breath, a barely audible oath about philistines; then he opened a bureau with swinging brass handles and lifted out a Tyrian robe of Chinese design.

He fumbled into it, rolled the sleeves to his elbows, then came tripping back to me.

"Well, *now* will you come in?" His voice was crisp. "Close and lock the door as you do, Mr. Calhoun."

I did as he bade me. "I've brought your dinner."

"And a report, I hope." He uncovered the food I set on his chart table beside a most curious glass container I'd not noticed before. Inside it was a 45-caliber ball flattened on one side. Falcon spread the napkin over his knees, used his fingertips to tweeze a strand of hair off a potato, and handed his fork to me.

"You first, Mr. Calhoun."

"You want me to eat some?"

"Eat a little of *everythin'*, if you will."

Actually, I was happy to oblige. I hurried from one item to another, then back again, trying to stuff myself before the skipper snatched the fork from me and said, "At *ease*." He squinted at me for several moments to make sure I didn't gag or change color or collapse face down on the floor, at last seemed satisfied and sat back, his head bent in prayer, then poured himself coffee. At some time in his childhood, I suspected, he'd learned to drink hot coffee the same way he ate soup, with a spoon, slurping up the black stuff like broth. So he did now; his father's habit, most likely. In between steaming spoonfuls he asked:

"D'you think I'm overly cautious?"

"Well—a wee bit, yes."

"I gather you trust, even *like*, other people, don't you?"

I was a little startled by his question. Was he joking? I laughed a second too late. "Yes, I do, sir. Don't you?"

"Not a bit. Never have. I suppose they've never been real to me. Only I'm real to me. Even you're not real to me, Mr. Calhoun, but I think you like me a little, so I like you too."

"Thank you, sir."

Falcon broke off a hunch of biscuit. "Your report, laddie."

Please don't think poorly of me if I confess that during the next half hour I unbosomed myself. I withheld nothing. Did I lack liver? Touching my side I assured myself this organ was there. Perhaps I simply needed to talk. Perhaps I was, at heart, a two-faced coward as bad as my brother when it came to betraying rebellious slaves to Master Chandler. (I'll tell of this treachery in my own good time.) However it may be, I outlined the mutineers' plan to deep-six him, citing each rebel by name, and described the central role they had assigned me in the takeover, the whole account spilling from me in fits and starts, for I feared Falcon's Jovian wrath more than theirs. More than once, his rages had sent men climbing to the crow's-nest for safety, and he'd turn to one of his officers, chuckling, "They think I'm loony." I told everything, talking louder toward the end because the ship's dogs began a howling brangle outside louder than before, belike timber wolves or wild coyotes. When, finished, I looked up, Falcon was smiling and picking his teeth with his thumbnail.

"So that's the way of it. They think settin' me adrift will solve everythin'? Hah! Hark you now. I'm not an *easy* man to eliminate, Mr. Calhoun. Not even for me." He tapped the container on his desk with his spoon. "I tried to kill myself once. That's what come of it. The ball bent flat on my skull. Naw, the peace they want's impossible, whether Cringle's at the helm or McGaffin or me."

"How do you mean?"

"I'm not the problem is what I mean." Apparently he felt the tightness of his gunbelt after eating; he took it off, placing his pistol and keys down on the table between us, a presence that made me all the more uncomfortable. I tried not to look at the gun, fearful that if I stared it might suddenly go off. "*Man* is the problem, Mr. Calhoun. Not just gents, but women as well, anythin' capable of *thought*. Now, why do I say such a curious thing? Study it for a spell. You're a boy with some schoolin', I can tell. Did it include the teaching of Ancillon, de Maistre, or Portalis? You recall each says war is divine, as much a child of the soul as music and poetry. For a self to act, it must have somethin' to act *on*. A nonself—some call this Nature—that resists, thwarts the will, and *vetoes* the actor. May I proceed? Well, suppose that nonself is another self? What then? As long as each sees a situation differently there will be slaughter and slavery and the subordination of one to another 'cause two notions of things never exist side by side as equals. Why not—I put it to you—if both are true? Books live together in the library, don't they, Teresa of Avila beside Aristippus, Bacon beside Berkeley? The reason—the irrefragable truth is each person in his heart believes *his* beliefs is best. Fact is, down deep no man's democratic. We're closet anarchists, I'd wager. *Ouk agathón polykoíranín eis koíranos éstos.* We believe what we believe. And the final test of truth is war on foreign soil. War in your front yard. War in your bedroom. War in your own heart, if you listen too much to other people. And in each battle 'tis the winning belief what's true and the conquerer whose vision is veritable."

"No—nossir!" says I, louder than I intended. "By my heart, sir, if something is true, it can't be suppressed, can it, regardless of whether all the armies of the world stand ready to silence it?"

"You're a smart boy. What d'you think? Is truth floatin' round out there in space separate from persons? Now, be frank."

"No, but—"

"Conflict," says he, "*is* what it means to be conscious. Dualism is a bloody structure of the mind. Subject and object, perceiver and perceived, self and other—these ancient twins are built into mind like the stem-piece of a merchantman. We cannot *think* without them, sir. And what, pray, kin such a thing mean? Only this, Mr. Calhoun: They are signs of a transcendental Fault, a deep crack in consciousness itself. Mind was *made* for murder. Slavery, if you think this through, forcing yourself not to flinch, is the social correlate of a deeper, ontic wound." He could see I was squirming and smiled. "Let 'em put me over the side. Before my dinghy's out of sight, they'll be arguing and pitching daggers till there's only one tar left alive. Such are my views." He pushed back from the table. "D'you still plan to help the rebels set me adrift?"

"No."

"That means you *submit*, doesn't it?"

"I guess so."

"See, 'tis always that way."

On deck the dogs kept snarling, as if they'd cornered something. I sat for a moment in misery and methought myself outdone. I stank. I could smell myself, and stood, wanting a defense against Falcon's dark counsel and arguments that broke my head. To my everlasting shame, I knew of none. As my fingers curled around his empty plate and passed over his keys, pausing there, then over his pistol, he pulled his robe tightly around him.

"Don't think I'm not grateful for what you told me. You'll be rewarded. Tomorrow break in that door, as you promised, but leave my things as they are. I'll arm a few mates on our side and we'll chain the rebels in the hold with the blacks."

"That's all? They won't be harmed?"

"I'll set them free. They'll forfeit their shares, of course, and I might bastinado the bunch of 'em to teach the others a lesson. But aye, I'll set 'em free. If all goes well, I'll double your lay from the cargo. You'll be in the lolly soon, I can promise. There'll be a bonus—hatch money—for the find we've got below."

"Can you tell me what that is?"

"I suppose I can now. We're past keeping secrets from each other." A soft burp forced its way to his lips. The hounds quieted some, leaving a silence in which I could hear only whimpering and Falcon's voice, as he leaned toward me, beckoning with one crooked finger that I tip my head toward his own. "Sit down here beside me, Mr. Calhoun. You shouldn't hear what I've got to say standin'."

Entry, the fifth [20]
JUNE 30, 1830

"'Tis a god." Falcon kept his voice low; he looked round furtively, as if the furniture might be listening. "We've captured an African god."

I said nothing. Surely you can understand why.

"Oh, I'm not one to believe in heathen gods, but I know 'tis different from anythin' seen back in the States. The Allmuseri have worshiped it since the Stone Age. They say it sustains everythin' in the universe. It never sleeps. Night and day, it works, like a weaver—like rust, or an Alabama field hand—to ensure that galaxies push outward and particles smaller than the eye dance their endless, pointless reel. It is the heat in fire, they say. The wetness in water. Once a year the whole tribe stays awake all night so it can rest, then resume its labor of creating and destroying the cosmos, then creating it again, cycle after cycle. According to Allmuseri priests, it accomplishes this with only one-fourth of its full power. That alone is enough to, say, guarantee photosynthesis and keep the planet on its axis. Perhaps it uses the other three-quarters to sustain alternate universes, parallel worlds and counterhistories where, for example, you are captain of the *Republic* and I'm the cook's helper. Naturally, they do not speak its name. That takes too long. It has a thousand names. Nor do they carve its image. All things are its image:

stone and sand. Master and slave. When Ahman-de-Bellah raided their village two months ago, he found their Most High located in a shrine, for like the Old Testament god this one, far from receding into silence, delights in walking with and talking to its people. With me, it's a witty conversationalist, I can tell you that, though prone to periods of self-pity and depression. Knows a little of everythin', though not as we know things, of course, and seems slightly amused Ahman-de-Bellah put it in irons."

"You can do that?"

"Quite right, m'boy. 'Twasn't *easy*, of course. Sometimes it's physical, you know, like me and thee. But only for a few seconds at a time. Mostly, it's immaterial, the way gods and angels are supposed to be. Being unphysical means there can only be *one* of each kind of god or angel—one Throne, one Principality, one Archangel, 'cause there's only a formal (not a material) difference amongst 'em, so the one below is the only creature of its kind in the universe—*is* the universe, the Allmuseri say." He paused, cleared his dry throat, and lifted a teaspoon of coffee to his lips. "Another thing 'bout not bein' physical most of the time is that it can't understand any of the sciences based on matter, like geometry. Heh heh. It can't *do* geometry, you see, 'cause it's a god."

"Are you saying even a god has limitations?"

"That I am. And not only limitations, lad. I daresay it has downright contradictions. For example, a god can't know its own nature. For itself, it can't be an object of knowledge. D'you see the logic here? The Allmuseri god is everything, so the very knowing situation we mortals rely on—a separation between knower and known—never rises in its experience. You might say empirical knowledge is on man's side, not God's. It's our glory and grief both, a function of the duality of mind I mentioned a moment ago. Oh, 'tis a

strange creature we have below, Mr. Calhoun. Omnipres-
ence means it forefeits our kind of knowledge. Omnipo-
tence means, ironically, that it can create a stone so heavy it
cannot lift that same stone from the floor."

None of this was clear. Aphasic, I nodded anyway. My
brain had stopped functioning a full five sentences ago. Could
it be that in a dimension alongside this one I was a dwarf sitting in a Chinese robe, telling a white mate I had captured
a European god and, below us, the hold was crammed with
white chattel? Preposterous! Considering thoughts of this
sort was like standing on the edge of a cliff. "Cap'n," I said,
swallowing, "you've got a god on ship?"

"You shouldn't goggle," says he. "Makes you look weak-
minded, Mr. Calhoun. We're not only shipping Allmuseri
on this trip, we're bringin' back their deity too. I'd wager
this freight's worth at least a footnote in the history books,
wouldn't you say? Better'n stumblin' on Lemuria or findin'
the source of the Nile. Most nations will pay a pretty whack
to possess a creature such as this. It's a tricky rascal, though,
if you ain't careful."

"Tricky, sir?"

"I mean what it did to Tommy O'Toole. Legend has it the
Creature has a hundred ways to relieve men of their reason.
It traps them, tricks them into Heaven. It's Loki and Brer
Rabbit together. That's why no one goes near it but me."

"You, I take it, are immune to Heaven?"

He gave me a look, then stood, placing his hand on my
arm to bid me rise, then eased me outside. "Do as I said
tomorrow. Tell no one we've talked—and, for Christ's
sake, see what's spooked the dogs."

I closed the door by leaning against the muntin, and
frowned (I hated it whenever anyone used the word "spook"),
my head on the frieze rail, listening to blood thrum in my

temples. I waited for my second wind. It never came. Forth I went anyway through layers of mist toward the animal pens, holding Falcon's tray close to my chest, squeezing it for no other reason than to have something concrete and stable to hold on to, and holding as well a key I'd taken off his table. I couldn't help myself. Stealing was a nervous habit for me sometimes, a way to shake off stress and occupy my hands. And I *had* felt nervous in his cabin because so little on this ship seemed solid, reliable. If before my report to Falcon I had felt unsure whom to trust, now I distrusted my own eyes and ears. A godhead in the hold? Closing my eyes, I made myself consider the consequences of the being that sustained the world falling into the hands of an American soldier of fortune. No explorer could touch Falcon now. He had won his deepest wish. From the Vatican to political circles in Virginia he would be pursued, maybe given the presidency or the personal empire he had dreamed of since the Revolution. Once his cargo was in captivity, under lock and key at some college (or more likely a military camp), history would change. History, as we knew it, would *end*, for there would be no barriers between the secular and sacred. I was starting to scare myself now and figured I'd better stop. Gods only appeared, Reverend Chandler had said, on Judgment Day. For my part, I wanted to live a little longer. I was only twenty-three years old. The Apocalypse would definitely put a crimp in my career plans. I needed the world as I knew it, as evil and flawed as it was, to *be* there for a while. On the other hand, if Falcon had not lied, there were easily half a dozen questions I wanted to put to who—or whatever maintained the cosmos second by second. Shaking my head to clear it, I pushed on to the pens, the trembling of my hands rattling silverware on his tray, for I could not imagine all the implications of Falcon's discovery, or what shocks at sea awaited me next.

Instantly I got my answer.

The dogs were howling, a slobber like sea foam spilling from their mouths, because Meadows was beating them viciously with a sjambok. In the glow of a deck light, I could see he was wearing my clothes. The killing part was my blouse looked better on him than on me. Lashing the ship's dogs, he spoke to them in an unerring imitation of black English, his accent passably southern Illinoisan, his speech sprinkled with my quirky, rhetorical asides, which I swore right then I would never use again. For a moment I was fascinated. It was like watching a voodoo priest manipulating a lock of your hair. Impaling a doll effigy of you with pins. Meadows even managed to mime a few of my physical eccentricities, like the way I tugged my right earlobe when perplexed—I caught myself doing it then, glanced back at him and gasped—or sometimes rubbed my nose with a quick flick of my thumb, boxer style: gestures that were quintessentially Rutherford Calhoun and delivered now to the frothing dogs with profound, heartless doses of pain. Meadows peeled off my clothing, let the hounds smell and snap at it one last time; then he pulled a pair of Cringle's breeches over his own, rolling up the cuffs. Again, he whipped them, wrenching his voice toward higher registers to sound like the master's mate giving orders. It laid me low, seeing Meadows vanish and a devastating caricature of Peter Cringle emerge, boiled down to his broad outlines. The barber-surgeon was a born thespian. Knowing each mate medically, I guessed, gave him this gift for brutal satire. After rubbing the crotch of Cringle's smelly trousers into their noses to drive home his strongest scent, Meadows draped a few articles of brightly colored African dress—Abo Po and abada—around his broad waist, unleashed a new, stinging round of stripes, and spoke those haunting words the All-museri men and women used, like a fragrance, breathed into the air. For the dogs, though, these were hated words, intertwined with twenty lashes. They would throw themselves, fangs unsheathed, with no thought toward their safety upon anyone speaking Allmuseri, scratching his brow like Cringle, or blending the languages of house and field, street and seminary, as I often did.

Fingers of sweat dripped from Meadow's face, his whipping arm was sore, and he rubbed it, then peered round in my direction. I pressed myself down between the topsail bitt and foremast, the skin on my back crawling. He shrugged, picked up his laundry basket, and headed for the fo'c's'le. Long minutes passed before I moved. My head went turngiddy. I was unsure of what I had witnessed. But I knew what it meant. This was not a ship; it was a coffin. The morrow would bring catastrophe because Meadows was one step ahead of the Old Man, giving a living weapon to Falcon's loyalists in case the mutineers seized the ship's guns or the Africans could not be controlled. Targeting Cringle to be torn apart I understood. But why me? Were all loyalties here a lie? We would be sunk to the bottom of the briny unless unbeknownst to these camps someone played a trump, a hole card, none knew existed.

I realized that I held that card. Before doing anything, though, I needed to rest. To return to the galley I was forced to maneuver slowly aft over and around human and nautical debris sprawled at the ship's waist, larboard side. The storm had flooded berths below. So several hands brought their gear topside to bed down in the open air beside slave women and the children. Cluttered with bodies, wooden crates blown apart earlier, their contents strewn every which way, and draped with dangling sheets of sail, the sunken portion of the *Republic* from tiller to stern felt like a makeshift refugee camp, a smelly, chaotic strip of shantytown where the injured and ailing were tossed helter-skelter together. In mist-softened light mutineers, Africans, and able seamen could not be distinguished. Brief as this moment might be, no stations were evident among the ship's company. Could these people slay one another after sunrise, as some planned? It hardly seemed possible. Or necessary. On the water, leagues from culture or civilization, I saw no point in our perpetuating the lunacies of life on land. Just for a spell the sea had swept some of that away. No one had the strength to sustain idols of the tribe or cave. Even the caged chickens were tired. Every so often walls of spray faffled on deck, much in the fashion of showers I remembered in New Orleans during the spring that were refreshing and brief, and just as suddenly were gone. Our sails were asleep. Beneath a damp blanket McGaffin slept beside the cabin boy. A Chinese mate and Ngonyama, who was officer of this night's watch, bandaged the arm of a boat-puller bruised during the storm. Cringle dozed with Squibb's parrot on his left shoulder. His back was against the topgallant rail, both his eyes shuttered, and his head all on his right shoulder. I saw he was sweating. The armpits of his coat were stained, which was odd. Things were cooler now at eight bells and, since Meadows had left the pens, quiet but for an occasional cough and the sound of the ocean, spongelike in the way it absorbed, even trivialized, the noises we made. Crew and cargo, so exhausted—by events and their own fierce emotions—appeared content to lie together a while in various postures of fatigue, barely lifting a finger, as if they were frozen, or maybe soldiers who had fallen after a battle, too drained and dead of brain to do anything more than listen to their own lungs; and the frail, in-and-out sigh in each man's chest was only the faintest of notes beside the brooling waves and wind of the Atlantic.

I came through the hatchway, holding the tray in front of me with one hand. Squibb, resting on the galley table, roused awake when he heard me, swung his feet over the side, and blew the overhead lantern back into brilliance. Stretching wide like a bear, then yawning, he placed his left palm over his lips. "Sounded like the storm put a scare into them dogs." I decided to say nothing about the dogs; Meadows had not included Squibb in that. Then my eyes drifted to the corner and Baleka, beautifully disheveled in her sleep. In her left hand she was holding an empty wineglass, one of Falcon's, from which she enjoyed drinking water or goat's milk in imitation of the ship's brain-sotten crew. As with other children I'd seen, she looked boneless in sleep, her body limp, one hand (the right) on her brow like a society woman about to swoon. But she wasn't breathing right. When I bent to brush my lips on her brow, I saw dark spots on her cheeks.

"She's a bonny lass," said Squibb. "I didn't want to put too many covers on her."

"Guess not," I said. "She's burning up. Did she wake while I was gone?"

"Once. I give her a glass of milk. Listen, Fletcher come down heah a minute ago and gimme his sea chest. Said he wouldn't need it anymore, seeing how it was the end of the world. He was scratchin' a coupla spots on his arm like the ones on her. I think she give all them boys somethin' when they was heah. How yuh feelin', Illinois?"

"I feel I've been on this boat so long my toes are growing webs between them . . ."

Squibb cautiously let his tone lighten to console me. "Sometimes the slaves bring their sickness with 'em. They won't last that long. We'll live to see worse and tell about it. Still"—he winked—"it wouldn't hurt, I suppose, if you've made out yer will. Yuh got family back in Makanda?"

"A brother, if you can call him that."

He noticed the wobble that came into my voice whenever I spoke of Jackson, and he paused. "Bad feelin's between yuh, eh."

"You could say that."

"Well, that's a shame, 'specially since yer kin's liable to get anythin' yuh leave."

The thought made me laugh, painfully. "You don't know him. Because of him I've got nothing *to* leave, Josiah."

"He cheat yuh out of it?"

"In a way."

When I said no more, he finally asked, "Yuh gonna tell me about it, or do I have to wait fer yer biography?"

"No."

"Yuh'll feel better, love. C'mon now. No point in carryin' round old cargo like that. All along yuh been tellin' people he betrayed yuh. Ain't that so?"

"Me, yes—only me."

"Didn't treat yuh like a brother, yuh're sayin'?"

"Yes. I mean, no! He treated everyone the same, and that was the trouble. Kin meant nothing to him. Do you remember that strange flower we saw in Senegambia? I forget what it's called, but one of the chaps pointed out how lovely a scent it released when you admired it and held the petals close to your nose. And that when you didn't notice at all and brought down your boot, it offered like a gift that same remarkable perfume. Do you remember?"

"Aye."

"That's Jackson."

Squibb nodded. "Yuh think 'bout him a lot, don'tcha?"

"Too much. And each time it's different. I go over what he did so often and from so many angles that it makes no sense anymore. He is like Ngonyama, or Baleka there. I didn't know that until the skipper brought them on board. Hell, Squibb, he could *be* from their tribe, for all I know."

"That'd make you one of 'em too, wouldn't it?"

This I doubted. The more I thought on it, the Allmuseri seemed less a biological tribe than a clan held together by values. A certain vision. Jackson might well have been one of their priests. Against my better judgment, I let Squibb wheedle me into talking about Master Peleg Chandler, his will, and my day of manumission, which I remember right enough because we were the only family he had. He was a tobacco planter living on southern Illinois land his great-grandfather cleared himself, a painfully shy man from a long line of pious homesteaders, hardly a man to go in for politics, or even raising his voice in a conversation. His daughter, Maggie, died at seven from scarlet fever; his wife, Adeline, took a fatal spill from a horse. Thus, Jackson, who was Chandler's nurse and aide since the time he could fetch and carry, and I stood to inherit everything he had. It was in the wind one morning—May 23, 1829—that he would be generous with his slaves for their years of devoted service. Among his holdings was a commodious, clean-timbered manor house, with sturdy pine furniture, heavy and square and still blond, and grounds that were beautiful in the springtime, bordered by berried woods and trees in bloom like half a hundred bouquets. Inside were glass-fronted bookcases, a quarter-turn stair with a landing space, and well-stocked cupboards in a kitchen full of DeGroot silverware. His stables were full of Morgan horses and Appaloosa; he had Berkshire and thin-rind hogs, and vast investments clear up to the state capital in Springfield. No, we hadn't suffered all that badly, I'm almost ashamed to say, and Jackson was troubled by this too, for now it seemed we would never want, if he included us in his will, which I knew he would because my brother was all the good he thought there was in the world.

(Squibb squinted at me with one eye shut. "Yuh ain't spinnin' a cuffer now, are yuh?"

I assured him this was God's own truth.)

We could tell he was dying—or damn near dead—that spring. He'd never been hale, of course, what with tuberculosis and a curious blood condition that sometimes gave his skin a faint grayish tinge. Cottonlike tufts of gray hair flecked his head, as if he had just rolled over in a field of dandelions. Also he was hard of hearing in his right ear and damned near deaf in the left, his voice an octave louder each year as his hearing failed. Master Chandler always kept an ear trumpet by his side. When he was annoyed at what you were saying, he would lift his trumpet not to his good right ear but rather to his left, effectively relegating you to silence as he smiled and nodded in seeming agreement. At his age, sexual imagery only made him melancholy. He could listen to Jackson play Bach's *St. Matthew Passion* or Beethoven's A Minor Quartet—that deep work of renunciation—downstairs in the parlor for hours. A funny old man, I'd have to say, with the soul of a celibate or contemplative. Yet he was, in most senses of the word, a fair, sympathetic, and well-meaning man, as whites go. In all North America, if you searched up and down, you'd not likely find a more reluctant slave owner than he—one who inherited us and hated the Peculiar Institution—and we knew fortune could have treated us far worse.

As so often happens with sick people who can get no satisfaction from quacks and country doctors, he turned to theology and found in Thomas and the Pseudo-Dionysus a solace that eased his pilgrimage through a broken world. Confined as he was to his sickroom and in nerve-racking pain, he suffered cheerfully, he read over and over Jan van Ruysbroeck's *Flowers of a Mystic Garden*, taking notes on blank margins he'd clipped from newspapers and magazines (he hated waste of any sort). Long passages from these works he made Jackson and me read to him, as he made us reel whole cloth from our heads the words of the English mystic William Law: "Love is infallible; it has no errors, for all errors are the want of love." What he didn't know about theology was, I guess, not worth knowing. Still, he knew lots of queer arcana too—rags of dubious learning, like how many divisions were in Hell (four), the number of devils there (7,405,926), and all this he passed along to his servants, the Calhoun brothers, when we attended to him.

Needless to say, I set no store by these matters. But Jackson listened. Some of the old man's aspects (but not all) he admired. He took the role of manservant seriously, but only after twisting it around, even turning it against the various definitions of the South until he became Chandler's steadiest caretaker of things on the farm. He had, I remember, an uncanny way with livestock. With birds, it went beyond uncanny to downright astonishing. Jackson would toss a pan of hard bread crumbs into the backyard after we had eaten, then walk inside and sit at the window. Minutes later, the yard was blanketed with birds from God knew where, a whole aviary thick enough, I always believed, to walk on if he'd wanted to. They would let him lie down upon them— he was so gentle, so self-emptied—then take off in formation like a magic, feathered rug. Yes, he had a way with birds. And plants as well. They'd explode into bloom from the blink of Jackson's eye.

He was, I should mention, eight years my senior, so we didn't exactly grow up together, and to this day I can only guess at what made him tick. To a degree, he viewed me as one more child he must see feed and keep from killing itself by climbing trees or playing too close to the well. And who was our father? How I wish I could say; he ran from slavery when I was three. I have searched the faces of black men on Illinois farms and streets for fifteen years, hoping to identify this man named Riley Calhoun, primarily to give him a piece of my mind, followed by the drubbing he so richly deserved for selfishly enjoying his individual liberty after our mother, Ruby, died, thus leaving me in the care of a brother like a negative of myself. He was (to me) the possible-me that lived my life's alternate options, the me I fled. Me. Yet not me. Me if I let go. Me if I gave in.

Let me explain.

My older brother, who was tall—maybe six feet three in his stocking feet—with a thick shoebrush mustache, a Julius Caesar haircut, and freckles that ran right across his forehead, had known our father and saw more deeply than I ever could into the rituals of color and caste. He spoke affectionately of our Da, wished him well wherever he had run to, but he could not forgive him for abandoning us to save himself. Riley sent no one to fetch us. As far as we knew, he wasn't working to buy us out of bondage or living nearby with the Indians, as some black men did, descending on farms to raid and sniper slavemasters the way the colonists did the British. No, he'd cut and run. I know Jackson pondered long on this dilemma: Stay in slavery to serve those closest to you or flee. Run or do your best in a bad situation. To his credit, he stayed, thereby assuring me of having *some* family. Other bondmen, though, saw his choice as obsequious. On occasion, I saw it that way myself. Rightly or wrongly, he thought it possible to serve his people by humbly being there when they needed him—whites too, if they weren't too evil, and he was incapable of locking anything out of his heart. There can be, as I see it, no other way to unriddle why my brother, more than any other bondman, was generally faithful to Reverend Chandler, laying out his clothes each morning, combing his dry, brittle hair, fetching his nightly footbaths, and just as regular in the performance of his appointed tasks for the other servants, standing there by everyone's side through family death and sickness; Jackson was a Sunday preacher in the slave quarters, the model of propriety, and had twice the patience of St. Francis. As you might guess, I was *his* shadow-self, the social parasite, the black picklock and worldling—in whom he saw, or said he saw, our runaway father. He was ashamed of Riley Calhoun. And of me. Hearing our master was near death that Saturday in May, my brother called me from the grainbin in Chandler's barn, where I had just managed to get my forefinger inside a gap-toothed, rather delicious-looking Negro girl named Dorothy, our laundress's daughter. He gave me a sad, scolding preacher look. Scrambling into my clothes, then brushing hay off my calfskin boots and my yeoman's cap, I pecked Dorothy on the cheek, then followed him up the footpath to the house.

On this day I speak of, Master Chandler was old and full of days. As pale as a parsnip. If I remember rightly, it was raining pitchforks. Isn't it always on a day of gloom? And the climb behind my brother to the top-floor chamber was the slowest I have ever made. Some part of me loved my brother. Yes. But we couldn't get along or see things the same way. If you are born on the bottom—in bondage—there are only two ways you can go: outright sedition or plodding reform. I chose the first, expressing my childhood hatred of colonization in boyish foul-ups and "accidents" (setting Peleg's barn on fire once, breaking things, petty theft, lies, swearing, keeping bad company, forgetting to bathe, fighting, all the things "problem children" normally do), but in the context of the Old South, for a colored boy in Makanda, they were really small acts of revolt—blows against the Empire—though I was too young at the time to know them by their proper name. These things Master Chandler dismissed as youthful folly, then, later, as irredeemable parts of the "Negro character." But Jackson went the other way: a proper Negro, he was, a churchgoing boy who matched my every irresponsibility with a selfless deed as if he wanted to shame me, or subvert each bigot's lie about blacks by providing a countertext, saying to the slaveholding world, "Not even this can make me miss a step." If that was what being a "gentleman of color" amounted to, then I decided I wanted none of it.

And let it be known that I hated that cramped low-ceilinged room. Nor was I eager to look into Chandler's face as the light there flimmered, then failed. His chin hung like a turkey wattle. His mouth was fishlike, all collops and pleats, caved in, his dry lips sunk inward as if his gums had grown together. Seeing him, Jackson breathed a deep sigh. Half irritation, half fellow feeling. He went to his bedside, then poured water for him from a hobnail pitcher. Though my brother spent hours in this sickroom (Chandler had a bell on his night table, which he jangled to call Jackson, and to this very day the tang of every bell reminds me of the one in his bedroom), all I felt then was its oppressiveness. There were no windows. The air inside was yellow, the floor damp. It smelled violently of medicaments, lotions, and disinfectants. Outside the wind howled, shaking the latch and hinges on doors downstairs. Timbers in the room shook.

"Sir." Jackson leaned toward Chandler's iron bed, then turned his head away from the smell. "Do you know me?" He sat on a painted fiddle-back chair, his dark hands folded.

Weakly, the old man took a deep-chested breath. He seemed touchingly glad to see my brother, who said, "Rutherford is here too."

Reverend Chandler frowned at that, thinking perhaps of how I'd disappointed him, that I was and would always be pretty light timber. The look he gave me was severe. I stayed a respectful distance from his bed, watching them from one side.

"Did you want to see us?"

"Bring me the Bible. And something to write with . . ." He coughed miserably. His breathing was noisy. Jackson came back from a trestle table in the corner, carrying the book and a goosefeather pen, which he handed to our master. Slowly Chandler began scrawling our names alongside those of Maggie and Adeline on the riffled pages of the book.

"I should have done this years ago, seeing how you've kept things going here for me and the others when I couldn't . . ."

Jackson bowed his head formally, his eyes on his spit-shined shoe buckles. "As the oldest, it was my duty."

(For Christ's sake, I thought, get *on* with the goddamn will! That very next morning I figured on starting off the day with a breakfast of egg bread; of sleeping until noon, hunting until dark, wearing a pair of skilts and a stylish cap, then dining on potted salmon from England and preserved meats from France.)

Master Chandler lay back. Jackson readjusted the old man's nightcap on a skull that looked thin as eggshell. I shivered, the chill of the room taking hold of me. After several moments, Chandler's breath rolled out again; "As of today, I release you both, if you wish to go." I stepped closer, listening with every nerve as Jackson lifted our master's head a little to adjust his pillow. "But Jackson—good Jackson— dear Jackson," he whispered, "let us come down to cases.

You *are* the oldest, and I daresay I am in your debt. Whatever you want for you and Rutherford is yours. Tell me how you wish to be rewarded and I shall see that you have it."

I breathed a sigh of relief, believing all our burdens had lifted. But my brother looked pained. Never before had anyone asked him what *he* wanted. He hesitated. A knot gathered in my throat; I wanted to speak, but Chandler cut the air with the side of his hand to silence me.

"You have *no* requests, then, Jackson?"

"Oh, yes, of course," said Jackson. "I've thought about it, sir. There's so much my people need."

"There's a lot *I* need," I said.

Jackson sent a scowl my way, then closed his eyes to help his words along. "I know Rutherford has thought about this too. But it don't seem *right* to ask for myself. I *could* ask for land, but how can any man, even you, sir, *own* something like those trees outside? Or take that pitcher there. It's a fine thing, sure it is now, but it kinda favors the quilts the womenfolk make, you know, the ones where everybody in the quarters adds a stitch or knits a flower, so the finished thing is greater'n any of them. Well, I been thinking on this, sir, and I wonder: What *ain't* like that? Nothing can stand by itself. Took a million years, I figure, for the copper and tin in that pitcher to come together as pewter. Took the sun, the seasons, the metalworker, his family and forebears, and the whole of Creation, seems to me, sir, to make that one pitcher. How can I say I *own* something like that?" He scowled to stop me from interrupting. "I'm sure I speak for both of us, sir, when I say the property and profits of this farm should be divided equally among all your servants and hired hands, presently and formerly employed, for their labor helped create it—isn't that so?—the fixed capital spread among bondmen throughout the county—I can give you their names—and whatever remains donated to that college in Oberlin what helps Negroes on their way north."

"There'll be less for you and Rutherford then," said Chandler.

My brother nodded. "Our needs are small, sir, or should be."

"Jackson!" My voice jumped. "You fool!"

"That'll be *enough*, Rutherford." A deep crease split Master Chandler's wrinkle-grooved face. He patted Jackson's hand, then twisted out a dour, disapproving look at me. "You'd do well, you young reprobate, to end this light-minded life you've been leading and improve yourself by listening to your brother's counsel. He is wise for his years. Wealth, you know, isn't what a man has, but what he *is*, Rutherford. Your brother, I daresay, has been an inspiration for me—"

"As you have been for me, sir," said Jackson.

The floor beneath my feet seemed to fall away. Do what I would, I could not move. They sat there for the longest time, complimenting and smiling at each other. I could have strangled them both. I felt like smashing things. Instead, I shrank from the room, feeling sacked and empty, wondering if I would ever get on in this world. It took me five days to stop shaking. For the rest of my short stay on Chandler's farm before I struck south for New Orleans, I felt angry at anything that moved.

It was nearly daybreak. Josiah Squibb sat staring, his eyebrows raised. "Great day!" He sucked his teeth. "Give it *all* away, did he?"

"Would I be here serving hardtack if he hadn't?"

"What'd yer share come to, Illinois?"

"About forty dollars. Also, I got the family Bible and his bedpan."

The cook snorted, one of those sounds impossible to decipher, then lay back on his table. Two or three breaths later he was asleep, somnambulized by my life's story (I never knew it was that dull) and playing dueling snores—so they sounded—with Baleka. I reached to touch her hair, then drew back my hand from the heat enveloping her like an aura. I could not let her die, a dark pawn, caught between Falcon and the ship's proletariat. I knew that now. I rose stiffly, stretched out the stiffness in my spine, and climbed back on deck where all slept except Ngonyama.

Leaning against the rough-tree rail, parts of him rubbed out by morning mist (his left arm, his legs), he stared back toward Bangalang. There was something in this, and the way he canted his head, that reminded me so of how my brother sometimes stood alone on the road leading to Chandler's farm after our father left, looking. Just looking. Seeing me, Ngonyama turned and smiled.

"You couldn't sleep, Rutherford?"

I shook my head. "Can I ask you a question?"

He waited.

"If you were captain of this ship, what would you do?"

"Me?" he laughed. "If I were master?"

"I mean, if your tribe could take the helm."

He took a moment to think, rubbing his chin, as if this were a Yankee riddle. "Brother, my people have a saying: Wish in one hand, piss in the other, and see which hand fills up first. But if this could be, we would set sail to Africa. All that has happened in the last few weeks would be as a dream, a tale to thrill—and terrify—our grandchildren."

"And the crew?" I asked. "Would you harm them?"

"What is the point in that? Once home, we would return their boat to them. Anger, we say, is like the blade of a sword. Very difficult to hold for long without harming oneself."

Behind me, I heard the morning hack of McGinnis. A few of the children on deck were starting to awaken. From the pocket of my breeches I withdrew a few loose crumbs of hardtack and the key I hoped might open their chains. Like a magnet, it had clung to my palm when I lifted Falcon's tray from his table the night before.

"Here," I said. "This is for you."

Entry, the sixth 22
JULY 3, 1830

Twenty blacks were brought from below to dance them a
bit to music from Tommy's flute and let them breathe. They
climbed topside and stood crushed together, blinded by
the sun, for that morning the weather was fair, yet hushed.
Meadows and Ngonyama searched the fusty spaces between
decks for Africans unable to come up on their own. There
were always a few of these since Ebenezer Falcon rearranged
their position after the storm. He was, as they say, a "tight-
packer," having learned ten years ago from a one-handed
French slaver named Captain Ledoux that if you arranged
the Africans in two parallel rows, their backs against the lin-
ing of the ship's belly, this left a free space at their rusty
feet, and *that*, given the flexibility of bone and skin, could
be squeezed with even more slaves if you made them squat
at ninety-degree angles to one another. Flesh could con-
form to anything. So when they came half-dead from the
depths, these eyeless contortionists emerging from a shadowy Platonic cave, they were stiff and sore and stank of
their own vomit and feces. Right then I decided our captain
was more than just evil. He was the Devil. Who else could
twist the body so terribly? Who else could enslave gods and
men alike? All, like livestock, bore the initials of the *Republic*'s financiers burned into their right buttock by a twisted

wire—*ZS*, *PZ*, *EG*, a cabal of Louisiana speculators whose names I would learn soon enough.

Meadows snapped his head away, his nose wrinkled, and he splashed buckets of salt water on them, then told Tommy to play. The cabin boy, taking his place on the capstan head, had not stopped smiling since seeing the Allmuseri god. Snapping together his three-piece flute and touching it to lips shaped in that strangely mad, distant smile unreadable as a mask, he let his chest fall, forcing wind into wood that transformed his exhalations into a rill of sound-colors all on board found chilling—less music, if you ask me, than the boy's air alchemized into emotion, or the song of hundred-year-old trees from which the narrow flute was torn.

One side of Falcon's face tightened. "Methinks that's too damned melancholy. Even niggers can't dance to that. A lighter tune, if you will, Tommy." The cabin boy obeyed, striking up a tune of lighter tempo. Falcon, pleased, tapped his foot, stopping only to stare as Ngonyama and Meadows carried an African's corpse from below. As with previous cases like these, Falcon ordered his ears sliced off and pre-served below in oil to prove to the ship's investors that he had in fact purchased in Bangalang as many slaves as prom-ised. This amputation proved tough going for Meadows, for the last stages of rigor mortis froze the body hunched for-ward in a grotesque hunker, like Lot's wife. Hence, after shearing off his ears, they toted him to the rail as you might a chair or the ship's figurehead, then found him too heavy to heave over.

"Lend us a hand here, Mr. Calhoun." Meadows wiped sweat off his upper lip.

I stayed where I was. Beside me, a moan burst from a car-penter standing too close to the slaves. They danced in place like men in a work-gang, but one had slipped when the ship rolled, falling on his back and accidentally, it seemed, kicking the sailor in his stomach. And a good kick it was, knocking the wind out of him. The mate looked puzzled; he ran two fingers over his forehead.

"You should earn your keep, my boy." Falcon nudged me toward them, then brought a handkerchief to his brow. "One hundred bars overboard. Gawd, I hate waste."

Ngonyama was holding the boy—for so he proved to be when I stepped closer—under his arms. Meadows had him by legs cooled to the lower temperatures of the hold. Though he was semistiff, blood giving way to the pull of gravity, motionless in his veins, was settling into his lower limbs, purplish in color as he entered the first stages of stench and putrefaction. The young rot quickest, you know. The underside of his body had the squishy, fluid-squirting feel of soft, overripe fruit. If you squeezed his calves, a cheese-like crasis oozed through the cracks and cuts made in his legs by the chains. It was this side of him Meadows wanted me to grab, providing him and Ngonyama the leverage they needed to swing him past the rail. I cannot say how sickened I felt. The sight and smell of him was a wild thing turned loose in my mind. Never in my life had I handled the dead. It did not matter that I knew nothing of this boy. Except for Ngonyama, the males had generally been kept below, but I'd seen him among the others when Falcon made the Africans dance. Judging by what little was left of his face, hard as wood on one side and melting into worm-eaten pulp on the other as rigor mortis began to reverse, he was close to my own age, perhaps had been torn from a lass as lovely as, lately, I now saw Isadora to be, and from a brother as troublesome as my own. His open eyes were unalive, mere kernels of muscle, though I still found myself poised vertiginously on their edge, falling through these dead holes deeper into the empty hulk he had become, as if his spirit had flown and mine was being sucked there in its place.

"'Ere now," said Meadows, "come about, Calhoun. I'm gettin' tired of holdin' him." I gripped the boy from below, slipping my right hand behind his back, my other under his thigh, so cool and soft, like the purple casing of a plum, that my ragged, unmanicured nails punctured the meat with a hiss as if I'd freed a pocket of air. A handful of rotting leg dropped into my hand before I was able to push hard enough for the others to swing him, just before his limbs disconnected like a doll's, to sharks circling the hull. That bloody piece of him I held, dark and porous, with the first layers of liquefying tissue peeling back to reveal an orange underlayer, fell from my fingers onto the deck: a clump from the butcher's block, it seemed, and the ship's dogs strained their collars trying to get it.

Ngonyama wrapped it in a scrap of canvas and pitched it as hard as he could into a wave. My stained hand still tingled. Of a sudden, it no longer felt like my own. Something in me said it would never be clean again, no matter how often I scrubbed it or with what stinging chemicals, and without thinking I found my left hand lifting the knife from my waist, then using its blade to scrape the boy's moist, black flesh off my palm, and at last I swung it up to slice it across my wrist and toss that into the ocean too. "No." Ngonyama placed his fingers on my forearm. He must have felt me wobble. His hands steadied and guided me to the rail, where I gasped for wind, wanting to retch but unable to. Saying nothing, he waited, and as always his expression was difficult to decipher. Weeks before I'd felt that no matter how I tried to see past his face to his feelings, the signs he threw off were so different at times from those I knew they could not be uncoded. It was said, for example, that the Allmuseri spat at the feet of visitors to their village and, as you might expect, this sometimes made travelers draw their swords in rage, though the Allmuseri meant only that the stranger's feet must be hot and tired after so long a journey and might welcome a little water on his boots to cool them. Nay, you could assume nothing with them. But of one thing I was sure: There was a difference in them. They were leagues from home—indeed, without a home—and in Ngonyama's eyes I saw a displacement, an emptiness like maybe all of his brethren as he once knew them were dead. To wit, I saw myself. A man remade by virtue of his contact with the crew. My reflection in his eyes, when I looked up, gave back my flat image as phantasmic, the flapping sails and sea behind me drained of their density like figures in a dream. Stupidly, I had seen their lives and culture as timeless product, as a finished thing, pure essence or Parmenidean meaning I envied and wanted to embrace, when the truth was that they were process and Heraclitean change, like any men, not fixed but evolving and as vulnerable to metamorphosis as the body of the boy we'd thrown overboard. Ngonyama and maybe all the Africans, I realized, were not wholly Allmuseri anymore. We had changed them. I suspected even he did not recognize the quiet revisions in his voice after he learned English as it was spoken by the crew, or how the vision hidden in their speech was deflecting or redirecting his own way of seeing. Just as Tommy's exposure to Africa had altered him, the slaves' life among the lowest strata of Yankee society—and the horrors they experienced— were subtly reshaping their souls as thoroughly as Falcon's tight-packing had contorted their flesh during these past few weeks, but into what sort of men I could not imagine. No longer Africans, yet not Americans either. Then what? And of what were they now capable?

Ngonyama touched the pocket of his trousers, patting the key I'd given him. After that, he handed it back to me and turned down his thumb. As far as I could tell, the key was wrong for their leg-irons. Yet something in his look said keys and conventional means of escape did not matter anymore, that the mills of the gods were still grinding, killing and remaking us all, and nothing I or anyone else did might stop the terrible forces and transformations our voyage had set free.

He turned his back when Cringle, pretending to inspect a bracket on the topsail halyard, moved behind me. Along his neck I saw three bumps the size of berries. His voice, a hoarse whisper, said, "Go! We'll give you twenty minutes before we take them back down. Be prompt now." I proceeded on to Falcon's door. There I took a moment to steady the twitchy fingers on my left hand by stretching them until each popped. In my waistband I carried a six-inch length of wire. This I wormed slowly into the lock face, letting it clear barriers I could see only in my mind until I felt it push against the pins of the bolt, thus releasing the bolt from the jamb. In less time than it takes to tell, I was inside.

Falcon's cabin was as I remembered it from my previous visits. Perhaps a little messier. Closing his door I bent down on all fours and began feeling with the tip of my knife for the hair-thin wires closest to the entrance. And then suddenly I could not breathe. I felt caged. Wrong if I did as the first mate asked. Wrong if I sided with Falcon. I began hiccuping uncontrollably (my body's typical response to dilemmas that had no solution), a worse fit of this than when Isadora and Papa tried to blackmail me into marriage: a palpable feeling of dread I cannot describe unless you have been, say, in the hayloft of an old Illinois barn during an earthquake and feel the rafters tremble, and wonder how near it is to crushing in and the loft collapsing and beams raining down upon your head. That is how I felt. With so many men at odds, each willing something so different from the others, like the factions at war during the French Revolution (my own velleities included), and some not even fully aware of their will, the result could only be something unforeseen that *no* one willed or wanted. A change not in the roles on ship but a revolution in its very premises. On my knees, I did nothing, though it felt as if the room, and ship even, fell away. Some part of me was a fatherless child again. Alone in an alien world. Wanting to belong somewhere and to someone. Five minutes passed. Maybe fifteen before I could move. Then, involuntarily, my hands clamped together in a bedside, precynical posture I'd not taken since boyhood, one of surrender and bone-felt frailty in the face of troubles so many-sided my mind trembled to think of them. "God," I asked, "is this some kind of *test?*" My worldly wits were gone, and I knew, there on my aching knees, the personal devastation that was my brother's daily bread: burning for things to work out well, knowing the lives of his loved ones depended on this, but having no power or techniques or strategies left except this plea for mercy flung from an inner wasteland into the larger emptiness, the vast silences, the voiceless shadows *out there.* But no answers came. Only an inexplicable calm, as if I were the sea now, and the dam of my tears—the poisons built up since I left southern Illinois—burst, and I cried for all the sewage I carried in my spirit, my failures and crimes, foolish hopes and vanities, the very faults and structural flaws in the blueprint of my brain (as Falcon put it) in a cleansing nigh as good as prayer itself, for it washed away not only my hurt after hurling the dead boy overboard but yes, the hunger for mercy as well. My hands were moist from this hoarse weeping. My face was swollen and, searching myself, I discovered I no longer cared if I lived or died. The passion for life in me, that flame, was dead. Such was my position, and the windless state of my soul, when the Old Man's door flew open, flooding light into the darkened room, and I looked up, and through stinging eyes saw:

The mate named Fletcher. One side of his head was battered in. The bone of his nose was broken. Nailing me with his gaze and noticing only that I was a Negro, he raised his fist and started to swing.

"Fletcher, it's *me*, Calhoun!"

He stayed his arm in mid-swing. "The cook's helper?"

"The same."

He drew a great breath and, snorting, sent columns of blood cascading down the front of his blouse. I could see he was about to keel over and steadied him. "You're too soon," I said. "Cringle set the takeover for tonight, didn't he?"

He shook his head, then tried to swallow. "Me'n Daniels was in the storerooms, just went down for one bloody minute, when eight of 'em come pourin' in the slop chest like roaches when you open a wall—"

"Falcon's men?"

"Daniels was skivered from navel to nose quick as a butcherin', but I run up here and—" He gagged. His eyes flew wide to take in the semidark room. "Are the guns in that cabinet?"

"Aye, but—"

Before I could finish, Fletcher shoved me aside, behind the door, which saved me when he lurched toward the cabinet, caught his foot on a wire no more than an inch from the floor, and set off two explosions fainter than the pop of firecrackers. Still, I was splattered with bits of his scalp and a thousand needles of splintered glass from the cabin windows. He gave a cry I heard from a great distance, as if I'd gone deaf. Nay, I *was* deaf after the explosions. And blinded by the smoke, the smell of black powder flung like soot onto the broken furniture and Fletcher himself. Heavy as he was for me, and unable as I was to hear, I dragged him toward the door, and bumped into someone in the entrance. Turning, I looked straight ahead and saw no one. Then down, and there was Captain Falcon, cursing silently (since I was deaf), holding a saber in his right hand and, in his left, a bloody scalp of hair. Like Fletcher, he shoved past, dodging round his own traps, and it was then, as I stood trying to read his lips whilst he shouted, that the *Republic* must have run onto half-hidden rocks, or struck an isle, or the father of all waves fell upon us, for the walls buckled from a tremendous, rolling crash and rumbling that smashed the beams of the ceiling and threw us to the floor. The impact laid back strips of skin on my arms. Outside: the confused noise of men on deck. Then gunshots. Heavy feet thundered forward, some aft, and now and again something fell to the deck. I called to the skipper, "Have we run aground? What was that?"

Faintly, as if from far away, he said, "There's something 'cross my legs!" For the first time since I'd known him, the captain's voice sounded frightened. "They lit a cannon, Calhoun. Fired right into us. Kin you hear me? Give me your hand!"

From where I lay, he was impossible to reach. I knew only that I must find Baleka and Squibb. Two pistol reports, like the work of a whip, rang out—*crack! crack!*—and my stomach froze solid. There was heavy thumping on deck. A creaking of the blocks. Tacks and guys, sheet and braces rang loud against the wind. I pulled myself free of debris in the cabin and collapsed on a deck boot-deep in blood. As my sight sharpened, I saw through the curtains of smoke a squat, broad-shouldered slave named Nacta, who sprang toward me, cleaving the air with a marlinespike. A foot from my head he checked his swing. His chest was heaving. He kicked me aside, then disappeared into the skipper's quarters. Backing away, I sensed then that not Falcon's loyalists but the Africans had overcome Fletcher and Daniels, though how in God's name I could not guess. I skidded over shattered barrels, the carcasses of dogs ripped open like charnel-house swine, and cedarwood blocks floating in deckwash. There was damage to the lower rigging and jigger staysail, which hung in rags from the mizzen lower mast. In disfiguring smoke that stung my eyes, someone from the world below, the hell of the hold, hunched over a sailor, who lay on his side like a body washed onto the shore, beating him about the head with a deckscraper, and when this blotched and spectral figure saw me, he faded back into the smoke. The ship swung, pitching me forward. I fell, flopped around, and rolled. Righted myself. Briefly, in the corner of my eye, I caught movement by the lifeboats, what seemed in those fibrous seconds to be two men—one black, one the barber-surgeon—working quietly, single-mindedly at the uphill chore of killing each other. The African, still in chains, was stone still, holding at waist level a rusty saw. As Meadows moved, bringing his sword down in an overhead strike, the other brought his saw straight up, his fingers steadying the handle, guiding the teeth straight into the barber-surgeon's belly in a clean, swift, diagonal stroke that left Meadows frozen in mid-swing before his bowels spilled at his feet. I swung my head away. When I looked back they were gone, or had turned into two barrels. Impossible!

I rubbed my eyes and waded forward cautiously toward the cookroom. The helm was unattended. The wooden

steering wheel, with its spokes that favored a Hindu man-
dala, revolved slowly in winds that spun the crippled ship
in a circle, without direction. Without destination. We were
dead in the water. Adrift. A creaking hulk of coppice oak
tossing about on a sea the color of slate. Finally, I heard
motion. Even fainter still, a madhouse cackle that seemed
to come from the crow's-nest. Then more shapes, like figures in a shadowgraph, appeared gathered by the foremast.
Many of the sailors were face down and knocked for seven
bells. Some had surrendered after a one-sided battle that
appeared to be overweighted, strange as this sounds, toward
the Allmuseri who used the slippery deck to their advantage. They had been in chains before, I remembered. Taken
in raids by other tribes. Consequently, *capoeira*, or their
close-quarter version of it, was based on doing battle after
they were bound: knee-shattering kicks thrown after they'd
fallen. Ankle-breaking footsweeps. Chokes designed to use
their chains until one of them found the key to their shack-
les, and those freed swung the ship's cannon back toward
her bridge. Engaged as they were in disarming the remaining sailors, none had seen my approach. I eased backward,
and felt fingers dig painfully into my arm.

"Come to the fo'c's'le," said Ngonyama. He was wearing
Captain Falcon's cap. "If you wish to plead for the lives of
any of these men, that time is now."

"You plan to kill them?"

"That decision isn't mine, Rutherford."

"This morning you said you'd set them free!"

He thought for a moment, his left hand bandaged, I saw
then, a bloody mess where the dogs had torn away three of
his fingers. "As I said, the decision isn't mine."

I followed him to the forecastle. Then I heard first the
low voices of men whispering, then loud ones in disagree-

ment, and soon two lanterns blinked as someone moved across the room. Ngonyama stepped to one side, bidding me enter first. Stepping inside, placing my hand over one eyeball—as children do—I peered past the door rail to see what was inside, and when I saw what *was* inside I moaned. Everything was in ruin. Sea chests had been smashed open. Cabinets overturned. Inside, Cringle was seated amidst this debris on a straight-backed chair close to the east wall, with hieroglyphs of lamplight dancing on his scarred forehead. He bled from a gash that trenched open skin by his nose then deepened and disappeared into his hairline. His head drooped. His hands, I noticed, were bound with luff rope, his ankles with shreds from his waistcoat. His bare chest was crosshatched with scars. And, no. He was not alone. I saw three Allmuseri sitting on the benches; I recognized two more named Babo and Francesco passing a bottle of the skipper's best bellywash, and still another called Atufal, a big man who had an iron collar around his neck and stood behind the mate arguing—if my hasty translation could be trusted—for them to toss him over the side.

My entrance stopped all conversation. I stepped forward and came as close as I durst from the doorway.

"*All* the way in—*njoo hapa.*" Ngonyama smiled two rows of black-veined teeth. "No one will hurt you here, Rutherford. These men are your brothers."

How I wished I could believe him! Cringle tried to speak, but the one called Atufal seized his hair, yanking back his head. The strands stood out like stalks. His throat was bared. Against this white stalk the little black named Babo placed an English handsaw. Atufal said again that the mate should be killed. Ngonyama listened. He began to pace, and prime a horse pistol. The others tossed Cringle's life back and forth among them, some grumbling aye—*yebo* in Allmuseri—to his execution, then making a clean slate of the crew; some like Ngonyama saying *la*, or nay. Contrary to what I'd expected, they were in no mood to celebrate their victory. They were too tired and frightened for that, as well they should be. This battered rag-wagon was home until they found land. And what then? A firing squad, most likely. Whether they put to in Bangalang, or Louisiana, or any New World port, they would be cut down like wheat. No Yankee court would free them. They were still chattel, according to white men's law. Ngonyama, who was nobody's fool, knew this to be fact. He wanted the killing to end. They were not free men yet, he told the others, only free of the stinking hold. Gently he pulled me toward a chair. "You must help us," he began. "There is so much to unravel. . . ."

My fingertips on the seat, I sat lightly, tipped forward and ready to spring, for still I did not trust him. Yes, I was black, as they were, but they had a common bond I could but marvel at. The little black Babo, who had always seemed so servile before, sat sharpening a hatchet with cloth and stone, a strip of some sailor's coat bandaging half his head so that only one eye was uncovered. The other, Atufal, whom Falcon often shackled to the ringbolts on deck, had gone kill-crazy during the mutiny, shooting and stabbing our sailors and his own tribesmen as well, striking down in his fear anything that moved toward him. He'd taken a musket ball in his left shank, which was mangled, white bone visible through the black flesh of his thigh, but still he seemed more pleased than pained. All of them were injured and exhausted, but transfigured by their victory. Was it my victory as well? Or was Ngonyama only saving my life for some scheme? "Start with Falcon," I said. "What have you done with the skipper?"

Ngonyama bit down his lip and walked to a window, righting overturned chairs as he went. He kept his back to me. "Nacta is guarding him in his cabin. Don't plead for *him*, Rutherford." His shoulders drew in. "It would be a sin to let him live. He is responsible for every death on board."

"That's a lie!" flashed Cringle. "'Twas *he* set them free during the fight. I saw him! We were exhausted, some of us sick, and that one"—he flicked his head at Babo—"killed Daniels, who had keys to their leg-irons, and let the others loose. They clubbed us with the wood we gave them for pillows and tossed the dead like Tommy into the sea. And he—"

Atufal's hand stifled the rest. Babo placed his hatchet down on the mate's neck. He slanted his eyes toward Ngonyama, seeking the sign for them to kill him. Ngonyama shook his head. No. But he was alone in his decision. Three of them I recognized as warriors named Ghofan, Diamelo, and Akim urged Babo to open the mate's throat. And they had reason, good reason, for seeing the last of the *Republic*'s officers dead. Akim, a wide, dark-fired man who was short but had the strength of three, squatted on his hams; he made them relive his sister's death five days after we set sail. Ghofan, a black who had been gelded, and then suffered the torture of the brand, pulled his shirt down to show them how Falcon had burned in the initials *ZS* not once but three times until the impression was as clear as stigmata, or the markings on cattle. Each man had his atrocity to tell. If not brutality to them then a beadroll of humiliations the midshipmen had inflicted upon the women, two of whom had been raped, or on their children, and to this list Diamelo added the small but nonetheless violent assaults on their spirit—parading them naked for bathing before their own children, forcing them to eat by ramming fingers down their throats, answering their wild clawing from the hold with gales of laughter. On and on the charges came, and with each accusation a finger was stabbed toward the mate. Mercifully, he understood none of what they said. He was quietly whispering to himself the Lord's Prayer. Against this evidence of American crimes perpetrated on the Allmuseri, Ngonyama was helpless. His plea for sparing Cringle's life was shouted down. I felt my face kindling. My stomach made a turn. Glaring at Babo, Akim slashed the air with his hand. Therewith, Babo's fingers tightened the blade on Cringle's neck. The mate closed his eyes.

"Wait." I was on my feet. "Listen to me . . . please!"

Irritably, Babo hung fire.

"You need him," I said, gathering my wits, sailing close to the wind. "Kill Falcon if you want, but if you kill his helmsman, you'll *never* reach land. Never! None of you can read English maps. Nor keep this ship full and by once she's fixed, provided she *can* be fixed, and only Peter can help you do that. He's the only officer left."

Cringle spat blood and broken teeth onto the floor. "They'll see hell quicker'n they'll see help from me."

"Will you *please*"—I ground my teeth—"shut *up!*"

"No, you shall hear this! As God is my judge, I'll see every murderer here brought before a firing squad. Turn your back a second on me," he said to Ngonyama, "and you shall have a foot of steel in it."

Ngonyama frowned. "He should not have said that."

"He *will* help you," I said. "If he doesn't, I'll drag him to the rail myself."

Diamelo took a step toward me. He rubbed his finger, very dark, along my face, which was a shade or two lighter than his own. "Do it now." His voice had a clean monotone like metal. "Prove what you say." Then to Ngonyama: "On whose side is he? I wouldn't trust this one." He took the hatchet from Babo and forced it into my hand. "Not until he has broken away from them."

[133]

Four others agreed, chiming in that I was a crewman like the rest, an American, a risk unless I joined them by spilling blood, as criminals like Papa Zeringue demand a crime before you enjoy their protection. After this stiff exchange, the Allmuseri were eager now for *me* to execute Cringle. They waited, their eyes following me minutely as I gripped the hatchet, which felt heavier in my fist than a handspike. Now I had endangered my own neck. Why in heaven's name had I not kept my mouth shut, or choked my luff, as sailors say. If I refused, both Cringle and I would be pitched overboard. A long moment passed. I felt my head going tighter. I drew a deep breath, stepping toward Cringle, the hatchet lifted over my head. How long their silence lasted is impossible to say; I heard only the rasping of wheel ropes. Waters lapping. A ruffling of sails and the stormlike sound of wind. The kerosene lamp burned low in its bracket. Cringle sat motionless, waiting to hear his own head hit the floor. My fingers opened. The hatchet fell.

Diamelo ordered me to pick it up.

"Nay," said I. "You can kill him, and me too. But without his help, and mine, you'll wander the mid-Atlantic until the ocean swallows you, or some man-of-war heaves to and puts you in irons again."

Ngonyama considered this. Diamelo did not buy it. There was an eye battle between them for a moment, and the boy won, quietly pleased, I think, that I'd given him a way to end the slaying. "You speak well, Rutherford." His face sharpened: lean and pointed like a cat's. "I've no doubt you were a good confidence man in New Orleans."

I had to sit again and squeeze the seat of my chair to hide the shaking of my hands. Ngonyama spoke to his former yokefellows in a voice too fast for me to follow. Reluctantly, they saw the wisdom in releasing Cringle. Still, I was not done. I made bold to say, "Spare the captain until you sight land."

Ngonyama made a 180-degree turn. "No!"

"He can't escape, you know that! Use him to take us to safety. After that, do with him as you will."

"You ask us to let him live?"

"Nay," says I. "I ask you to make him *your* slave."

That thought stopped Diamelo. I could tell the taste of it intrigued him. "All right, then. As you say, he will serve us, and then we can slay him." Begrudgingly, Babo followed Diamelo's order to untie Cringle. His other bravos the boy sent outside to see to the wounds of their women and children, and to prepare a sacrifice to ensure their safe passage. In spite of himself, Cringle said, "They'd better steady the booms and yards by guys and braces, and lash everything well down."

Ngonyama said, "Thank you."

Then he took me to one side and told me to bring up any mates who had fled to the storeroom, his face older-looking now, grave, his shoulders giving way to gravity or the crunch of some secret grief he could not share. "Rutherford"—his brow tightened—"I have done as you advised. But, as you see, Diamelo is very strong with the others. You know, in our village I was a poor man, like you, but his father was well-to-do. Diamelo is used to getting his way. I worry less about your captain now than how Diamelo can sway my people."

Once outside, as we made our way down the ladder to the storeroom, the mate, who was above me, looked down and sneered, "Savages! And silver-tongued ones at that! Was it you who taught him English? You made a mistake there, Calhoun. He'll have you servin' his dinner, and wipin' his arse next, that one, if you listen to him."

"Maybe . . . but suppose he meant what he said."

Cringle kicked at me in rage. "Will you wake *up*, boy! Can you take his side after what they did? They were about to kill *you* too, Rutherford, or are you so wet you've forgotten that?"

"I'm not on *anybody's* side! I'm just trying to keep us *alive*! I don't know who's right or wrong on this ship anymore, and I don't much care! All I want is to go *home*!"

"Well"—he backed off a bit—"I'm not snapping at you. I owe you my life. I doubt if anyone would thank you for saving me, certainly not my family, seeing how I've failed them, but I'm grateful none of my sides were knocked off tonight, and I'll do whatever you say, God help me." He clapped me on the back. "That much I owe you."

The Allmuseri prepared their ceremony to sanctify the ship, to make it a kind of church, and enlist their gods as guides in our seafaring. Cringle and I canvassed the ship's storerooms and underbasements, looking for survivors, and to no avail until we descended into a tiny shotlocker full of saltpeter barrels in the lowest cell of the prow. I heard moaning—it was distinctly moaning—from the tiny cubicle, and called Cringle, who squeezed inside with an old Swedish poop lantern, then crawled back out, his free hand leading two figures I had given up as food for the sharks: Baleka, Squibb. Immediately, the girl squeezed me around my waist, both her hands bunching my shirt in the back.

"You're all right, Josiah?"

"Passable, Mr. Cringle. We come down heah soon as the fracas broke out." He folded his arms across his chest. "The others, I was wonderin' . . . Are they . . ."

"Dead? All but four of us. The Negroes have the ship now. It's their move. The only protection we have from them, I'm sorry to say, is Calhoun."

I mustered a smile. "Y'all better be nice to me."

The mate frowned, clambering back up the ladder. We sent Baleka up next, followed by Squibb, but I tarried below for a time, feeling a wave of dizziness wash over me, and I noticed spots on my forearm, which I dismissed. Once the wooziness passed, I pulled my sleeve down to my wrist and wearily climbed back into open air.

Thus things stood on the *Republic* for the rest of the day. Come nightfall, the fifteen Allmuseri who had survived the ship's takeover gathered on the starboard side. Their women had fashioned loose, baggy gowns for themselves from old sail. Although they had given better than they got in the fight, many of the men were injured. Six were carried to the ceremony, another five hobbled on crutches cut from topmast timber. Baleka pulled the skipper's goat to a hastily built altar inside a red circle they had splashed by the foremast. The sky was full of sea gulls, the sea calm now, shimmering as brightly as a mirror the way it reflected the moon. Cold, light breezes fluttered in the lower sails, so light you needed to wet your finger to feel them. Rags of gray vapor played round the topmost spars. Sitting on a crate beside Squibb and me, the mate shivered and pulled his peacoat close around him. He was jumpy from lack of sleep, his face ashen. "Mark my words, all of you. We're going to need that animal in a few days." Out of tobacco now, he sucked his pipe, which made a gurgling sound from spittle backed into the steam. "The storerooms are flooded. There's nothing left to *eat*." He grinned sourly, then coughed. "Unless we're ready to start eating each other."

Squibb stiffened. "Sir?"

"There'll be none of that," says I. "Only Falcon speaks of eating flesh, and he's under lock and key in his own cabin."

Squibb's belly rumbled. He looked down the deck to where Nacta stood with a rifle outside the skipper's door. "Who's gonna be captain, then?"

"Cringle, I guess. He's next in line. And one of their people to watch him."

The mate looked straight at me.

"Would to mercy I *do* get my hands on the helm," said he, rocking his head, "then I plan to steer us to America, so help me. We could steer the ship toward Africa during the day, as the blacks want, then toward the States at night when they're sleeping." Again, he sucked his long pipe. "We'll be docking on Long Island before the Negroes know what hit them."

"Can we do that?" asked Squibb.

I left a silence.

"What if we *don't* find land?"

Again, I could vouchsafe no reply.

"Mr. Calhoun . . ."

"Rest *easy*, Josiah. Whatever we do, the Allmuseri have the next move."

Which was now, I saw, to complete their peculiar cleansing ritual. From what I could understand, the blacks were not simply offering the skipper's goat to their god; they were begging him to wash the blood of the *Republic*'s crew off their hands. Perhaps even more important to them than freedom was the fact that no leaf fell, no word was uttered or deed executed that did not echo eternally throughout the universe. Seeds, they were, that would flower into other deeds—good and evil—in no time at all. For a people with their values, murder violated (even mutilated) the murderer so badly that it might well take them a billion billion rebirths to again climb the chain and achieve human form. Ngonyama wondered, I could see, if it had all been worth it, this costly victory in exchange for their souls, for that indeed was what was at stake. Ironically, it seemed that Falcon had broken them after all; by their very triumph he had defeated them. From the perspective of the Allmuseri the captain had made Ngonyama and his tribesmen as bloodthirsty as himself, thereby placing upon these people a shackle, a breach of virtue, far tighter than any chain of common steel. The problem was how to win *without* defeating the other person. And they had failed. Such things mattered to Ngonyama. Whether he liked it or not, he had fallen; he was now part of the world of multiplicity, of *me* versus *thee*.

And so they placed their foreheads on deck in shame and supplication, praying that the killing would not be carved forever into their nature, and that some act other than the traditional payment for murder—their own deaths in exchange—might be accepted to balance out their world again; that the *Republic* would be a ferryboat to carry them across the Flood to their ancestral home. When they were done and Ngonyama walked quietly to where we sat, his voice splintered as he spoke, his eyes hardly focusing on me at all.

"We are finished, *Ndugu*, my brother." He wiped his forehead with his fingers. "All is in order and ready for the return. We should start at once. My people have decided to sail for Senegambia. You must convince your captain to plot a new course for us."

Cringle sneered, "Good luck."

"If he does not," said Ngonyama, "I can guarantee that all of you will die."

This was no idle threat. Therefore, twenty paces found me at the skipper's door. Nacta would not step aside, his wide-legged stance a challenge of sorts as he jiggled in his left hand the ring Falcon wore to unlock his firearms. Down the deck Ngonyama ordered him to step aside. As Nacta moved away, I entered, limping a little on my left side, for the last interview anyone on this earth would have with Ebenezer Falcon.

Entry, the seventh
SAME DAY

In the shrunken air of Falcon's cabin there were secrets too scandalous for me to share with the ship's company. This was not a knowledge I wanted, but it waited to ambush me, like the Old Man himself, amidst sacks of drachmas, nuggets and bars of gold, and church boxes from sacked coastal towns, strewn along the floor. Anything not destroyed by the explosion, Atufal and Diamelo smashed because it windowed onto the savage world of their enslavers. Wheresoever my eyes ranged, aft toward the enormous upended bed, forward to his broken inventions by the larboard wall, his lodgings recalled abandoned manor houses raped and harried by brigands, and thus for a brief moment nothing here was familiar to me. A post-Christian roomscape, it struck me—me whose head was half full of Allmuseri words. The room swirled so for a second I had to plop my hands on my knees, put my head down, and wait until the ship's hull stabilized. But even then I felt culturally dizzy, so displaced by this decentered interior and the Africans' takeover, that when I lifted a whale-oil lamp at my heels it might as well have been a Phoenician artifact for all the sense it made to me. Yet in the smoking debris there was movement, a feeble stirring of Icarian man, the creator of cogs and cotton gins, beneath contraptions that pinched him to the splintery floor.

I found his legs trapped under timber. Therewith, I gripped wood with one hand, pushed aside with my other his torn sea charts, lire, egg-sized rings, almanacs, and his log, which he often sat upon to reach his table, then tried raising the beams off him without wrenching my own back. Falcon gave a gruntlike *oof*. Alow and aloft he was scuppered. When he crawled a few inches by grabbing the base of a bookcase and dragging himself forward, cartilage in his shoulder crackled like worm-addled wood—or, on deeper planes, the unhinging of his atoms. I saw half the ribs on his right side were broken, that he strained not only to deny a physical pain involuted and prismatic but deeper wounds as well. What were these? I could see that all he valued would perish from the indifference of Allmuseri who would no more appreciate the limits and premises of his life than he would theirs, whereby I mean his belief that one must conquer death through some great deed or original discovery, his need to soar above contingency, accident, and, yes, other pirates like John Silver and Captain Teach, his pseudogenius—to judge it justly—which could invent gadgets but lacked genuine insight, which rained information down on you like buckshot, but in the disconnected manner of the autodidact, which showed all the surface sparks of brilliance—isolation, vanity, idealism—but was adrift from the laws and logic of the heart. All at once I found that I was still ensorcelled by a leader who lived by the principle of Never Explain and Never Apologize. But I pitied him too, for his incompleteness. I pitied him, as I pitied ourselves, for whether we liked it or not, he had changed a people simultaneously for the better and worse, made himself the silent prayer in all their projects to come. A cruel kind of connectedness, this. In a sense we *all* were ringed to the skipper in cruel wedlock. Centuries would pass whilst the Allmuseri lived through the consequences of what he had set in motion; he would be with them, I suspected, for eons, like an ex-lover, a despised husband, a rapist who, though destroyed by a mob, still comes to you nightly in your dreams: a creature hated yet nevertheless at the heart of all they thought or did.

"Cap'n, this is Rutherford. Do you know me?"

"The galley swab?" His mouth opened horribly in a face as flat and foul-looking as a sea boot.

The skipper's nervous system, that deep structural mechanism none of us can reason with or *talk* to, was so damaged from the percussion of falling beams he could not control his bowels or the spastically dancing muscles of his face. Thus, smiles followed morose expressions. These were replaced by petulance, surprise, delight, then grief, as if behind the tarp of his skin several men and women were struggling to break free. I suffer you, then, to consider my shock at seeing him this way, fighting to the end to appear singular and self-reliant when, inly, all Nature in him was seditious. Although dazed by this reel of involuntary emotional masks, I'd seen enough of shipboard surgery to know his only hope was a stiff shot of rum, a sterilized knife to hack off everything below his knees, and henceforth precisely the sort of dependency on others a swashbuckling sea rover—a man so *fixed* and inflexible in his being—would find intolerable. "Aye, I know you. Is it the end of the world, Mr. Calhoun?"

"Sir?"

"It came to me as I lay here, a nightmare that this was the last hour of history. Nothing else explains it. The breakdown. I mean, how *thorough* it is, from top to bottom, like everything from ancient times to now, the civilized values and visions of high culture, have all gone to hell in fine old hamlets filled high with garbage, overrun with Mudmen and

Jews, riddled with viral infections and venereal complaints that boggle the mind and cripple whole generations of white children who'll be strangers, if not slaves, in their own country. I saw families killing each other. People were living in alleyways. Sexes and races were blurred. I saw riots in cities and on clippers. Then: the rise of Aztec religion and voodoo as credible spiritual practices for some, but people were still worshiping stage personalities too. On and on it came to me. Crazy as it seems, I saw a ship with a whole crew of women. Yellow men were buying up half of America. Hegel was spewing from the mouths of Hottentots. Gawd!" His whole body shuddered from stem to stern. "I was dreaming, wasn't I?"

"Maybe, Cap'n. Things'll never be that way."

One or two moments went by as he creased on his left side, still as the ship's figurehead, his skin paggly and scabbed, one of his sock suspenders broken (he had invented, I should record for this record, suspenders that ran from your shirttail to your socks so you never had to pull them up and always had a shirt that looked crisp, smartly starched, and capable of passing military inspection, including after a battle), his face relaxed and voice low, calm as island currents.

"You're uncommonly quiet 'n' calculating tonight. Is it 'cause you betrayed me, Mr. Calhoun—"

"Nossir. I did exactly as you asked."

"True?"

"Your plans, and those of the mutineers, got on the wrong side of the buoy and beached. I'm sorry, sir."

"Then we underestimated the blacks? They're smarter than I thought?"

"They'd have to be."

He nodded, wrinkling his nose at, I presumed, his own fierce odors. "Mr. Calhoun?"

"Here, sir."

"What's not changed is that I still need you to be my eyes and ears. I cannot write, so you must keep the log. No matter what becomes of me, I want others to know the truth of what happened on this voyage. Will you do that?"

"Cap'n, I'm no writer. I don't know how a ship's log is done."

"Doesn't matter. You're a bright lad. Do your best. Include everything you can remember, and what *I* told you, from the time you came on board. Not just Mr. Cringle's side, I'm saying, or the story the mutineers will spin, but things I told you when we met alone in secret."

To this I reluctantly agreed. I took his logbook from the ruins. But I promised myself that even though I'd tell the story (I knew he wanted to be remembered), it would be, first and foremost, as I saw it since my escape from New Orleans.

"Now, then," he said, satisfied that I would be his biographer, "can you tell me how the situation stands?"

"The Africans have the ship. We're steamin' blind. They want us to lay a course for Senegambia, whereupon the remaining crew will be released, if you can guide us there."

As I spoke, color faded out of his face. His fists, small-knuckled, squeezed open and shut at his sides. "They don't own this ship."

"Captain, they *do*. You can't change that."

"Naw, *you* don't understand. Neither do they. The slaves think they've wrested the *Republic* from the crew, is that it?"

"So it would seem."

"They're wrong." Muscles round Falcon's eyes tightened. "She wasn't *our* ship from the start, Mr. Calhoun. Every plank and piece of canvas on the *Republic*, and any cargo she's carrying, from clew to earring—including that creature below—belongs to the three blokes who outfitted her in New Orleans and pay our wages. See, someone has to pay the *bill*. I'm captain 'cause I knew how to bow and scrape and kiss rich arses to raise money for this run. I didn't come up in the last bucket, you know. I knew how to reach 'em, which wasn't easy, 'cause they don't like to be seen. Each one of 'em expects his investment to be returned. Mebbe tripled, like I promised. If we fail, they won't be forgiving. These are the men we have to appease, not them whoresons and rowdies outside. Oh, I know what you're thinking. We suffered the unexpected. Surely they'll understand. But I'm telling you they won't see nothing 'cept that I took their money—a lot of money, lad—and they'd just as soon see us drown, if I sail home empty-handed, as hear me report their fixed capital seized control of this brig and swung her back to Bangalang."

The ship's finances was a field where my ignorance was complete. On economic matters my heart was simple, my mind slow. I kept quiet. But was Ebenezer Falcon telling me that he, at bottom, was no freer than the Africans?

"A month before we left I visited one of these brahmins, my hat in my hands. Oh, I grinned and all but gave him my backside to pat. If any of the hands'd seen me I'd never be able to show my face in public, let alone raise a crew that wouldn't laugh at me. But it worked, Mr. Calhoun. I was just the crab he wanted, says he, to bring back blacks as valuable as the Allmuseri. I remember going over the crew list with him in his parlor. A simple room, you understand, but long as the main top bowline, filled with pale, eastern light in early morning and simple furnishings such as men of modest means might select. He came to breakfast in a waistcoat cut deep in front, not a wrinkle in his breeches, and his hair combed in a négligé style. A perfect gentleman of taste and proportion is what his toilet told you. All that was to hide the fact he'd made a bloody fortune running slaves and supplies for the British during the last war. See, only poor men put on a show. Which is what I did, 'cause I wanted this contract bad enough to beg for it. I figured this run'd be money for old rope. That easy, you understand? He let me do most of the talking, complimented me on my Latin, my expeditions down the Nile, my schedule for self-improvement, my travels and diverse translations, a few of which (unread) were on his bookshelf behind us 'cause he had a controlling interest in the Boston publishing house that produced them. He let *me* talk—get it—'cause even though the lubber could barely write his name he didn't have nothing to prove in this world. He could buy men such as myself with his pocket change. Buy beauty, if he couldn't produce it. Buy truth, if he was too busy to think. Buy goodness, even, for what blessed thing on God's earth don't have its price? Who ain't up for auction when it comes to it? Huh? Tell me that? All the while I gabbed, squirming in my seat beneath his family's coat of arms (the head of a Negro), sipping hot coffee from a cup that kept shaking in my hands, he was just smiling and studying me. Not as one man studies his equal—and I was *more'n* his equal on water or in the wilderness—but the way I've seen Ahman-de-Bellah appraise blacks fresh from the bush. I did not like the feeling, Mr. Calhoun. Nor did I like him. He ain't been at sea for half a dogwatch. I felt closer, if you must know, to the illiterate swabs and heathens I'd gone through hell with on ships and in the heart of stinking jungles. Thing is, he made this voyage possible." The Old Man was quiet for a long time, his eyes like bits of ice, his complexion paly, whiter than lamb parchment. When he spoke again, his voice was hushed, like a man in church. "His name is Zebediah Singleton, and a third of this tub is his."

"And the other two-thirds?"

"Elihu Griswold, a Georgia planter, owns a big slice, but I don't expect you'd recognize these names. Like I said, these blokes don't like to be seen. For good reason too, given all the crimes they've committed. The last one is a Creole speculator named Philippe Zeringue."

"Ngonyama won't listen to any of this, Captain. There are fifteen Africans now, but only four Yanks. They have the arms and we do not, nor any chance for regaining our course if you—*Philippe Zeringue, did you say?*"

"You know him?"

"No, but—uh, I believe I've heard the name."

"Well, three of these rebellious Allmuseri are *his.*"

"Which three?"

The Old Man shrugged off my question, talking on about an invisible economic realm—a plane as distant from me as the realms of religion and physics—behind the sensuous one I saw. Suddenly the ship felt insubstantial: a pawn in a larger game of property so vast it trivialized our struggles on board. My months on the *Republic* seemed to dissolve, delivering me back to Papa Zeringue's smoky restaurant, which I'd never left, and then it was he talking in front of me and not Falcon, laughing at my Illinois country-boy ignorance of how the world worked, telling me there was no escape from the webs he had woven in New Orleans, across the sea, and even into the remotest villages of Africa. But how could he do this, I wondered? Buy and sell slaves when he himself was black? Was this not the greatest betrayal of all?

"Of all what?" asked Falcon.

I'd spoken in my reverie without knowing it. "Nothing," says I. "Captain, I think I'd better go to my bunk and lie down. But you *must* promise to do as the Allmuseri say. Our lives depend on it."

"I'll tell 'em what I told you. But first I must ask you for one last favor. Have you the gun-ring I gave you at the fort?"

I held up my left hand.

"Give it to me, please."

He waited, pensive, staring past me to Nacta's back in the doorway, his features like fog, remembering his nightmarish dream of things to come. I could not tell whether he accepted the Africans' conditions or if he was hatching some new treachery and, frankly, after learning that Papa was my real boss, that his reach extended this far, that I still had to answer to *him*, I felt too defeated to say more. I handed over the ring. He shipped a face suddenly full of scorn, one that told me Get Out. I did, glancing at the brand on Nacta's shoulder, then at the others as I went, perplexed and perversely fascinated by which of the blacks belonged to a black. Making my way aft, I saw Ngonyama and Diamelo enter the captain's room. Part of me knew Falcon was sifting through the wreckage for a weapon. I knew if he found one he would shoot them, but I thought this possibility slim until, as Cringle leaned over the rail near me, his Protestant stomach perpetually knotted and belly full of wind from Squibb's baking, we heard a single shot like the crack of doom on Judgment Day. I felt that shot in every fiber. My scalp began to crawl. The mate spun on his heels and sprang in four steps to Falcon's door. Nacta pushed him back. Then I couldn't see clearly as the other Africans clewed up at the entrance. Someone, Akim said, was dead. I clawed through the crunch of bodies, hoping it was not Ngonyama, that Falcon, in his stupidity, had shot Diamelo instead. Inside the room I was restrained by Ghofan. He held me with both hands. Said, "This one gave him the gun." He was shouting at Ngonyama, who made answer that "Rutherford came in unarmed. Let him go."

Released, I stumbled forward and found myself beside Diamelo. He was peering down at Captain Falcon, whose ringed hand, his right, was tight on the trigger of a Philadelphia derringer that had blasted away half his head, painting the wall behind him pink with kernels of bloody scalp big as peppercorns, a pâté of brains and blood, and left us—as all in the suddenly silent room knew—alone and sightless on strange waters, our chances for reaching home and dropping hook dashed by his death like driftwood.

As runaway slaves follow the North Star, having no guide to their homeland but a single light overhead, so the *Republic* steered by the stars for a fortnight. No matter, as Cringle told me, that the source of this fire in the heavens had likely died a millennium before the earth cooled, or that all our dreams were pinned upon an illusion of light, a trick of perception: we sailed on. And on, the clipper now a crippled Ark of blacks bandaged in canvas, begging for attention, calling night and day for food, medicine, and consolation. Petty fights and rumors broke out like disease itself, causing divisions we did not need, for our first priority was getting the ship into trim. If decks did not need scrubbing, then headstays needed tarring; if not that, then slack-standing rigging had to be overhauled, replaced, and repaired, for you cannot touch a single rope without altering the intricate tracery of the whole design. Poor old ship! She was not worth a powder shot now. At times, late at night on calm waters, I almost thought I heard her weeping for herself and our pitiful skeleton crew of half-starved ex-slaves. Without much water, without good canvas, and almost without an experienced crew, we were buffeted about by contrary winds, thrown off course frequently, so that often we flew in circles, retracing our path, or fell into a trance of sea and wind too frail to propel us, drifting aimlessly like men lost in the desert, our sails mere rags and ropes in ill repair.

Oddly enough, Diamelo spun leeward and suffered the greatest loss when the Old Man's body, weighted and bundled in sailcloth, was brought on deck and pitched into the Ditch. He watched nervously as Cringle and I cracked open the skipper's sea chest and distributed his gear before the mast among the slaves to lighten ship, and because it just made your duties too damned hard to have reminders of a dead shipmate sculling underfoot. But Diamelo wanted these reminders. All along I had tried to steer small when near him and not cross his bows, because he never spoke to the Americans except through a third person. Whenever he had to hand anything to Cringle or Squibb, he threw or slid it toward them with his toe. Deeply, deeply he hated us. Daily he led a whispering campaign against Ngonyama, accusing him of treason against his own people by serving as Falcon's liaison to the slaves. I said that wasn't so. He called me a Cooked Barbarian and told me if I spoke out of turn again I would be thrown in irons. Physically he was thin as a drainpipe, so lubberly I could have taken him down in two, maybe three seconds. Weeks below had left him bony, with large, froglike eyes that fastened onto you like fingers; swollen feet; and a tight skullcap of crinkly hair that could easily double under the boiling African sun as a natural pith-helmet. So it was not so much his stature that sometimes swayed and stoked up the others when he spoke as the purity of his racial outrage. This he kept close to him like a possession—imagine how one holds a cat—a point of reference that made every event prior to his enslavement pale by comparison. After hearing him plead earlier for our heads, it was easy to see his bondage in the barracoon, then in the ship's hold, as the most significant, the most memorable, even the finest hour of his life, a memory to safeguard and strengthen, to designate as the anno Domini demarcation since his birth two decades before. Prior to his imprisonment, said Ngonyama (who knew him since childhood), Diamelo had been a soger who drank palm wine and drifted indifferently from one occupation to another; been the village wastrel; the first at every dance, the last to leave; the boy who peeped at women when they went off to pee; the bully who proved himself on smaller boys; the hunter who hung back until the prey was dead or declawed; the sleepy student bored by muscle-banging field work, contemptuous of the doddering elders, impatient with the painstaking years required to master one of the complex Allmuseri crafts. But there in the crowded barracoon Diamelo found his long-delayed focus: Ebenezer Falcon, a true (godsent) devil to despise. A dragon so exquisite in his evil that Diamelo, never a boy to impress his people by his skills or social contributions, discovered no one spoke of his flaws and personal failings when all their lives were wreckage. He had but to breathe one two-syllabled iambic word, *Falcon*, to hold their ear and magically control their emotions. If the Old Man had thrown Ngonyama's sense of direction into doubt, he had inadvertently handed Diamelo's to him on a plate. In three weeks the wastrel previously cool toward his tribe's culture became its champion, a change the older Allmuseri, like Ngonyama, found unconvincing, opportunistic at times, even false, though none could afford to criticize him during their crisis below. But a champion must keep his dragon alive. It must not disappear, as the skipper did when he slipped his cables. Nay, retired dragon-slayers tended to be as directionless as soldiers after a war.

Although we'd flung half the skipper's things into the

Drink, shrewd Diamelo told the others his presence was still dangerously alive inside and out, fore and aft, in the steerage and forecastle, bulwark and waterways. Perhaps in *them* now as well. The evil had not been exorcised. The dragon was not simply a man but the spirit behind his ship, his way of seeing and speaking the world. Therefore he proposed new, emergency conditions for our conduct. The master's house must be dismantled. Only Allmuseri was to be spoken by the crew when in contact with the newly empowered bondmen. Cringle was to use maps Ghofan was preparing; he did not trust the ones Falcon had left. In addition to this, he forbade us to sing songs in English, his oppressor's tongue, whilst we worked. He said we must learn their stories. Nurture their god. Allmuseri medicine was to be used to treat sickness and injuries. We were not, of course, to touch their women; in fact, we were to lower our eyes when they passed to show proper respect for a folk we did not understand, had abused because of that, and now must come to for a wisdom we'd ignored. Last of all, until we reached Senegambia we were to dine only on dishes familiar to the Allmuseri—six upon four, since our rations were low.

Little of this lasted, except for each of them going below to feed their god. On both sides, African and American, survivors of the revolt felt too battered to embrace an entirely new regime. When Diamelo offered his proposal, they voted with their feet. Why? Brother, some days we ate candles. Oil. Leather when we had to, saving scraps of dandy funk (or biscuits) for the women and children, who warmed a bit toward Squibb and me. Nevertheless, Diamelo continued to wash himself in salt water whenever Cringle's shadow fell upon him, cleaned utensils if I touched them first, and took an unusual interest in the operation of the ship's cannons.

To make matters worse, Death climbed in through

[153]

every portal. Falcon had left us a drifting laboratory of blood-chilling diseases. That figured, in a way. I mean that blacks would not take the helm of the *Republic* until the ship was damned near damaged beyond repair, a shadow of her former self, her days of greatness gone—in other words, a vessel you couldn't give away, even if you tossed in a thousand-league guarantee. We dragged contaminated, pungled bodies to the rail. Two of the Allmuseri had Guinea worms. Being no surgeon, and not feeling all that good himself, Squibb was obliged to improvise as best he could. His prior shipboard experience served him well. He could detect plague by its sweet scent; scarlet fever by an odor like biscuits; insanity (he swore) smelled like rats. Most wounds required amputation. After lopping off the limb, the bloody stump was swathed in a strip of leather, which Squibb left until the whole thing dried out; then he scalded the nub with hot oil or tar, and this meant three of our hunger-bitten deck hands—the newly liberated Africans—were lurching about their tasks minus one leg, or with only two fingers on one hand, or without an arm. To any observer it would seem that a crew of invalids staggered upon the deck. The best dental work Squibb could muster was extraction. He destroyed the exposed nerve with arsenic. Atufal spent his free time carving false teeth for these unfortunates, sometimes using the frontal teeth of the dead to strengthen these crude replacements for the living. As might be expected, every mother's son on board had lice and eczema, was continually scratching, covered with red blotches, complained of fever, constipation, fatigue, and the bloody flux. Most went barefoot and, therefore, bled about the feet and calves from scratches that ulcerated almost overnight. Besides this, there were cases of distemper, a sort of maddening fever degenerating into a frenzy so violent that the victim ripped away his clothes, shredded his skin, or that of the man next to him, to hanging ribbons, then leaped into the sea. And these, I must add, were the milder cases aboard ship.

Far more dreadful were the sufferers from Black Vomit. This affliction attacked the nervous system and brain. Those so infected took on a yellowish tinge. Fell comatose. Their pulses sank almost too low to feel, and then came fits of delirium. Screams that kept the rest of the crew on edge or near nervous exhaustion, because the victims of Black Vomit went from apparent health to rot in a period of two days. In addition to this, and to crown it all, a handful among us showed signs of tetanus from wounds we had received during the fight. Squibb made heavy water helping them, and remarked sadly, "We'll be quarantined afore any port lets us put to. Yuh know that, don't yuh? This bloody ship smells like a pesthouse."

That stench, I noticed, was on Cringle. When not at the helm, navigating by guess and by God, he lay in Falcon's cabin, poring over maps and pulling his hair, his skin rucked and sagging, burned down to half his weight. His body jumped with fever. His head was full of bald patches, the remaining tufts of brown hair being starched, bleached, and brittle. Squibb diagnosed his affliction first as typhus, then scabies, and finally as sea scurvy. Actually, it was all three. His legs were swollen. Two wisdom teeth were loose in his head, wobbling in gums going putrid, but he would not stop riffling the skipper's cabin for sea briefs and old logbooks, or clues—anything!—that would show us the best route back home. "'Twas that storm," he speculated, his topsail-yard voice tightened to a throaty rasp. "I've not seen the like of it. Grayback waves over the gunwale. Lightning in the sails. Sky and sea were torn for a spell, or that was what I felt from the bridge." Leaning back in a busted three-legged chair, nearly tipping it, he pushed away his maps so as to ease his eyes. "You should never have gone for a sailor, lad. If you'd stayed home, you and that lady'd be spliced by now."

I did not wish to think of Isadora. I rose, felt the sea fall, then my belly, and sat back down. "Have you no running fix on our position?"

"None. Could be near Martinique or São Miguel, for all the bloody charts tell me. We've strayed off course, left the sea whose ways I know, and come into a rogue sea I know not."

"Forget the charts, then. The stars—"

"The heavens are all wrong. That's what baffles me. They've not been in the right place since that gale gave us a dusting. We should never have taken on Allmuseri. They're foul-weather Jacks. The world tilted because of it, or someone switched the sky on us. You tell *me* what happened. I'm a simple sailor, Rutherford. All I know is Castor and Pollux aren't where they should be for another thousand years, or maybe where they were when Copernicus was watching the sky." He gave a sigh. "Maybe it's me . . ."

"Then we are lost?"

He cleared his throat, but nothing came out. Cringle pinched the bridge of his nose to relieve pressure on his eyes, hesitant to answer me now, and as he rested I remembered the tales spun by old tarpots barely able to hobble up and down the wharves in New Orleans, about cursed ships that sailed forever and were damned never to touch shore. All were created by some catastrophe, they said. After a captain poisoned his crew. Or a high-seas riot. Or when the mates slit a master's throat in his sleep. Sometimes she was seen off ports struck by plague. Had we become such a phantom ship? As one throws out a net, I pitched him a question, hoping to break his silence and bring something back:

"Why did you sign on?"

He started. "What?"

"Why did you sign aboard the *Republic*?"

"It wasn't my decision." Now he was rubbing his forehead. "My father is a very influential man, as people remind me often—a father to be proud of, I suppose. When he was fifteen he came to America from a poor fishing village near Dorset, came in the belly of a steamer, like the blacks, with two shilling and a half crown in his pocket, and in twelve years he turned it into a fortune that'd buy his family's village twice over. And people love him, yes, they do, because he is charitable and helps anyone who started out with nothing, as he did. He holds contempt only for the privileged, but ironically that is precisely what his fortune has produced." Cringle laughed brokenly, his pipebowl bobbing from his mouth like a buoy. "McGaffin was right. I don't belong here. Like my other appointments, this one was . . . arranged."

"For what purpose?"

"Not mine, I assure you. If I understand his reasoning, it's because I've made a bad show of everything else. He's arranged many jobs for me, you know. I've been a bookkeeper for his company. Papa's heir secretly despised by the employees who smile because he's the boss's son, then whisper behind his back about how unfair 'tis he's standing in the way of someone who's been there forty years. That sort of thing—do you see?"

I didn't, but I didn't admit it.

"I *tried*, of course; I wanted to prove to him that I could make a go of things on shore, as he did, but men like him or Falcon have always made me feel contrary. Sooner or later I find myself disagreeing with them, or doing something to defy their smugness, or saying, 'No! Your way of doing things is not the *only* way.' Before this I was a clerk, a customs inspector, a higgler, an apprentice to a tailor, then a cabinetmaker, and twice engaged to women he thought suitable for me and, well . . ." The mate smothered a belch. "None of them panned out. He was disappointed. *I* was disappointed." He squinted at me. "D'you know what it's like having a father such as this?"

"Hardly." I tried to laugh to lighten his spirits. "I don't even know who my father *is*. Mine was never there to expect anything of me, or to make me expect much from myself. I *have* no family traditions to maintain. In a way, I have no past, Peter. At least that's how I've often felt. When I look behind me, for my father, there is only emptiness. . . ."

"Then you're luckier—and freer—than you know. You can never make a man like *my* father accept you on your own terms. Nor can you argue other alternatives with him, because material success is a pretty tyrannical proof for one's point of view. Truth is what *works*, pragmatically, in the sphere of commerce. You can't surpass him, because he's done everything, been everywhere before you got there, knows everyone, judges everything in terms of profit and how wide an impression it makes in the world, and hasn't left you any room to *do* anything except join his legion of admirers. And, worst of all, you *must* admire such awesome success as his, even though he feels, of course, that your mother corrupted you too much with books and crafts when you were young—it's always the mother he blames, you know, for spoiling you with poetry, or . . ." He lost track of his thought and rubbed his bladelike nose. "I'm here, Rutherford, because if he can't have a son who's a captain of industry, like himself, or a forceful personality like Falcon—they were old friends—or his favorite aide in his company, one William Jenson by name, who is *really* his son in spirit, I believe, one of those orphans who fashioned himself by his own hand, as my father says he did, and don't even *ask* me to tell you how it feels to see him grooming this lad, who looked at me with such self-satisfied smirks that I could have strangled him . . . if he can have none of these, then he wants, I suppose, a ship's captain. Should I fail at this, there's nothing else, because I shall *not* go crawling back to work in his company."

"And you?" I asked. "What do you want?"

"Right now, I want to be left alone." He laid his head on the table, cradling it in the crook of one arm. "All right? Just for a few moments before the first dogwatch begins . . ."

I urged Cringle to sleep and helped him to his hammock. Across his shoulders, neck, and backside there were boils and chancres, some hard, some softened to the point that pus drained from the sores. The smell of him was terrible. A cheesy odor, which spread thick and palpable on the air when I leaned closer to cover him with a stiff stretch of sail-cloth. His gums were infected too, bleeding down his throat, breaking his sleep with a rattling cough, like maybe both his lungs were riddled with holes.

And how did your narrator fare? Little better than the ship's bravos, I confess. Whenever Baleka cried bitterly for her mother and no one could calm her, when Diamelo threatened to beat Squibb because the Falstaffian cook couldn't decipher orders he gave in Allmuseri, or when one of the Africans was too weak to work and fell behind, the first thing I was forced to do was forget my personal cares, my pains, and my hopes before repairing to the deckhouse where the sufferers were sprawled. I placed a hand on each of their foreheads and listened. Though tired and sleepless, I clowned and smiled for the children; I told American jokes that failed miserably in translation. I prayed, like my brother, that all would be well, though I knew the ship was straining at every seam, making water, that beneath the thrashing waves there was only bottomless death, the extinction of personality, with not a sliver of land on the horizon, and perhaps all would *not* be well, as I told them until I worried the words into meaningless blather, perhaps only disaster lay ahead of us, but the "useful fiction" of this lie got the injured through the night and gave the children reason not to hurl themselves overboard before the first blush of whiskers had a chance to appear on their cheeks. If you had known me in Makanda or New Orleans, you would have known that I doubted whether I truly had anything of value to offer to others. Obviously, my master thought I did not. Once in Illinois when I felt jealous of Jackson's chumminess with him and wanted to get on his good side, I asked, "Sir, what do you think *I* can do for others?" Peering up from under his brow at me, wearing a pair of Ben Franklin wire-frame spectacles, he replied, "Yes, that *is* the question, Rutherford. What *can* you do?" That helped my morale not at all. It made me feel as if everything of value lay outside me. Beyond. It fueled my urge to steal things others were "experiencing." Believe me, I was a parasite to the core. I poached watches from Chandler's bureau and biscuits from his kitchen; I pirated from Jackson's trousers the change he made selling vegetables from his own garden; I listened to everyone and took notes: I was open, like a hingeless door, to everything. And to comfort the weary on the *Republic* I peered deep into memory and called forth all that had ever given me solace, scraps and rags of language too, for in myself I found nothing I could rightly call Rutherford Calhoun, only pieces and fragments of all the people who had touched me, all the places I had seen, all the homes I had broken into. The "I" that I was, was a mosaic of many countries, a patchwork of others and objects stretching backward to perhaps the beginning of time. What I felt, seeing this, was indebtedness. What I felt, plainly, was a transmission to those on deck of all I had pilfered, as though I was but a conduit or window through which my pillage and booty of "experience" passed. And momentarily the injured were calmed, not by the lie—they weren't naïve, you know— but by the urgent belief they heard in my voice, and soon enough I came to desperately believe in it myself, for them I believed we would reach home, and even I was more peaceful as I went wearily back to help Cringle at the helm.

Not so with Ngonyama.

"This evil is visited upon us," he said testily, stepping over his injured tribesmen, giving them water, which we had to ration closely, "for the crewmen we killed."

"Do you think Diamelo sees it that way?"

He shot me a stare so fierce, like sparks from a blacksmith's forge, that I had to look away. "Who else is there to blame? All well and good for *you* to blink at sin, Rutherford. You're a *Yankee*." His wide lips curled a little in contempt. "None of us were brought up to *accept* failure, or laugh it off, as you do." Crabby, he rubbed his chin, then said an English swear word I never dreamed he knew. "I shall never understand you, *Ndugu*. We were forced onto this ship. Why have *you* wandered so far from your home?"

He really meant all that. As will happen with a man of his beliefs, he saw the sickness upon us as a moral plague and held himself responsible for our suffering. The aftermath of the mutiny stopped his spirit cold. Riveted it. Nailed him fast. He had slipped into relativity. He could not move forward, and thus lost ground to Diamelo day by day. (But I must add he kept us alive by not telling Diamelo all he had learned at the helm.) It all had to do with an old Allmuseri belief (hardly understood by one Westerner in a hundred) that each man outpictured his world from deep within his own heart. A fortnight ago he had thought *murder* and lo! the mutiny was manifest, as if a man's soul was an alchemical cauldron where material events were fashioned from the raw stuff of feelings and ideas. That meant an orthodox Allmuseri, as he was, had to watch himself twenty-five hours a day and police his heart. As within, so it was without. More specifically: What came *out* of us, not what went in, made us clean or unclean. Their notion of "experience," I learned, held each man utterly responsible for his own happiness or sorrow, for the emptiness of his world or its abundance, even for his dreams and his entire way of seeing, so that an Allmuseri pauper might be rich if his heart was clear, and their kings impoverished if they harbored within themselves hunger, grievances, or hatred, as Ngonyama had done toward the crew, wishing misery and death upon them. All that, it seemed, had flown back upon him like spit hurled at an enemy against the wind. And now Ngonyama grieved less over what lay ahead of us than what lay in the immediate past, this rift, this vast rupture he had caused within himself by permitting the execution of so many.

Never a night passed but I entered the quiet, disheveled fo'c's'le—full of mildewed clothing and rusted weapons covered with fungi—and, standing at the room's center, imagined I heard those murdered tars: McGaffin's snarl; fetching music from Tommy's flute; the yammering of Fletcher and Meadows; and the nerve-jarring *Har! Har!* of forty pirates in a gin-duel. As I struggled to describe every detail of our passage in the captain's log, I longed for the crewmen lost to fill the ship's room again, for our lonely drifting to disappear, and, as in a dream, delivering me back to Isadora's sitting room, where I would set my teacup clicking down on her candlestand, cross the carpeted floor on my knees, and bury my face in her skirts, begging her to take me in and forgive my idiot blathering about wanting excitement and saying all the beautiful things I'd meant to tell her to balance how I'd hurt her sometimes. Like a wife she would watch me closely to see my reactions to the portraits of women in popular magazines, or on the street, faintly jealous if I stared at them too long, but never showing it, wounded but too proud to let on that I had brought her pain, this woman who, I knew, had paid my bills back home. And it came to me, there in the darkened room, that perhaps Papa was right and there were only two kinds of people in the New World: debtors such as I had been all my days and those who, like Isadora, paid the rent for all the rest. But the dream never doorwayed into her rooms, and the furnishings of the fo'c's'le took on a grim finality or gave me such a feeling of there being nothing beyond these groaning timbers, this endless sea, that I wept shamelessly like a child.

"Ruth'ford," said Baleka, catching me like this. "Can I get you anythin'?"

I blew my nose. Croaked: "Dry socks."

She hung back, a little rattled to see me blubbering and biting my nails, her hair tucked under an African headwrap or *gele*, as their women called them. As with all Allmuseri children, Baleka never displayed her feelings directly. Frankness was a Western virtue that offended the blacks a time or two. She policed herself from doing or saying anything that might displease others. Thus Baleka could only be read at angles by paying attention to the subtlest of vibrational shifts in her voice, the slight emotional spin she put on ceremonial action, the nearly imperceptible imprint her feelings left, like heat from hands on glass, upon Tribal behavior so ritualized, seasoned, and spiced by the palm oil, the presence of others it virtually rendered the single performer invisible—or, put another way, blended them into an action so common the one and many were as indistinguishable as ocean and wave. I wondered if she thought it weak for a grown man, a Westerner, to weep. Turning my back to her, I blew my nose on the hem of my blouse, and said, "Yes?" My voice croaked. "What is it?"

"It's your turn to feed it."

Baleka looked at her bare feet. Instantly, I knew what she meant: the creature Falcon had captured had to be fed. Every day it had to eat. Heretofore, the more pious of the Allmuseri had done this, but eventually the duty fell to everyone. I was the first of the Americans luffed in for the chore. But on what did it feed? None of the Africans who went alow had been with it for more than fifteen minutes. None had taken food. It was a duty I dreaded. Still, I felt compelled to see what sort of cargo Falcon had believed would make his fortune shoreside and, just maybe, hasten the millennium.

Weakly, then, feeling unsteady in my spine, fearful that perhaps I, too, had the first signs of sickness, I descended into the chamber with a glim and rope tied at my waist. The darkness there was blacker than chimney soot. There, where the scuttles were closed, the smell rivaled stagnant water in a swamp. The air was stale, potted. The silence was so heavy I swear you could hear a maggot pump ship on sailcloth. No wind stirred within these walls, but the flame of my lantern swayed violently as if things were stalking to and fro. My chest began to ache. Feeling the urge to vomit, a backwash of fluids in my throat, I bent forward, but nothing came, and now I was so weak I could neither stand nor sit, and simply lay still. About five paces to my right was the box. Otherwise, I saw nothing. Something was off, my nerves told me. I felt an edge on the air, a skin-prickling charge like that before an electrical storm, the chamber releasing an elemental whiff of something just spoiling to happen: catastrophe hunkering, fleetingly visible in the corner of the eye. And then, as if cued to the gathering chaos I felt within, the crate opened and from it stepped a dark man, his features striking in the stylized way of Benin sculpture, the bone in the bridge of his nose boldly cut, his cap of short hair a mosaic of burls. This, I knew without noting another detail, was the dangerous, shape-shifting god of the Allmuseri. And I knew the infernal creature—this being who delighted in divesting men of their minds—had chosen to present itself to me in the form of the one man with whom I had bloody, unfinished business: the runaway slave from Reverend Chandler's farm—my father, the fugitive Riley Calhoun.

Entry, the eighth
AUGUST 1, 1830

Visiting the village of the Allmuseri, the Spanish explorer Rafael García was driven mad. I now knew why. I glimpsed the creature, coal black and squatting on stubbly legs, as you might see objects through clouded glass. This blistering vision licked itself clean, as cats do, and had other beings, whole cultures of them, living parasitically on its body. Do I exaggerate? Not at all. It stood before me mute as a mountain, preferring not to speak, I suspected, because to say anything was to fall short of ever saying enough. (Within its contours my father's incarnation was trapped like a ship in a bottle, contained in a silence where all was possibility, perfection, pre-formed.) It was top-heavy. All head. Luscious hair fell past protruding eyes and a nose broad as a mallet, and framed a grin stretched in hysterical laughter, bunching skin on its cheeks into a hundred mirthful folds: a ceremonial mask from Gambia, I guessed, but it's safe to say I was hardly in my right mind. Nausea plummeted from my belly straight down to my balls, drawing tight the skin along my scrotum. I came within a hair's-breadth of collapsing, for this god, or devil, had dressed itself in the flesh of my father. That is what I mostly saw, and for the life of me I could no more separate the two, deserting father and divine monster, than I could sort wave from sea. Nor something more phantasmal that forever confused my lineage as a marginalized American colored man. To wit, his gradual unfoldment before me, a seriality of images I could not stare at straight on but only take in furtive glimpses, because the god, like a griot asked one item of tribal history, which he could only recite by reeling forth the entire story of his people, could not bring forth this one man's life without delivering as well the *complete* content of the antecedent universe to which my father, as a single thread, belonged.

All my life I'd hated him because he had cut and run like hundreds of field hands before him. He was a dark man and fiercely handsome, to hear Jackson tell it, and even when he was tired after a day's work he could whip a guitar like nobody's business and sing until it made grown women cry. They liked him, the womenfolks, but Da wasn't so popular with the men who sometimes found his old, wired shoes next to their pallets. A couple tried to kill him, said Jackson, and lost because Da was big through his chest and could lift a cow his damnself, then afterward he'd bring stump whiskey to whomever he'd whooped, saying he was sorry for all the bedswerving and scrapping and gambling he did—that he couldn't help it, and besides, it wasn't really *his* fault he acted thataway, was it? "Looka how we livin'," he'd say. "Looka what they done to us." You couldn't rightly blame a colored man for acting like a child, could you—stealing and sloughing off work when people like Peleg Chandler took the profits, and on top of that so much of their dignity he couldn't look his wife Ruby in the face when they made love without seeing how much she hated him for being powerless, even with their own children, who had no respect for a man they had seen whipped more than once by an overseer and knew in this world his word was no better than theirs. Each time Da talked like this, checking off cankers and cancer spots of slavery on his porch in the quarters, the other men listened, even those who hated him for pestering their wives, their eyes rage-kindled and drifting away to old angers of their own. "We was kings once," he would say, scrawling with one finger on the dusty porch a crude map of an African village he remembered vaguely (and neglecting to add that in his tribe his own family was not royalty but instead the equivalent of Russian serfs or Chinese coolies). "We lost a war—naw, a battle. So now we's prisoners. And the way I see it we supposed to keep on fightin'."

Most of the time Da did fight. Never Reverend Chandler, though. Rather, he fought his family and others in the fields, chafing under the constraints of bondage, and every other constraint as well: marriage and religion, as white men imposed these on Africans. Finally, in the light of my slush lamp, I beheld his benighted history and misspent manhood turn toward the night he plotted his escape to the Promised Land. It was New Year's Eve, *anno* 1811. For good luck he took with him a little of the fresh greens and peas Chandler's slaves cooked at year's end (greens for "greenbacks" and peas for "change"), then took himself to the stable, saddled one of the horses, and, since he had never ventured more than ten miles from home, wherefore lost his way, was quickly captured by padderolls and quietly put to death, the bullet entering through his left eye, exiting through his right ear, leaving him forever eight and twenty, an Eternal Object, pure essence rotting in a fetid stretch of Missouri swamp. But even in death he seemed to be *doing* something, or perhaps should I say he squeezed out one final cry wherethrough I heard a cross wind of sounds just below his breathing. A thousand soft undervoices that jumped my jangling senses from his last, weakly syllabled wind to a mosaic of voices within voices, each one immanent in the other, none his but all strangely his, the result being that as the loathsome creature, this deity from the dim beginnings of the black past, folded my father back into the broader, shifting field—as waves vanish into water—his breathing blurred in a dissolution of sounds and I could only feel that identity was imagined; I had to listen harder to isolate him from the We that swelled each particle and pore of him, as if the (black) self was the greatest of all fictions; and then I could not find him at all. He seemed everywhere, his presence, and that of countless others, in me as well as the chamber, which had subtly changed. Suddenly I knew the god's name: Rutherford. And the *feel* of the ship beneath the wafer-thin soles of my boots was different. Not like any physical surface I knew, but rather as if every molecule of matter in her vibrated gently, almost imperceptibly, and the effect of all this was that from bowsprit to stern she seemed to *sing* like the fabled *Argo*.

Then I fainted.

Or died.

Whatever.

A long, long interval passed in the most unimaginable quietude. Silence as deep, as pervading as the depths of the sea. There was stillness, the sweet smell of growing things, then their stench. I heard screaming, felt it barreling out of my bones. I was thrashing and two Josiah Squibbs were holding me down in the fo'c's'le—my sight was distorted, I saw everything in doubles—mopping my brow with his kerchief. Apparently he had been feeding me from a bucket by his left elbow. Feeding me the choicest cut of medium-raw *steak*, unless the meat on the fork in his right hand was a product of my prolonged fever. Once he saw me awake, Squibb set down his fork and began fooling with my arm.

"Lie back now, bucko. Yuh need to bleed," said he. "And pray."

Beside him were instruments of venesection that made me cringe: fleams, thumb lances, and a copper bleeding bowl. I was not, I should mention, an advocate of bleeding, cupping, or leeches, though these medical practices still lingered on ship when all other methods had failed. I wondered: Was this necessary? And, more to the point, was Squibb capable of carrying it off without killing me? Nay, I was not eager for this, but I knew the cook, so tired, was ready to try everything he'd seen to save us. Squibb's cold hands rubbed my right arm vigorously; he consulted astrological charts to confirm that the hour was right for an incision and tightened a rag just below my elbow to enlarge the vein.

"Josiah, half a moment—"

"Don't talk. Ain't nothin' to say." The cook's face was pale as a scrubbed hammock, his eyes as red as a pigeon's. He shoved a stick into my hand and demanded I squeeze it. "This'll balance the humors, though Gawd knows I don't know what happened to yuh. We pulled yuh hup from below. Yuh been out of yer head fer a long time. Christ, lad, yer hair's sugah white."

"How long?"

"Three days full. Ever since yuh went below. But lissen. We spotted a *ship* this mornin', boy!"

"Whereaway?"

"Two miles to leeward in the southeast corner."

"Her flag?"

"None. Leastways none I kin see, but I think she's American. She's been following us hank fer hank, tryin' to eat our wind. I think her skipper knows we're in trouble. If she's British, we're sunk. They'll search us and charge you 'n' me with murder!"

"Peter hailed her, then?"

Squibb stiffened, shipped a long face, then looked at the bucket from which he'd fed me. "Yuh had Mr. Cringle fer supper, m'boy. We all did. Now, lie back, dammit! This was what he wanted. I was sittin' with him toward the end, which he knew was comin'. Yuh know, when a body goes the bladder 'n' bowels fly open—I seen it happen a hundred times—and yer mates have to clean yuh hup and all. He wanted to spare us that, so he asked the blacks to he'p him to the head. After he was done, he had a few mates gather round him. By that time we was eatin' our shoes, barnacles, 'n' the buttons off our shirts. The women and children had chewed every shred of leather off the pumps. So Cringle says, in a voice as calm as a chaplain's, 'My friends, I have no inheritance to leave my family in America. They'll not miss me, I'm sure, but I wish to leave you something, for no man could ask for better shipmates than thee. You're brave lads. The lasses have given their full share as bluejackets too, and methinks 'tis scandalous how some writers such as Amasa Delano have slandered black rebels in their tales. Of course, I fear you'll get ptomaine if you put me into a pot, but I've nothing else to give. I hope this will help. Please, leave me a moment to pray. . . .'

"He took mebbe fifteen minutes. After that he called me in and give me his knife. Cringle closed me fingers round the handle. He instructed me that if I preferred not to kill him face-to-face, he'd turn his back to me. Don't you know he told me to cover his mouth, plunge the knife between his shoulder blades, then pull it free and cut his throat from behind. If that was too difficult for me, he said I should stab into the soft flesh behind his ear, pokin' straight through the brain. If not that method, then I was to grip the blade with both hands and strike just below his collarbone, workin' the knife back and forth so it wouldn't break when I withdrew it. He told me we was down to only four or five knives, so I couldn't afford to have this one snap off inside him when his body pitched forward.

"At first I couldn't do it, Illinois. I started to ask if it wouldn't be better fer us to die like men, but I checked meself before sayin' a thing so foolish, 'cause what could I mean? What was the limit of bein' human? How much could yuh take away and still *be* a man? In a kind of daze I done what he wanted, standin' back from meself, then unstringin' him, and it was in a daze that I lay back, short-winded and watchin' the Africans cut away Cringle's head, hands, feet, and bowels, and throw 'em overboard. Next, they quartered him. They skinned him and cut the meat into spareribs, fat-back, bacon, and ham. It was then I reckon it hit me, that I'd killed a man." Squibb's eyes darted toward the cabin door, as if the mate's ghost might be standing there. "I can't sink no lower, laddie, and I 'spect Mr. Cringle's won his wings. After what he done, I don't plan to lose yuh. Yuh kin count on that. . . ."

Cringle's death silenced me. By any measure, he had been the best mate among us, the most magnanimous and gentle during our ordeal, the most generous in the face of hopelessness—in fact, a sailor who gave hope, steadied the ladder for others, and solved more problems than he created. I could not long straddle the thought that Providence had taken him so brutally. I wanted Squibb to deny it, but as I watched him work I saw, as he could not, how thoroughly his own life had been altered by our voyage. As our mates perished, Squibb was pressed into service not only as the ship's cook but also as our surgeon, and was often obliged to search his rum-pickled memory for nautical knowledge when a helmsman was needed. More than anyone, I think I knew how these demands and duties, all in the face of probable death, tested him. Now, what I am about to say must go no farther than the pages of this logbook. Five or maybe six days after the mutiny Cringle caught Josiah Squibb stealing rations reserved for the children. He was that hungry. That afraid. When the mate called him on the carpet he cried. His parrot too. It behooves me to explain how great a crime this, more than murder and man-eating, seemed to him. Until those days of sin, the darkest for him in the calendar of our cruise, he had believed the Almighty would safely deliver us to shore. But no longer. Distinctly, I remembered the Old Man saying, "A ship is a society, if you get my drift. A commonwealth, Mr. Calhoun," and Squibb, after snatching food from the mouths of infants, felt too ashamed to speak to me or anyone for a few days after Cringle caught him stealing. What was the use? Every day since leaving the fort we had lost something. Now there was nothing more to lose. Being that far down he was no longer afraid to fall. In this new condition, the concepts of good and evil, sinner and saved, even of life and death, falsified the only question of significance aboard ship, which was this: What must he do next? If asked to double-breech the lower decks or batten hatchways, he quietly did so, lifting himself above likes and dislikes, dwelling on the smallest details of his chores to deflect his mind from brooding—a Way, perhaps, to solder that deep schism Falcon believed bifurcated Mind. When someone had to fit a strap around the main topmasthead, it was Squibb who swung the block, a coil of halyards, and a marlinespike round his neck and, oblivious to the ship's swinging hard to starboard, to the fact that he had a bad foot and might fall from the crosstrees, climbed aloft and finished the job in Bristol fashion. Whatever was needful he did, including the learning of a little conversational Allmuseri when Diamelo demanded his former captors ease back from English. It would have been helpful to know if he still sought perfection in women who looked like his late wife. . . . Don't care about that? Okay, we shall push on. . . .

The result of Squibb's sea change was that his touch, as he worked the lancet, reminded me of Ngonyama's (or that of a thief), as if he could anticipate my pain before I felt it, and therefore move the other way. His breathing even resembled that of the Allmuseri, the proportion of inhalation, retention, and exhalation being something like 1:4:2, like oil slowly flowing from one vessel to another. I felt perfectly balanced crosscurrents of culture in him, each a pool of possibilities from which he was unconsciously drawing, moment by moment, to solve whatever problem was at hand.

"Josiah, that ship . . ."

"Ah was the one signaled her. I cried, 'Ho there, the ship, ahoy,' then Diamelo stopped me with a cat. He's afraid she's a man-o'-war that'll put the blacks back in irons. Things are bad. I have to tell yuh that. Ngonyama can't help us now. He's pissin' blood, bleedin' inside, I figure, so I don't give him much time. I don't give *any* of us much time. We're comin' into dirty weather again. The ship won't wear. This boat's mebbe our only chance to get home. Diamelo wants to fire on her, then abandon this tub—and us—fer that one. Y'know, I'd say that boy's a li'l slack in the stays . . ."

"No question, but has he convinced the others to become corsairs too?"

The cook sighed. The lines of his face were all vertical, those on his forehead flat, like currents. "Can't say. It's all touch 'n' go from heah, Illinois."

"Josiah—"

Squibb shushed me. The telling of this left him looking squally and shivering so badly, like a man lost in snow, that he took himself duckfooting from the room, splashing through water, after removing the tourniquet from my arm, and I cannot say I heard him rightly through the natter and babble of voices in my head. More weakened than before from bleeding—he had drawn a pint of purplish blood—I could only rest quietly, thinking of the ship that might be our savior, my heart whamming away like a drum as our own boat convulsed.

I slept. Deeply at first, then in pools of my own milky perspiration. Slept through the passing of light and patches of darkness in the portal above my head, and came awake into a conscious nightmare. Never ill a day in my life, thanks to Master Chandler's Saturday morning doses of castor oil, I now found that my gums were bleeding. I could not stop the flow. Rags of bedclothing stained with blood began to pile up beneath the berth where I lay. Crisp pain coursed through all parts of my body—stomach, head—and I would have felt pain in my spleen and pancreas too, but I wasn't exactly sure where they were. There came a knock at my door. Twice, I think, but I was unable to answer. The catch was turned. The door eased open. Someone looked in, saying nothing, then passed on. In the cavity of my chest a fire burned like camphor. I lay sprawled in purging fever. A quivering mass of jelly. My eyes felt filmy, and so I tried to keep them closed, sleeping again and shivering violently, though, as I say, I felt that I was on fire.

When I opened my eyes again—I do not know the day—the cabin had a twisted feel, the surface of objects warped, the planes and lines of the room falling away to a point in the corner millions of leagues away. I closed my eyes, only to experience a vertigo like the vortices that suck ships to the bottom of the briny. Slowly I pulled myself to the floor, feeling nothing under my feet, though I knew well enough I must be standing, feeling, in fact, no physical tie to the other objects in the room at all. Then I gave at the knees and keeled over.

How long I lay at the foot of the berth I cannot say. Again, daylight burned from ruby to blue in the portal, then shaded down into night. I wobbled to the door, intending to call for help, sideswiped a table, which caused me astounding pain, and fumbled with friction matches to light the lantern, burning myself several times, I could see, but I felt nothing in my fingers. I stumbled into my trousers, then made my way outside onto the deck, a slight paralysis pinching my left side, so that I dragged that leg a little, then stumbled down to the orlop, its tainted air filled with buzzing insects like floating plankton, burning my lungs. As I squatted there, my head swung into this cesspool of swishing fecal matter, I brought up black clumps I can only liken to an afterbirth or a living thing aborted from the body—something foul and shaped like the African god, as if its homunculus had been growing inside me—and voiding this was so violent a thing I was too weakened to rise again, and lay jackknifed for a long time with my face flat against the splintery hollow rind of the hull, listening to the swash and purl of waters below me.

Then, as before, I desperately dreamed of home. I'm sure the Allmuseri did the same, but home was a clear, positive image to them as they worked on the ship. As *I* remembered home, it was a battlefield, a boiling cauldron. It created white rascals like Ebenezer Falcon, black ones like Zeringue, uppity Creoles, hundreds of slave lords, bondmen crippled and caricatured by the disfiguring hand of servitude. Nay, the States were hardly the sort of place a Negro would pine for, but pine for them I did. Even for *that* I was ready now after months at sea, for the strangeness and mystery of black life, even for the endless round of social obstacles and challenges and trials colored men faced every blessed day of their lives, for there were indeed triumphs, I remembered, that balanced the suffering on shore, small yet enduring things, very deep, that Isadora often pointed out to me during our evening walks. If this weird, upside-down caricature of a country called America, if this land of refugees and former indentured servants, religious heretics and half-breeds, whoresons and fugitives—this cauldron of mongrels from all points on the compass—was all I could rightly call *home*, then aye: I was of it. There, as I lay weakened from bleeding, was where I wanted to be. Do I sound like a patriot? Brother, I put it to you: What Negro, in his heart (if he's not a hypocrite), is not?

I was lying where I had fallen when Baleka came below, saw me, then rolled me upon my back like a beetle. She was speaking, I knew that much, but my ears were stopped completely. Her face seemed fathoms away, or perhaps it was that my own eyes had shrunk back into my head, receding inward to some smoking corner of the brain. Try as I might, I could not remember my full name. She and one other I did not know lifted me up the gangway to the deck, and dropped me back on the bed in the fo'c's'le. I tried to sit. The room spun. I fell back again, lying half off the bed, and wept at my helplessness. I had not known before that everything, within and without, could break down so thoroughly. For all I knew I had already lived through many afflictions and survived them, too busy at ship's business to know I was afflicted. And then they were gone. No, they did not walk out. One second they stood beside me, then they dematerialized like phantoms. All that day and night I lay in a dissolving, diseased world, unable to find a position comfortable enough to remain in. My bowels ran black. The pain was quick. Everywhere at once. Then, at some point in this river of sickness, I saw Ngonyama crack open the cabin door. He was alone, his eyes like sea mist, a breath of ice in his matted hair.

For a moment he stood above me, keeping his own counsel. He cupped my hands together in his to warm them. He was feverish too. A blue tinge stained his lips. And, more's the pity, he could not straighten out the fingers on his right hand or stop shivering, as if someone stood upon his grave. He was in pain, but tried not to show this, because he was disassociating himself from the misfortunes of his body, as he'd done when the Old Man put a brand to his backside, going out to meet his suffering, you might say, as a proud African king meets a king. With him sitting hard by, I could not help but remember the practice his people had of setting aside one day each month for giving up a deep-rooted, selfish desire; the Allmuseri made this day a celebration, a festive holiday so colorful, with dancing and music and clowning magicians everywhere, that even their children were eager for the Day of Renunciation, as they called it, to arrive. Would such a four-dimensional culture perish with him and the others? During all this time I tried to speak, but felt my throat to be phlegmed, my lips soldered together, a crusty material caking my mouth. Ngonyama put his hand on my chest, urging me to lie back, and I did, feeling another flicker of panic. Even though we had come through much together—mutiny, storms, meetings with gods—my friends could help me no more than a man who falls overboard during a gale, the sea taking him instantly. I gave myself up for lost. Even as he watched me, I sank farther away, his face dislimning, the room fading in a frightening way that made me realize how dependent its appearance was upon the workings of my own nervous system, how in this sickness my faculties that gave it shape were loosened, shut down, switched off, and for all purposes nothing in my sight could sustain itself without me, how *I* was responsible for *all* of it, the beauty and ugliness; and I thought of how the mate was righter than he knew, and of Blake, a poet Master Chandler had me read, his beguiling, Berkeleyesque words, "I see the windmill before me; I blink my eyes, it goes away," and so did the cabin, and so did the world. In the black space behind my eyelids I saw nothing, and knew I was dying, no doubt about that, and I did not care for myself anymore, only that my mates should survive.

At six bells Ngonyama left, and I lay, as in a chrysalis, until I could hear no longer, then fell again through leagues and leagues of darkness, the paralysis of my legs spreading upward toward my groin, deadening and numbing as it went. There came tremors, as if I were bursting or splitting apart. For a few seconds I was blind. Huge, frosty waves pitched the *Republic*, rolling her so prodigiously the floor shook and the cabin walls panted. Thrown open by deckwash blue as floodwater, the cabin door banged loudly against the wall. The storm outside, for certainly it was that, changed pressure inside the cabin and further troubled my breathing. I lay eager to question Ngonyama again, and lifted my head when I heard footsteps enter the room.

"Ngonyama," I said too quickly, for it was not him but Squibb, looming over me, knee-deep in water, his face pooled in wet hair.

"Kin yuh stand, Illinois?"

I pushed myself up. "Help me get dressed."

"No time fer modesty. We've got to use this storm as cover till we gets a boat over the side."

"How many are left?"

"Twelve, countin' us. I've already got the gel in one of the longboats. Smack it about now, 'less yuh plan to follow this bastard into the briny!"

Furniture was floating as high as Squibb's hams. He guided me through the door, but no sooner did we reach the deck than an explosion rocked the ship: I was stunned, thrown back against a bulkhead, Squibb falling beneath me. The ceiling caved in, raining planks and boards that buried us and broke the cook's left arm. Somehow, with a strength I cannot explain, he shoved them aside and, upon gaining the deck again, stepping over a body I recognized as Diamelo's, we found the foreyard broken in its slings, the larboard railings torn away, and the orlop deck fallen into the hold. From what I could tell, clinging to the remains of the masthead, Diamelo had gone the wrong side of the buoy by popping off one of the cannons, unattended for weeks, and with unstable powder. The ball ignited but failed to fire, and moments later when it eventually blew, spraying the deck with bricks and burning metal, not a man, African or American, in the line of fire was left standing. Smoke was burning my face, blinding me again, but I was able to make out Ngonyama at the wheel. There on the flaming bridge he seemed preposterously alone, black flesh and wood so blended—he had lashed himself to the wheel and now could not break free—it was impossible to tell where ship ended and sailor began or, for that matter, to clearly distinguish what was ship, what sailor, and what sea, for in this chaosmos of roily water and fire, formless mist and men flying everywhere, the sea and all within it seemed a churning field that threw out forms indistinctly. I tried to make my way to the helm and add my hands, weak as they were, but Squibb restrained me. The wind was high. I could not hear his voice, but knew he was saying the ship was hogged, falling to pieces around our heads. The mizzenmast had snapped. The ship began bilging at her center, a heart-stopping grind of timber as her waist broke in half, the decks opened, her beams gave

way, her topsides broke from the floor heads, and heavy
sea swamped all the forward compartments. With a knife
Squibb cut off his boots, stripped away his stockings, shirt,
trousers, and, naked as a fish, pushed me toward a jolly boat
where he had earlier sent three of the children. Judging this
to be their last hour on earth, the little ones wailed. Every
new wave lifted the ship, which again dropped so low water
combed forward, then aft, dragging yet another hand away.
And it was as I fought to keep the children in the boat that
I felt the deck slam upward suddenly, pitching all of us into
the sky, then dashing us into a feather-white sea.

You cannot know the feeling, nor words deliver the fact,
of how I felt once flung into the Cupboard. My eyes were
logged, full of freezing water. Still, I was able to make out
the ship rolling onto her beam ends. Her stern sank foremost. I slipped underwater, the sea filling my throat, bal-
looning my lungs—it was a feeling of inversion, as if I'd
mistakenly touched a harmless-looking wall, thinking it
solid, then tripped, falling through into a shadowy realm
of mist and specters on the netherside. Drowning, I saw my
past spool by me, a most unsettling experience, there being
in my case precious little of value to review. My lungs were
bursting. I found myself following the broken ship; she was
clearly before me, only ten cables below, her carcass sus-
pended like an antique bark hung from a museum's ceiling,
as were my shipmates, their lips bubbling ribbons of air. I
batted my hands frantically to get back, my fingers scratching at the bottomside of the Atlantic and, surfacing, shaking
water from my eyes, I saw chests, water casks, and debris
crowded with quaking bilge rats floating near me and threw
myself upon a hammock lashed in the orthodox way, with
seven hitches. Likewise, some of the Allmuseri were gripping loose deckboards, furniture, and shrouds awaft round

the hulk of the *Republic*. But not for long. The speed of the ship's descent quickly dragged them down at the rate of knots. Husbands, fighting to keep afloat, called their wives, but in the black bowl of sky, and blacker sea, no one could identify another, and soon their chins flipped up and disappeared in a sparge of foam.

In principle, the hammock should have kept me floating for a full day. It did not. During the night, the shipwrecked went under, one by one. Who lived, I could not say, for the hammock beneath me grew heavy and at last, filling with salt water, surrendered its weight and mine into the Atlantic's dancing, lemon-colored lights.

Entry, the ninth ²⁴
AUGUST 20, 1830

Here the log of the *Republic*—and my life—might have ended. Stouter men than myself, even eighteen stone, might have proven more buoyant, but seeing how thin I'd become, and weakened by bloodletting, I found myself floundering until, miraculously, I was fished from the sea. Arms stronger than mine pulled me over poop-deck beams. Someone's hand seized me by the hair, and my half-drowned body was hauled aboard what looked like the deck of a ship built for Andrew Jackson himself. Fingers on both sides of me pushed forward, forcing water through my lips, and unless I was deceived there were crewmen and elegantly dressed passengers gathered round me, the cook, and three children yanked from the waves—a ring of pale, insubstantial faces, one of which peered through a lorgnette and asked in Creole patois, "What kind of fish are they?" for our condition was so horrible our own mothers would not have known us. By contrast to these spectators, we must have seemed like wharf rats and wretches. We smelled worse. Our scalps were full of worms. Although these passengers appeared to be polite society, I had no inkling of the sort of vessel we were aboard, which was just as well, as I shall soon explain, and my gratitude at being rescued was so great I would not release their

captain, a kindly old shellback named Cornelius Quackenbush, for nigh half an hour, and once he uncoiled my fingers
from his cuffs I clung, legs and arms, to the cathead until I
slipped into a swoon.

When my senses returned or, if that is saying too much,
when I again opened my eyes, I discovered Captain Quackenbush's crew had carried Squibb and me to a comfortable
berth, and the children to another nearby. Little by little, I
learned that this ship, the *Juno*, was a floating gin palace,
as some sailors called them, with gold plates in the galley
and Royal Wilton carpets that cost five dollars a yard, and
that when she sighted us during her return to New Orleans from the West Indies our wreck was adrift only a few
leagues southwest of Guadeloupe. Captain Quackenbush
received us with a welcome that spoke well of his sympathy for all sailors, closing his eyes as Squibb recounted the
tale of our misfortunes, then bowing his head to thank the
Author of All Things for selecting him to be the agent of
our rescue.

So yes, Quackenbush fed, bathed, and treated us kindly
for days after our deliverance, but I still felt myself to be
thousands of miles from anything I felt sure about. Furthermore, I never dreamed how the full weight of all we'd
endured would hit me like a falling masthead: I felt like a foot
soldier home from a foreign campaign. As a crew member
on the *Republic*, I'd learned to live each day as if it might be
my last. Anyone who served under Ebenezer Falcon woke
each morning with a prayer on his lips, preliving his final
hour and different ways he might die. During a storm, you
could never relax, be overconfident, or let fear show upon
your face. You developed what Cringle called a "flood men-
tality"—that is, you were always prepared to have water
high as your waist. During each crisis, every action had to

be aimed at helping your fellow crewmen. You could not afford to tire. Your duty was always to insinew your ship; if you hoped to see shore, you must devote yourself to the welfare of everyone, and never complain, and constantly guard against showing weakness. Looking back at the asceticism of the Middle Passage, I saw how the frame of mind I had adopted left me unattached, like the slaves who, not knowing what awaited them in the New World, put a high premium on living from moment to moment, and this, I realized, was why they did not commit suicide. The voyage had irreversibly changed my seeing, made of me a cultural mongrel, and transformed the world into a fleeting shadow play I felt no need to possess or dominate, only appreciate in the ever extended present. Colors had been more vivid at sea, water *wetter*, ice *colder*. But now . . .

Ah, now, I felt shock waves long postponed. I could not stop shaking. I wept easily, and found this involuntary exercise so refreshing I promised to empty myself and wet my handkerchief this way every week, say, at elevenish on Sunday evenings, so don't bother to call on me then. Yet the simplest tasks defeated me. When called upon to select from bedclothing volunteered by the passengers and brought by the ship's boy, who asked, "Do you prefer white bedspreads or blue?" I was paralyzed, first because he reminded me of Tommy, and second because I could see no difference between the two choices after our travels, or how the distinction mattered in the Grand Scheme of things, and I pondered this astonishing question for a quarter-hour, incapable of choosing until Squibb said, "Blue," and bailed me out. These embarrassments did not abate. Trays of food brought to our room each morning—all those culinary options— gave pause to a man who had lately dined on his first mate and quartermaster.

But that was not the worst of it.

I could not sleep for more than four hours at a stretch, not after being trained to catnap by Falcon, who kept me up for midnight watches. Nightmares of the African god pestered my sleep. Now and then I felt the *Juno* was sinking, and I fell to the floor, forcing a laugh when I got to my feet so Squibb wouldn't worry, but he saw the state I was in all the same. Saw it when I fabricated excuses for not leaving our cabin the first week, and the week after that. Saw it when I stood naked, having forgotten to dress, behind the long curtain at our porthole, which I kept drawn, peeping out at carefree people dining and courting on deck and, Lord help me, I wondered how they might taste—people, I heard, preparing for a shipboard wedding; people who hungered and hated, plotted and schemed over a thousand inconsequentials. Hardly trivial to *them*, I knew, because not all that long ago such matters as getting a good-looking woman into bed and making a Big Killing and keeping up with the latest stage play and buying clothes and cutting a swell figure had consumed my energies as these activities did theirs; but I simply could not *do* this now. None of it made sense after the Middle Passage. And I wondered: How could I ever live on land again? Often the depression was so great I felt guilty simply for being alive. By surviving, I sometimes felt I'd stolen life from Cringle, or was living on time belonging to Ngonyama and the other mates; I felt like a thief to the bitter end. Sometimes late at night, after Squibb, his arm in a sling, went rummaging outside for a horn of rum, I considered how easy it would be, and perhaps just, to join my drowned shipmates by hanging myself. And of course it didn't help that passengers, partying after the storm passed, chose to sing a chantey called "Have You Ever Been in New Orleans."

". . . If not you'd better go
It's a nation of a queer place; day and night
      a show!
Clergymen, priests, friars, nuns, women of all
      stains;
Negroes in purple and fine linen, and slaves in
      rags and chains.
Ships, arks, steamboats, robbers, pirates,
      alligators,
Assassins, gamblers, drunkards, and cotton
      speculators;
Sailors, soldiers, pretty girls, and ugly
      fortunetellers;
Pimps, imps, shrimps, and all sorts of dirty
      fellows;
White men with black wives, *et vice versa* too,
A progeny of all colors—an infernal motley
      crew! . . ."

Only the hours I spent hunched over the skipper's log-book kept me steady. Along with his sea chest, it had been salvaged after the shipwreck, and once its pages dried I returned to recording all I could remember, first as a means to free myself from the voices in my head, to pour onto these water-stained pages as much of the pain as I could until at the end of each evening, after writing furiously and without direction, I at last felt emptied and ready for sleep. Then, as our days aboard the *Juno* wore on, I came to it with a different, stranger compulsion—a need to transcribe and thereby transfigure all we had experienced, and somehow through all this I found a way to make my peace with the recent past by turning it into Word. Consequently, when I wrote I was incapable of venturing forth into the social world, so Baleka did this for me, begging passengers for things I needed, such as a wig.

Because I'd lost most of my hair, you see. Where once I had had a thick, bushy helmet that only a dogbrush could unkink, I was now almost as bald as Martin Van Buren, though a damned sight less tubby: a kind of old kid I seemed in the cabin's mirror as I squeezed on a raven-black headpiece, one tight at the temples like a stocking cap. My beard was Biblical in length, my joints Job-like in their creaking. Each morning when I rose, my ribs felt like iron rods. Our travels through several time zones had played badly with the metabolic cycles of my body, according to the ship's surgeon, causing a loss of nitrogen and sulfur, and confusing my inner ear. And, given the diseases I'd lived through, I feared I was probably sterile. No matter what I did—hairstyling, mud facials, or fancy perfumes—I could not hide what I was: a wreck of the *Republic*. The girl, as dear to me now as a daughter, brought fresh clothes for me, a cane I needed badly, plus a set of wooden teeth so I could smile without looking like the Grand Canyon or the Kali Gorge.

"Ruth'ford," she said two Saturdays after our rescue, "you can't stay in this room writing *forever*! Please go out with me—we don't have to walk far, or stay out very long."

"Tomorrow maybe."

"But you should thank the rich gentleman who gave us these things, shouldn't you?"

She had a point there. Among the women on board, Captain Quackenbush found the loveliest linen for Baleka, round-toed shoes fastened with bright ribbons, and a turbanlike bonnet very French in design. "I suppose you're right. Did he tell you his name?"

"Uh-huh." She nodded. "Mr. Zeringue."

Suddenly I could not breathe. I fumbled with the cabin

window until it flew open, and hung out my head. Old fears flooded back, particularly when my gaze fell again on the girl, because if she had not misspoken herself, and if the wig I wore—burning my scalp—belonged to Papa, then Baleka and the other children were legally his property, pure and simple, which was a thought I could not abide. But was it he? Had Providence hurled me to Africa, then pulled me from the Drink, only to place me—and these innocents—again at his mercy? "Baleka"—I threw on my jacket—"you're sure he said Zeringue? What did he look like?"

She puffed her cheeks, poked out her belly, and, with her right hand, flicked ashes from an invisible cigar. There could be no mistaking the model for this pantomime.

"And tell me, child, where is he now?"

"There's a big room on the ship. He was going there."

"Can you show me the way?"

It was now Baleka who skiffled me along the well-scrubbed deck, but I soon slowed, weaving from the bite of cold wind. Every few feet I listed to port, supported only by my cane and the girl who, after such excruciating progress, at last brought me to anchor at a huge messroom abaft the main-mast. From just left of the door, I heard someone at a piano, practicing a wedding march. In the room's quiet, planked interior, embellished for some festive occasion, the noise on deck did not intrude. Toward the rear, Captain Quacken-bush stood on a makeshift platform with a Bible, consult-ing in whispers with—yes, by crimus, below him was Papa, looking, if you can believe this, profoundly sad, beat down around the ankles like a man loaded with chains. He seemed to me poorer in both pocketbook and spirit, and doubtless shaken by his devastating losses when the *Republic* went down right before his eyes. His face was pasty, his posture a little stooped, and about him was the air of a man confused by his barrister, his lover, or both. He was involved in some kind of rehearsal. Wedding flowers were everywhere. Yet I sensed something else, an internal signal that once warned me shifting winds bore watching, and—as Papa's fiancée walked toward him in a blue silk dress, beneath a Kitty Fisher bonnet—it was blasting away. Her legs were wobbly from motion sickness; Papa and the captain seemed worried she might bring up her last meal on the lush carpet leading to the altar. She did not fully turn, but in my bones I knew this was Isadora. But an Isadora I could not believe. In the mess-room's hushed light, which created soft overtones on her lips and a warm cast to her skin, her beauty was heart-stabbing. Added to that, she had lost about fifty pounds. (Soon I would know why.) I started to speak, but could not; I wanted to enter, but my will began to wither. For an instant I must have gone blank, the room blurring and turning soft at the edges like the effect of four fingers of whiskey. Rubbing my face with both hands, my cane in the crook of my arm, I looked again, saw her step shyly beside Papa, and then I could stand it no longer. I was about to barge inside and separate them when a hand fell heavily upon my shoulder.

"Suh," said Santos, "this is a private function." He was as muscular and lumpy-looking as ever, dressed in a neckstock cravat and barrow-coat: the very portrait of misery. Modern styles in fashion clearly were not the best attire for a giant afflicted with that rare disease—gaposis—where nothing fits right. Pulling at his collar, he tilted his head left, studying me. Recognition flickered and burst into flame. "Say, hold on heah! Just one fuhcockin minute! By Gawd, you's a pitiful sight, but underneath that wig, ain't you that thief from Illinois?"

Our commotion was attracting onlookers.

"Papa, looka what just pulled into harbor!" Santos

reached with his right hand, planning to grab my left wrist, a move I'd seen McGaffin make during the mutiny, and something (I cannot say what) swept over me (I cannot say how), but I sidestepped as I'd seen Atufal do, snatched his wrist and allowed Santos's propulsion to pitch him forward whilst I took a half step closer inside his guard, dropped quickly to the ground directly below him, then scissored his waist with my legs and tipped him over backward, the back of his skull bouncing off the deck. I'd wager the deck was more damaged than Santos's head. Like the brontosaurus, snapping at something that bit it yesterday, it might be a full thirty minutes before the pain of that bump traveled from his skin to his central nervous system. Nevertheless, this elegant and unexpected eruption of *capoeira*, which now seemed as natural to me as lifting my arm, was enough to sting his pride and send him scurrying backward, startled, into a forest of legs. We were surrounded by spectators, among them Squibb, who had come running from our room when he discovered I was gone.

"Santos," Papa snapped, stepping outside, "who is this?"

Santos was staring at me in bewilderment. "That's that boy the schoolteacher was seein'." Deeply, he frowned. "Nigguh, how'd you *do* that?"

Isadora asked, "Rutherford?"

The captain peered over her and Papa's shoulders. "Mr. Calhoun, I'm glad to see you're taking a little air after your misfortunes. However, we're in the middle of an important ceremony—"

"He was on that ship?" Papa stepped back from me, scratching his jaw. "Calhoun? I don't believe it, but if you was there, I wanna talk to you 'bout why that ship went down and whose fault it was. In my cabin, son. Right now. Santos, you bring him along—and don't lose the goddamn ring."

His man sat where he was, leery of me. I used this second of uncertainty to pull Squibb to one side and ask him to perform one last duty for me, one my life and Isadora's depended on, then hurried her away from the others. Baleka kept following us, trying to listen. I shooed her away. And all the while Isadora gave me a once-over, pushing her head close to see if I'd switched my nose for a different proboscis, if I was the same person under my beard, and just as quickly she pulled back.

"Do I smell that bad?"

She shook her head. "You don't look or sound the same."

Of course, she was right. Sometimes without knowing it, I spoke in the slightly higher register of the slaves, had their accent, brisk tempo of talk, and occasionally caught myself incapable of seeing things in general terms. In other words, when I wasn't watching myself, each figure floating past me possessed *haecceitas* but not *quidditas*, a uniqueness so radical I felt I could assume nothing about anyone or anything, or now—in the case of Isadora—generalize about her from one moment to the next.

She began squinting, and not simply to shut out the sun, although we were on the ship's western side afore the windlass. Rather, it was the squint of slowly remembered rage, and suddenly her voice was full of frowns. "Where *were* you, Rutherford! I waited for hours and hours after everyone else left, except for him." She pointed in Papa's direction. "Do you know—have you any idea—how *humiliating* that was for me?"

"I'm sorry," I said. "If I could do it over, I would." Cautiously, I touched her left arm, hoping she would not pull away. "I'm not the same, as you say. There's someone else, a girl . . ."

I could feel Isadora's arm tense beneath my fingers. Quietly, with her lower lip caught between her teeth, she waited for me to explain.

"She's one of the children orphaned by the voyage. And no, I'm not her father, if that's what you're thinking, but I might as well be. Whenever Baleka is out of my sight I am worried. If she bruises herself, *I* feel bruised. Night and day I pray all will go well for her, even after I am gone. Sometimes she drives me to distraction with all the things she shoves under my nose for me to see—Yankee things she wants me to explain, but I cannot *eat*, if you must know, until I am sure she has eaten first, nor sleep if she is restless and, to make matters worse, if she is quiet for too long, I worry about that as well . . ."

Isadora placed her right hand over my fingers. "My goodness, you *have* changed, Rutherford."

"Aye, and what I'm saying is that in order to raise her I shall need your help."

"Is that a proposal?"

"It is."

"Then I'm sorry, Rutherford." She lowered her eyes, her hand left mine, and for a moment I felt like a ship unmoored. "I can't accept your proposal now."

"Why not? Is it because you accepted Papa's first? Isadora, how can you even consider marrying him?"

She hurried to the rail, gagged, her stomach unsettled by either the rocking of the ship or her scheduled marriage to a man who made Cesare Borgia seem like a milquetoast. And abruptly she was angry with me again, so angry after gagging her voice came in sputters and a spray of spittle I felt too ashamed to avoid by turning my head or by taking a step away. "Papa and that goon of his were there when *you* weren't, Rutherford! He might be a criminal, but he saw how I was hurting, standing there in front of all those people Madame Toulouse invited, so *everybody* who's anybody in New Orleans would know *no*body wanted me." I eased to one side, believing Isadora was drawing back her fist; instead, she pulled nervously at her earlobe, a new habit she'd developed since I'd been gone. "I could have died right there, really I could have. But then . . . he was *nice* to me. He took me home. The next night he came by with a whole carriage filled with my favorite flowers, and proposed, and then I didn't know what to do. You don't say no when you're being courted by a man who owns half the city, has underworld connections everywhere, and kills people for interrupting him."

"You did that?"

"Once," she confessed. "After that I was afraid to. He scares me, Rutherford! Sometimes I'm so frightened I can't eat or sleep. You don't know what kind of things he's been up to."

"I think I do. And I'm not surprised he wants you. You're beautiful," I said, to soften her anger, yet it was true. Her anxiety and loss of appetite had made her prettier. Up close, I could see she'd used the ash from matches to darken her eyes, the juice from berries to rouge her cheeks and lips. "You've twice as much education and culture as he has. Given the circles he moves in, marrying you might bring the lubber a little respectability."

"I suppose that's why he took me on this trip, to *force* me to accept his proposal. I've been holding him at bay, really I have, Rutherford, for weeks. He hates animals, you know, even though he maintains a few as bodyguards and personal friends. He says I'll have to get rid of my cats. Well, I told *him* I couldn't let them go, not out into the cold, before I'd knitted sweaters for each of them, and I've been doing that every day for two months, stalling him, I mean, because at night I undo them." She wanted something to dry her eyes; I offered the tail of my shirt. After blowing her nose loudly she said, "It was working until last month when Santos, that blot on the species, stopped by my room to deliver a present from Papa and saw me unraveling booties I'd made for one of the puppies. You remember Poopsie, don't you?" I nodded, the memory of dog fur on my clothing unpleasant, but I made myself smile, which prompted Isadora to lean into me so firmly I felt our bodies had been fitted at the factory.

"Rutherford, what am I supposed to do?"

I asked her to stay in her cabin for the next hour. After making sure she'd locked her door, I bade Captain Quackenbush direct me to Papa's quarters. Then I shook his hand, and turned to Squibb, who waited by the rail with Ebenezer Falcon's logbook.

"This is what yuh wanted, right?"

"Thank you, Josiah."

"And yuh're goin' in there with them swabs by yuhself, mate?"

"Aye, but I'd appreciate your staying close by and keeping a bright lookout."

With his good arm, Squibb gave a mock salute. "Whatever yuh say, Cap'n," which belied the fact that if any gob could be counted on during a storm it was he. And believe me, a storm was brewing. Poor Isadora! Papa now had her by the short hairs. Served her right, I thought, for bringing him into our lives in the first place. I knew I could not leave her in such a fix, that I had to confront him, much as David, his pitiful sling and shepherd's stick at his side, squared off with the giant of the Philistines. Whether Papa fit the image of Goliath best or Santos, I cannot say. Yet of one thing I was sure. I was not, nor could I ever be, his match. For some blacks back home, those who did not know the full extent of his crimes, Papa was, if not a hero, then a Race Man to be admired. His holdings were diverse (including a controlling share in the *Juno*, according to Isadora), and he carefully watched political changes in the country, even the smallest shifts in local government, so he could profit from them, sink a little cash into land here, a house there, which in twenty years would return his investment tenfold. Once he bought a business, he never—absolutely never—sold it back to white men, because he feared if it left black hands it might never return. Aye, for many he was a patron of the race, a man who lent money to other blacks, and sometimes backed stage plays written by Negro playwrights in New Orleans. Could evil such as his actually produce good? Could money earned from murder, lies, and slave trading be used for civic service? These questions coursed through me as I paused before his cabin, and I saw how a man such as Papa might hunger for an heir, particularly a son raised by a woman as refined as Isadora—a teacher, indeed, a nursery-governess by trade. As the boy matured, he might feel a twinge of shame at his father's bloody fortune, but he would toast his old man's portrait some nights, for those crimes had carried their family from the fields to the Big House, from the quarters to the centers of finance. Oh, Papa's heir might occasionally complain like Peter Cringle (surely Papa would nudge him toward politics) but, like those blacks in awe of the giant Philistine, he would feel that freedom was property. Power was property. Love of race and kin was property, and if the capital in question was the lives of other colored men . . . well, mightn't a few have to perish, in the progress of the race, for the good of the many?

Before I could rap on the door it sprang open. Santos had been eavesdropping at the porthole. He kept a distance of twelve feet between us as I entered; his eyes never left me when he slammed the door, turned the key in its latch, and retired to a corner opposite Papa, who was seated at a table with carved cabriole legs bolted to the floor. It came as no surprise that these accommodations contained all the comforts Papa enjoyed on shore. He did not travel without enough packages—dozens of shoes, two changes of clothing a day—to fill the hold of a merchantman, and these were cast about on ornate furniture, thrown over tripod tables, across a heavily cushioned sofa, and on his heavily draped bed, heaped into piles awaiting Santos, who would wash, press, and sort them the way my brother had served Reverend Chandler. Surprisingly, Papa apologized for this disorder, and then he took a cigar from a tortoise-shell box on the table and offered me one.

"Calhoun"—he leaned forward in his fruitwood chair to give me a light—"I won't ask how you got on that ship if you don't ask why I'm interested in its cargo."

"The slaves, you mean?"

He straightened, as if I'd poked his spine. "It was a slaver? They're illegal, aren't they?" He pondered this, thumbing one of the straps to his suspenders. "How many slaves would you say it was carryin' before that storm off the coast of Guadeloupe?"

"Fifteen," I said. "Before the storm and after the mutiny."

"Mutiny? By who—sailors or slaves?"

"Both, or I should say the ship's crew was planning to set their captain adrift before the slaves broke free."

"I see." Papa ritched back in his chair, his mind racing ahead of me, judging by the evidence in his eyes, as chess masters leap two moves ahead of your own. "Then it was *his* fault, wasn't it? Your captain? If there was—uh, an inquiry into all this, if Mr. Quackenbush was to file a report on the shipwreck from which you was saved, thank heaven, would you be prepared to, uh, testify before a maritime court that your captain, being mad, lost control of his vessel, and was maybe even unfit before the voyage began, that he, a barrator, added African slaves to a simple expedition intended only for the transport of butter, bullocks, and rice? Could you say that, Calhoun, if someone—a nameless benefactor, say—was to come up with the currency to reward you for such a tirin' public speech?" While he talked I opened the logbook you presently hold in your hands. The smell of the sea came off these pages so strongly I had to blink away images of the ship's sails and mainmast. Papa's fingertips nervously drummed the edge of his table. "What're you playin' with there, boy?"

"Oh, dates," I said. "Nothing important, just the ship's manifest, with names for each Allmuseri slave on board, payment rates for the ship's principal investors, including your whack, Papa."

"Naw, I can't be in that book." He frowned and bent closer, trying to look, and swallowed. "Can I?"

I tilted the book so he could see. "Naval authorities will find this document very interesting. Captain Falcon's logbook, I'm thinking, would be Exhibit A for any investigation into the loss of the *Republic*. On the other hand, it would be tragic, don't you think, if it fell into the hands of William Lloyd Garrison. Or maybe the runaway slaves living among Indians, up in the mountains, who periodically raid plantations and, dear me, *kill* slave owners."

"Santos," barked Papa, "take that book from him!"

As with pain, so too did thought travel slow as slugs in winter through the inner wiring behind Santos's brow. You may have noticed that he could not think and move at the same time. So he stood perfectly still, like statuary in the corner, and thought furiously, and finally brought out,

"Papa, is he sayin' you was dealin' in slaves?" Big as he was, the man was preparing his face to cry over this betrayal. "What was that name you used, Calhoun? All—museri? My granddaddy use to call hisself that." He thumped a step toward Papa, his tread shaking the floor, then realized it was too hard to talk, think, and perambulate all at once, and stopped alongside me, his voice cracking and hands flat at his sides. "My people on my grandpa's side is from that tribe." He wanted to think again, thus was silent for two minutes as we patiently waited. "Calhoun, why would Papa *do* something like that."

"Ask him," I said.

"Papa?"

If anyone knew the untapped power in Santos's top-heavy body, it was the man who had hired him. He never got sick, *couldn't* get drunk, no matter how he tried, and had such a high tolerance of pain he often injured himself accidentally. With each step his man took, Papa backed toward the corner behind his table, and was now squeezing himself against it, as if literally trying to force his way through the wall into the next room. "All right, lissen. Let me put my cards on the table. I made a mistake. Anybody kin do that, right? At first I didn't know that ship was carryin' anything more'n vegetables and hides. You got my word on that. Zebediah Singleton come to New Orleans to play at one of my tables, and told me 'bout a business investment he said was straight-up legal—an opportunity for a cullud man closed out of the shippin' industry. I thought it'd be a good thing for me'n my people, a chance to diversify, get a foot in the door, go up one more stairway into somethin' legitimate instead of bein' stuck in the kinda business—gamblin' and gun-runnin'—I been limited to all my life." Papa's scalp was rivering a screen of perspiration over his brow, causing him to rub both palms over his eyes. "I didn't mean no harm. But once I got in that was it. You kin see what I'm sayin', can't you? Sometimes the biggest curse in the world kin be getting exactly what you want, or think you want, 'cause there's no way to see all the sides when you sign your name or give a handshake. You don't always know what yo' business partners are doin', if they plan to cut yo' throat, or use yo' money—unbeknownst to you—for purposes that'll make you wish you was dead. Calhoun, if I'd known up front the real freight we was smugglin', I wouldn'ta had anythin' to do with it."

"I don't believe you, Papa." I turned, pitching my voice toward Santos. "And the Africans who survived this business venture of yours won't either. They only number three, all children ranging in age from eight to eleven. As cute as they can be too, like Santos here. You could ease your conscience a little, I guess, if you provided something for them—a full endowment, say, for each—until they come of age."

Santos said, "Damn right."

"Done!" The muscles in Papa's face fell loose, hanging in folds. "And you're gonna destroy that book, ain'tcha?"

"I'd rather keep it as insurance." I did not want to hear any more. Possibly, he was lying to me about his involvement in the slave trade. Possibly, he still had deep pockets and a web of criminal connections in Louisiana and planned to have me and the logbook conveniently disappear once we were on shore (I decided it would be best for me to return to southern Illinois); but possibly, too, his equating of personal freedom and racial pride with fantastic wealth and power had gotten the blighter in over his head. Needless to say, I had little sympathy for him. I wanted to give him a good drubbing, but I felt too weakened after learning that Santos might be Baleka's distant cousin, and *that* meant he might be my in-law and come to visit for family reunions. Santos, though, who knew nothing of these backroom dealings, seemed eager to volunteer for the chore. "You bought slaves, Papa? After all I told you 'bout how Ruffner treated me, you did that?" I had to stick out my cane, like a tree limb, to keep him on our side of the table. But yes, it felt good to have his 280 pounds on my side for a change.

Papa had one hand mashed over his heart. "What else is it you want from me, Calhoun?"

"For now, that you leave Isadora and me alone."

He stood glaring at the logbook, and I put it behind my back, thinking he might leap any second to grab it. Suddenly, the point of my proposition struck home. "Wait a minute." His eyes snapped level with mine. "That's *blackmail!*"

"Bloody right," says I. "I'm sure you're acquainted with the technique, Papa."

I was also sure he had no alternative but to accept. Because there was no reason for me to hear his reply, I closed the logbook and limped toward the door. His man tossed me the key. Neither Papa or Santos had changed position. However, as I closed the door behind me, I did hear, ever so softly, the former dirt-pit wrestler say, *Papa, I'ma kick yo' natural ass.*

Squibb, hearing this too, shipped a smile. "Musta gone all right, eh?"

"Aye."

"Whatcha gonna do now, Illinois? The captain tells me he kin use a coupla hands fer his next voyage. He's makin' a run to the South Seas. You interested?"

"Depends," I told him, looking aft to where Baleka, brandishing a pot, was chasing a cat; I wondered where the animal had come from. "Might go back to Makanda and look for some land to settle on—solid ground for once, you know?"

"Aye, but if yuh plan to raise kids 'n' chickens, it'd he'p if yuh had a wife, wouldn't it?"

I could not have agreed more.

Five turns around the deck, intended to walk off my worrying and my tendency to hiccup during times of stress, brought me to Isadora's door, in my hands a brilliant bouquet of roses I'd "borrowed" from Papa's arrangement in the messroom. My hands trembled. I felt precariously balanced between my old life in New Orleans and the first rung of another with Isadora, if she would still have an old, broken-down sea dog like me. But why should she, I wondered. She did not know me, as I was now. What was worse, I could not explain myself in a single day. Telling her all I'd endured since I'd seen her last would take a thousand more nights than Scheherazade needed to beguile King Shahryar. Darkness was coming on, the sea trembled as evening shaded down gently over far-reaching waves. I took a breath, then knocked, and Isadora called out, "Come in. It's unlocked." Anger flared in me again. Hadn't I asked her to keep her latch bolted? Entering, I was prepared to scold her, but when I saw Isadora, there from the doorway, I was certain I had come into the wrong cabin, and rubbed my eyes. Seated on her bed, she wore only a thin cotton gown designed for sleeping. I don't mind telling you this was a shock. I was even less prepared for the birdcage, two smelly dogs, and a cat, lightweight and doubtlessly warm, stretched across her knees like a comforter. The cat and dogs all wore mittens and mufflers. All watched me like bored deck hands waiting for something rich to happen. Quickly, as I shut the door so no one might see her, I realized she had prepared herself not for the man I was now but for the rogue in need of reforming I had been months ago.

"I asked you to lock this. Are you expecting someone?"

"Just you."

"But you look ready for bed. Are you feeling well?"

"Oh, a little tired, I suppose." She smiled. "Until you showed up I was worried, but I feel good now."

I started to ask her to let me feel some of it too, then stopped, knowing that was what the old Rutherford would say. I struggled for a few seconds, feeling my former ways tugging at me. This was the me Isadora remembered, that she was responding to, but in a way that struck me as contrary to her nature. Truth is, she simply wasn't all that good at acting seductive. Her model, now that I think about it, was a temptress in a play we had seen a year ago, and as Isadora tried to imitate that actress's come-hither expression I could only answer by covering my lips to smother a sudden urge to laugh. But I thought, God bless her for trying.

"Isadora, I spoke to Papa. There won't be any wedding, so you needn't worry."

"I'm not." She spanked a spot on the bed for me to sit, which sent her animals flying to the floor. "And my answer is yes, Rutherford. I will marry you and help you make a home for Baleka. I'm sure Captain Quackenbush will perform the ceremony. I mean, everything *is* ready for a wedding."

I stood where I was, relieved and smiling, but I wondered what to do next, where to begin, how to close the physical distance of the last few months. Furthermore, how could I tell her that Santos might stay overnight if he came to visit? How could we keep him away? More importantly, how in heaven's name would we *feed* him?

"Are those flowers for me?" she asked. Again, she flashed that foolish, fetching, teasingly erotic smile. "Bring them here."

[203]

I sat down beside her, kissed the cheek she turned up toward me, then sat twiddling my thumbs. Meanwhile, Isadora took a whiff of the flowers strong enough to suck a few petals into her nose. She let the bouquet fall to the floor and turned to me after moistening her lips with the tip of her tongue. Placing her left hand on my shoulder to hold me still, she used her right to grip the top of my slops, and pulled. Buttons popped off my breeches like buckshot, pinging against the bulkhead.

"Isadora," I asked in a pinched voice, "are you sure you want to do this? We can sit and read Scripture or poetry together, if you wish."

She made answer by rising to her bare feet, shoving me back onto the bed, and tugging off my boots and breeches. By heaven, I thought, still water runs *deep*. Who'd have dreamed these depths of passion were in a prim Boston schoolteacher? She was so sexually bold I began to squirm. I mean, *I* was the sailor, wasn't I? Abruptly, my own ache for detumescence, for a little Late Night All Right, took hold of me, beginning at about my fourth rib and flying downward. Soon we both had our hands inside each other's clothes. How long it had been since someone held me, touched me with something other than a boot heel or the back of their hand! And she, so much slimmer—pulling the gown over her head—was to me a figure of such faint-inducing grace any Odysseus would have swallowed the ocean whole, if need be, to swim to her side. I kissed the swale by her collarbone and trailed my lips along her neck. Then, afraid of what I might do next, I slid my fingers under my thighs and sat on my hands.

Isadora twirled slowly on her toes, letting me see all of her. Now that she had my undivided attention, she asked, "Well, what do you think?"

"I'm not thinking."

"Good."

"But the animals. Can't you send them outside?"

"Rutherford!"

"At least cover up the birdcage."

"Don't worry, he's blind." Her voice was husky. "Just lie still."

Knowing nothing else to do, I obeyed. Isadora climbed over my outstretched legs, lowered herself to my waist, and began pushing her hips back and forth, whispering, "No, don't move." I wondered: Where did she learn this? Against her wishes, I did move, easing her onto her side, then placed my hand where it wanted to go. We groped awkwardly for a while, but something was wrong. Things were not progressing as smoothly as they were supposed to. ("Your elbow's in my eyeball," said I; "Sorry," said she; "Hold on, I think I've got a charley horse.") I was out of practice. Rusty. My body's range of motion was restricted by the bruises I had taken at sea, yet my will refused to let go. I peeled off my blouse, determined to lay the ax to the root like a workman spitting on his palms before settling down to the business at hand; but, hang it, my memories of the Middle Passage kept coming back, reducing the velocity of my desire, its violence, and in place of my longing for feverish love-making left only a vast stillness that felt remarkably full, a feeling that, just now, I wanted our futures blended, not our limbs, our histories perfectly twined for all time, not our flesh. Desire was too much of a wound, a rip of insufficiency and incompleteness that kept us, despite our proximity, constantly apart, like metals with an identical charge.

I stopped, and stared quite helplessly at Isadora, who said, "I thought this was what you wanted?"

"Isadora, I . . . don't think so."

She studied my face, saying nothing, and in this wordless exchange felt the difference in me. It coincided, I sensed by slow degrees, with one in herself, for in her disheveled blankets we realized this Georgia fatwood furnace we were stoking was not the release either of us needed. Rather, what she and I wanted most after so many adventures was the incandescence, very chaste, of an embrace that would outlast the Atlantic's bone-chilling cold. Accordingly, she lowered her head to my shoulder, as a sister might. Her warm fingers, busy as moths a moment before, were quiet on my chest. Mine, on her hair as the events of the last half year overtook us. Isadora drifted toward rest, nestled snugly beside me, where she would remain all night while we, forgetful of ourselves, gently crossed the Flood, and countless seas of suffering.

ACKNOWLEDGMENTS

Many sea stories and histories of ships from many cultures went into research for this novel. However, special citation must go to W. R. Thrower's excellent *Life at Sea in the Age of Sail*, John A. Garraty's *The American Nation*, and the voluminous writings of Eknath Easwaran. I would also like to thank Seattle writer Mark Gray for letting me use his description of southern Illinoisan speech; novelist Richard Wiley for answering my questions about Africa; martial artist Gray Cassidy for providing me with several articles on the black fighting art, *capoeira*; filmmaker Art Washington for keeping me politically honest; Russell Banks for inspiration; scholar Werner Sollors of Harvard for sending me narratives of the sea; Scott Sanders for his encouragement; Gene Clyde for his books on shipbuilding; Janie Smith for her patience in typing my generally chaotic manuscript pages; *Callaloo* for publishing the first chapter and *F3* the second, when the book was called *Rutherford's Travels;* and the Guggenheim Foundation for a grant to complete the novel.